D1052267

JOAN WOLF

His Lordship's Desire

MIRA

ISBN-13: 978-0-7783-2330-3
ISBN-10:   0-7783-2330-7

HIS LORDSHIP'S DESIRE

Copyright © 2006 by Joan Wolf.

www.MIRABooks.com

Printed in U.S.A.

As always, for Joe.

One

Perched high on the Berkshire downs, five miles north of Lambourn, Standish Court rose out of the mist before the eyes of Alexander Devize. He had not seen his home in over three years and the sight of the large, spreading redbrick building, built around a graveled courtyard, caused a sudden tightening in his stomach. When he left home three years ago, his father had been alive and in charge. Now Alex was the Earl of Standish and he wasn't quite sure he was ready to assume the huge responsibilities that came with his new position. The change from the chaos of the battlefield to the settled sprawling acres of Standish Court would take some getting used to.

He left his phaeton at the bottom of the shallow set of stairs that led to the front door and walked slowly upward. He raised the knocker and banged it three times.

The door was opened promptly by a burly young footman who looked at him politely. "Yes, sir. May I help you?"

Alex had opened his mouth to identify himself when an elderly voice from behind the footman said, "You stupid dolt. That's his lordship!"

Henrys, who had been butler to the Devizes for as long as Alex could remember, pushed the large footman out of his way and said in a quavering voice, "My lord, my lord, how wonderful it is to see you home!"

Alex took the old man's hand. "It's grand to be here, Henrys. I hope I don't give everyone too much of a shock."

"Not at all, my lord. Not at all. Her ladyship will be so glad to see you! She and Mrs. Sherwood are in the Yellow Drawing Room. Will you go to them or do you wish me to announce you?"

"I'll go along myself, Henrys." He gestured to the door. "My phaeton is waiting. Will you see that everything is taken care of?"

"Of course, my lord, I shall see to it immediately."

Alex took off his hat uncovering his black curls, then walked slowly through the entrance hall. He went through the arch that Adam had created to replicate the Arch of Constantine in Rome and into the centerpiece of the whole house, a huge circular domed room lined with twenty Corinthian columns carved from a striking green-veined marble. The vast open floor was marble and on the walls were a series of *grisaille* panels depicting sacrificial and martial scenes.

Alex's father had designed the room to inspire awe and wonder from the onlooker, and it fulfilled that role admirably. Alex stood looking at it for a long moment, then he proceeded to the right, to the staircase that would take him to the second floor.

On the second floor he passed through the main drawing room, which had a magnificent plaster-work ceiling by Joseph Rose, an intricate Thomas Witty carpet which mirrored the ceiling's design, pale blue damask walls and Chippendale furniture, through the music room and into the smaller Yellow Drawing Room, which had windows looking out on the front and the west side of the house.

The two women were seated on matching Chinese-style sofas with a tea table set up between them. Both were holding fragile teacups in their hands. Alex focused on the woman with gray-blond hair drawn back into a smooth chignon, "Hello, Mama. I'm home."

Lady Standish looked at him and dropped her teacup on the Persian rug. "Alex? Good gracious, is that you?"

"Yes, it is Mama." He smiled. "I'm sorry to give you such a shock."

"You're home!" Lady Standish shrieked. She stood up and held out her arms. "You're home, you're home, you're home!"

He enveloped her in a giant hug. "Yes, I'm really home," he said. "You shouldn't be too surprised. You wrote me that I was needed." He kissed her soft cheek. "You smell good," he said.

"I thought you would come home by yourself

last year, when your father died," she said a little accusingly.

"We were in the middle of the campaign to push the French out of Spain, Mama. We've done that now, and I felt that my usefulness was over. So here I am."

Lady Standish sighed. "Well, I won't reproach you any longer." She turned to the woman who was sitting on the other sofa. "Louisa, is it not wonderful that Alex has come home?"

Louisa Sherwood, his mother's cousin, nodded her head. "It's good to see you again, Alex. We've all missed you."

Lady Standish returned to her seat and said, "Ring the bell, Alex, and I'll have this tea stain cleared up. Would you like to join Louisa and me for tea? Or perhaps you would care for a glass of sherry?"

Alex smiled. "Tea would be fine, Mama." He sat in a fragile-looking Chinese-style chair that was near the two matching yellow sofas. "Having a quiet Sunday afternoon, are you?"

"Yes. The girls went out for a ride and they took the children with them, so we have some time to ourselves."

A footman came into the room. "Clarence," Lady Standish said, "bring more tea. And come back with something to rub out this tea stain."

"Yes, my lady," the footman replied.

As he left the room, Lady Standish turned eagerly to her son. "How grown-up you look, Alex.

You were a boy when last I saw you. Now you are a man."

"Yes, well, war will do that to a fellow, Mama," he returned soberly.

"I almost died when I heard you were wounded at Vitoria. I thought for sure you would come home to recuperate."

"It was nothing more than a flesh wound, Mama. I wrote you that. It healed very quickly."

The footman returned bearing a tray with more tea and an extra cup and saucer. While the footman rubbed at the carpet, Lady Standish poured her son some tea.

Alex accepted the cup and turned courteously to the other woman in the room. "How are you, Cousin Louisa? You are looking very well."

Louisa Sherwood was a very pretty woman and she smiled pleasantly at Alex. "I am very well, thank you, Alex."

Alex turned back to his mother. "Now, what is so pressing that you sent me such an urgent letter?"

Lady Standish's face became serious. "The estate has been solely in the hands of our estate manager for a year now, and I think it is time that someone oversees what he is doing. He tells me the cottages by the river need reroofing, but I do not like to authorize such an expenditure without your approval. There are several other things that need doing. It was time for you to come home, Alex."

Alex thought that his mother, who had been living at Standish Court all the while that he was away, should know more about the necessity of reroofing the cottages than he did, but he didn't say so. He merely nodded and took another sip of tea.

"We can also use your help in another area," Lady Standish said. "I am bringing out your sister this season, and Louisa's daughter, Diana, is to make her come-out with Sally." Sally was the family's pet name for Lady Sarah, Alex's eldest sister. "It will be much more pleasant for us to have a gentleman to escort us than to have to go places by ourselves."

Alex put his cup on the table closest to him. "Dee is twenty," he said. "Hasn't she already made a come-out?"

"Well, she has been 'out' in the neighborhood, certainly. And she has had her share of proposals. But she's refused them all, so I said that when I took Sally to London, Diana could come along."

"An incredibly generous offer that we deeply appreciate," Mrs. Sherwood said softly.

Lady Standish patted her cousin's hand. "I have never forgotten how kind Diana was to Sally the year that she was so ill. And I will be very happy to have your company."

The two women smiled mistily at each other.

"So you are taking both Dee and Sally to London for the Season," Alex said. "Is this a husband-hunting expedition?" His voice was a little tense.

"Of course it is," Lady Standish returned. "That's the whole reason for any young girl to make a come-out."

At this point, the door to the Yellow Drawing

Room opened and a beautiful girl with coppery-gold curls and wearing a well-used riding habit came into the room. Alex's breath caught.

"I am sorry to have to tell you this, Cousin Amelia, but Maria fell off her pony and I'm afraid she may have broken her collarbone. She is asking for you. Will you come?"

Lady Standish got immediately to her feet. "Of course I will come. What happened?"

"A deer darted out on the trail and spooked Candy. Maria fell off. I am terribly sorry, Cousin Amelia. It all happened so quickly that there was nothing we could do."

"Have you sent for the doctor?" Lady Standish asked as she made for the door.

"Yes. I sent one of the grooms from the stable."

"Oh dear!" Lady Standish moaned. "What is it about that child that she is always in trouble?"

The door closed behind her.

Alex, who had stood up as soon as Diana entered, now said, "Hello, Dee. It's good to see you again."

The girl's dark brown eyes turned to him. Something flashed in their brilliant depths and then was gone. Her hand touched the back of the sofa. "Hello, Alex," she said. There was a pause. "Or should I call you 'your lordship'?"

He felt himself flush. "I will always be Alex to you. You know that."

She raised a perfect winged brow. "Do I?"

He felt his breathing coming faster than usual.

She had been beautiful at seventeen, but now, at twenty… "You should," he managed to say firmly.

She shrugged, a lissome movement of her slender shoulders. "It's good you've finally come home. Your mother has need of you. Standish Court is an enormous estate. You have responsibilities here."

The brown eyes that were looking at him were cold. He was not accustomed to having Diana look at him like that, and he set his mouth and said quietly, "I realize that. That's why I have come."

"The war is over anyway, is it not?" she said.

"Yes. The allies are ready to enter Paris, and Napoleon will be forced to sign an Act of Abdication one of these days."

Dismissing him from her attention, Diana turned to her mother. "I think I will go back to the stables and check on Candy, Mama. She didn't seem to take any harm, but I want to make sure."

"I'll go with you," Alex said quickly. "I'd like to see what horses you have. Monty is still here, isn't he?"

"Of course. In fact, I have been riding him, so he is in excellent condition."

He turned to Mrs. Sherwood. "Will you excuse us, ma'am?"

She looked from him to her daughter then back again to him. "Of course," she said after the briefest of pauses. "When you are done, return to our house, Diana. I want to finish fitting that new dress of yours."

"All right, Mama," Diana said, and the two young people went out the door.

They didn't speak as they went down the stairs and through the back hall to the door that was closest to the stables. The garden was still mostly bare from the winter and the great fountain with nymphs and cherubs was dry as well. The footpath to the stable led through the garden and down a grassy hill. At the bottom of the hill stood the brick stable building and the stable yard, which was surrounded by a stone wall. In the distance were the fenced-in paddocks where two horses were turned out.

As they passed under the stable arch, Alex finally broke the silence. "I wrote to you many times, but you never once wrote back. Not once, in all those years."

She raised her chin and kept walking. "Did you expect me to? You made your choice, Alex. I said it was either the army or me and you chose the army. It wasn't I who ended things between us, it was you."

He put a hand on her arm, forcing her to stop and face him. "You told me to go."

"It was so obvious that you wanted to go, Alex. I just said the words you wanted to hear. But I never said that I would wait for you."

"But you haven't married," he said.

She shrugged, a typical Diana gesture. "There is no one around here that I want to marry. But I am going to make my come-out with Sally next month and, hopefully, we will both find suitable husbands in London."

He looked down at her. He was two inches over six feet tall and the top of her head reached only to his nose.

He tightened his grip on her arm. "I thought about you all the time I was away. I missed you, Dee. I told you that in my letters."

"I never read them," she said, and pulled away from him and continued on into the stable yard. A tall, broad-shouldered man in his thirties was holding a horse in front of the stable, and his face broke into a huge grin when he saw Alex. "My lord," he said. "You're home!"

Alex forced a smile and went over to Standish Court's head groom. "Yes, Henley, I'm home to stay. How are you? You look well."

"I am very good, thank you, your lordship. We were all that worried about you when we heard you was wounded!"

"It was nothing," Alex said. "It healed very quickly. Miss Sherwood has come to check on the pony that threw my sister and I have come to have a look at the horses."

Henley called to a young boy to come and take the horse he was holding. "Monty is in fine fettle," he said. "Miss Diana has been keeping him fit for you."

"Why don't you show his lordship around the stable and I will take a look at Candy," Diana said.

"Fine!" Henley said enthusiastically.

Alex glanced at Diana but she was not looking at him. After a moment he moved off with Henley.

"We haven't made many changes since your father died," Henley said as they walked down the wide aisle and looked into the light, airy stalls. "We kept his two hunters and Master James and Master Jeremy ride them when they come home from school. The grooms keep them exercised and Miss Diana will take them out occasionally and put them over some jumps. Here is Annie, Miss Diana's horse."

Alex looked into the stall at the tall, rangy bay mare. Strictly speaking, Annie did not belong to Diana. Alex's father had bought the mare from an abusive owner and had allowed Diana to ride her, deeming the mare not good enough for any of his own children.

Alex said, "She must be getting on in years by now."

"She's virtually retired," Henley said. "Miss Diana has been riding Monty lately. Of course, now that you're home…"

"I have a horse coming," Alex said. "The horse I rode in Spain. There's no reason why Miss Diana can't keep riding Monty."

Henley beamed. He had always adored Diana. "You'd think that horse should be too big for her, but he's like butter in her hands. I think she can ride anything, Miss Diana."

They were standing at the stall of a stocky chestnut gelding, who came over to greet them. He looked at Alex with soft eyes.

"This one is new," Alex said.

"He belongs to Lady Sarah. He's a sweetheart."

They continued on down the aisle, looking at the

carriage horses and the ponies that belonged to Alex's two younger sisters, Maria and Margaret. Diana was in the stall with one of the ponies and she came out as they approached.

"There's no heat," she said. "I thought she might have kicked herself when she spooked, but she seems all right."

"She's a feisty little pony," Henley said. "Maybe she's too much for Lady Maria."

"She's new," Alex said. "I don't remember her."

"Maria outgrew her old pony and we got her Candy a few months ago," Diana said. "She was quiet when I looked at her, but she seems to have a habit of spooking."

"Having a deer jump out in front of her would spook most horses," Alex commented.

"True," Diana said. "But there have been other occasions…"

"Remember that hellion of a pony I used to have?" Alex asked.

For the first time a faint smile tilted Diana's lips. "You loved him because he would jump anything."

"He would buck at anything, too."

The smile disappeared from Diana's face. "I hope the horses meet with your approval," she said stiffly.

"Miss Diana has taken charge of the stable since your father died, your lordship," Henley said. "She has made sure that everything runs smoothly."

"I see that I must thank you, Dee," Alex said. "I appreciate your time and effort."

"It was nothing," she said dismissively. "Now I

think we had better return to the house and see what has happened to poor Maria."

She strode down the aisle toward the door and he lingered a moment, watching her slim figure clad in a serviceable riding skirt and a wool jacket. Her red-gold hair caught all the light in the stable.

After a moment, he followed her.

Two

Maria had indeed broken her collarbone and Alex bent to kiss his ten-year-old sister and commiserate with her.

"Have you ever broken your collarbone?" she asked. Her face was white and her blond curls were tumbled.

"No, but I broke my arm once."

"Falling from a horse?"

"Yes. My pony bucked me off."

Maria said, "I don't think I like Candy. She is always jumping at things."

"Then we'll get you another pony," he said promptly.

"She was good when I tried her. It was just when we got her home that she started to act spooky."

"Then she's not the pony for you," he said. "We'll get you something more reliable."

She smiled at him. "Thank you, Alex."

"Maria needs something like my Basil," said Margaret, Alex's twelve-year-old sister. "He's very steady."

"We'll see what we can find," he said.

Alex, Diana, Sally and Margaret were in Maria's room and Maria was in bed, where Lady Standish had insisted she stay for the rest of the afternoon. Maria's left arm was in a sling.

"At least it's your left arm," Margaret said.

"Yes," Maria said glumly. "Jeremy is going to make fun of me when he hears that I fell off and broke my collarbone."

Jeremy was Alex's brother who was at Eton.

"No he won't," Alex said. "I won't let him."

Maria's blue eyes looked hopefully at her eldest brother. "You won't?"

"No."

Maria smiled. "I'm glad you're home, Alex."

"I'm glad I'm home, too," he said.

"I think we should all leave and give Maria a chance to rest," Sally said.

Diana was the first one to turn to the door. She was followed by Margaret, then Sally and lastly Alex. He closed the door behind him gently.

Once they were out in the hall, his eighteen-year-old sister Sally smiled up at him. "We're so glad you're home and that you're safe," she said.

"I'm glad to be home," Alex said for perhaps the dozenth time that day.

"Did Mama tell you that Diana and I are going to make our come-outs next month?" Sally asked.

"Yes, she did."

"You can be our escort, Alex. Perhaps you will even find a girl you want to marry yourself."

Alex's eyes went to Diana. "Perhaps," he said.

Dinner that evening was a festive affair. It was a welcome home dinner for Alex and both Margaret and Maria were allowed to join the family at the table. Diana and her mother were also present. Lady Standish explained to Alex that since his father had died she had invited her cousin Louisa and her daughter to join her for dinner every evening. "It would have been too sad, with just Sally and me."

The Sherwood women lived in a cottage on the Standish estate and had done so for the past eighteen years. Lady Standish had invited her cousin Louisa to make use of the house when her husband had been called to military duty in India. Mr. Sherwood had eventually attained the rank of colonel and after India he had been called to the Peninsula, where he had perished in the Battle of Corunna.

The Sherwoods were not in the same social or financial class as the Earl and Countess of Standish, but because the two women were close friends, the Sherwoods had often taken part in the activities of Standish Court. The earl had been very tolerant of his wife's cousin, but he had been more aware of the gap between the two families than his wife had been. Both women knew that if the earl had been alive, Diana would not have been making her come-out with Sally.

So Alex sat around the table that night with six females. It was a distinct change for a man who for the past three years had known masculine companionship almost exclusively.

"You must sit down with Billings and go over the estate books," Lady Sherwood said to her son as the soup course was served. "I think he is a good man, but your papa was scrupulous about keeping up with all of the estate accounts. I believe there is also something that needs to be done with the property in Derbyshire."

How different my life is going to be, Alex thought. *All my life, all I wanted was to be a soldier. Now that's over and I'm an earl.* He let his eyes roam around the familiar but somehow strange-looking room. Then he looked back at his mother.

"I'll talk to him, Mama," he said.

Lady Standish gave him a grateful smile. "It is so good to have you home, my son."

"Alex said he would get me a new pony, Mama," Maria said. "Candy is too dangerous."

"Good, good," said Lady Standish. "We can't have you breaking your bones, Maria."

"What do you think is going to happen in France, Alex?" Mrs. Sherwood asked.

Alex looked at her. She was still very attractive but she had never been the beauty her daughter was. "We have Napoleon on the ropes, ma'am," he replied. "He is going to have to abdicate."

"Does that mean the king will come back?" Diana asked.

Alex turned his eyes to her. She was dressed in a simple ivory evening dress that set off the pure white of her skin. It gave him a shock of physical pleasure just to look at her. She was even more beautiful than the image he had carried in his heart for all those years. "He said Louis has been waiting patiently in England for this chance for a long time."

"Well, I hope they set up a government more like ours, with a parliament that gives the people some power," Diana said. "It would be a shame for France to have gone through all it has only to end up with the same old Bourbons again."

Alex smiled at her. "Still a revolutionary, eh Dee?"

"I wouldn't call it revolutionary to wish for a governing parliament," Diana replied soberly.

"I don't think France will ever be the same again," Alex said. "The revolution has left its mark, that's for certain."

"Well, I think that's a good thing," Diana replied decidedly.

Sally said, "When do you think we can leave for London, Mama?"

"I would like to have our ball before the end of April," Lady Standish replied. "That means we will have to be in London several weeks earlier, to make plans and to buy clothes."

Sally smiled. She had golden curls and sky-blue eyes like Alex. She said now, "It is going to be such fun, isn't it, Diana?"

Diana smiled back. "Yes, it is."

"What's all this about a ball?" Alex said.

"We must have a ball to introduce the girls to society," his mother said. "You will be the host, of course."

He frowned. "I don't know about this, Mama. I've been away at war for the last three years. I don't know anything about balls."

"You won't have to do a thing," his mother assured him. "Louisa and I will do it all. All you need to do is be there and stand in the receiving line with us. Oh, and dance with each of the girls, of course. And with as many other ladies as you can."

Alex's frown remained. "I had no idea when you called me home that I was going to be thrust into the middle of London's social whirl."

"It is your proper place," his mother said. "You are the head of the family now, Alex. You have responsibilities."

I know I do, he thought a little grimly. *I just didn't think that one of them was going to be to help Dee find a husband.*

The following week was a whirlwind of activity for Alex. His estate agent, John Billings, took him all over the property belonging to Standish Court and pointed out the things that needed to be taken care of. His banker came from London and spent many hours going over his assets and encumbrances.

The late Lord Standish had been a prudent man and the estate was in good financial order. His mother had a widow's jointure and use of the dower house should she want it. His brothers and sisters were Alex's responsibility, but there was ample money to fund the boys' educations and the girls' come-outs into society.

In fact, Alex was a very wealthy man.

Mr. Billings had a few pet projects—like a canal on the Derbyshire estate—that he had been trying to get the late earl to invest in, and he brought them up to Alex, who put him off, promising to think about them.

Alex drove over to Oxford and Eton to visit his two younger brothers, who each managed to cadge ten pounds off of him.

By the end of the week, the whole family was as comfortable with Alex as if he had never gone away. Everyone, that is, except Diana.

He had tried numerous times to be alone with her, but she had not cooperated. She didn't want to take a ride with him; she didn't want to take a walk out to the lake with him; she didn't even want to go with him to look at a new pony for Maria.

It was very frustrating.

He even stooped to trying to stir up a little sympathy from her by remarking that the damp weather was bothering his wound. She simply gave him a brilliant, dark-eyed stare. "What a shame," she said, and walked away.

It didn't help that she was so beautiful, that every time he saw her he wanted to catch her in his arms and kiss her until she couldn't breathe. It was quite clear to him, however, that such an action would only alienate her further.

* * *

"Why are you so angry at Alex?" Sally asked Diana suddenly one afternoon as the girls were sitting side by side in the Yellow Drawing Room looking at magazines of the latest styles in clothing.

Diana felt a stab of alarm. "I'm not angry at him. Whatever gave you that idea?"

"Well, you're very short with him, that's for certain. And he is trying to be so nice to you. It's not like you, Diana, not to be friendly. Especially to Alex."

"I'm friendly," Diana said defensively. She couldn't meet Sally's honest gaze so she kept her eyes on her magazine.

"No, you're not. Look at me, Diana. What's wrong?"

Diana looked up, her brown eyes meeting Sally's sky-blue gaze. The two girls were very close, and it was difficult for Diana to fib.

"Nothing is wrong," Diana said crisply. "You're imagining things, Sally. It's just that my mind is on things other than Alex right now. I'm very excited about our London come-out."

Pretty color flushed into Sally's cheeks. She was a lovely girl, the picture of innocent girlhood poised on the brink of becoming a woman. She had been allowed this last year to attend one or two local assemblies and house parties where she had encountered young men, but her experiences had not given her any hint of sophistication.

"I'm excited about it, too," she said. "It will be so different from our usual life here at Standish Court."

"I know," Diana said. She tried to focus her mind on their upcoming London visit. "Cousin Amelia says that there are places to ride. Hyde Park is evidently a popular venue. We will need horses. I wonder if Alex knows which ones he is going to bring."

"Ask him," Sally urged. "You will be miserable if you can't ride."

"I know."

"Then ask him. You know Mama is leaving the horses up to Alex. Find out from him what he is going to do."

Later that afternoon, Diana had an opportunity to ask Alex this important question. They were both at the stable at the same time. Diana was lunging Candy when a carriage came in with a jet-black horse tied behind it. Shortening up the lunge line, Diana went over to look at the black horse, which was standing quietly looking around him.

He was a large animal, with a beautiful arched neck, short back and long, strong-looking legs.

Henley came out of the stable and went over to the carriage. "This must be his lordship's horse from the Peninsula," he said to the driver.

"That's right," the driver answered. "This is Black Bart. I've brought him all the way from Bordeaux."

"I'll send to the house to tell his lordship you are here," Henley said.

While they waited for Alex, Diana introduced

herself to Black Bart. He took the piece of carrot she offered and pricked his ears forward when she began to talk to him. Then, once they were acquainted, she proceed to run her hands down his legs and over his nicely sloping shoulders.

"Bart!" It was Alex's voice. "How are you, fellow? I've missed you!"

The horse nickered when he heard the familiar voice. Alex went over to rub his forehead and scratch under his mane in a place he clearly liked.

Diana said, "He's a beautiful horse, Alex."

He turned his head to grin at her. "He saved my bacon a few times, I can tell you that. Unlike many cavalry horses who simply gallop forward out of control, Bart always listened to me." He turned back to the gelding. "You're a good boy, aren't you fellow?"

Bart tossed his head in reply.

Alex turned to Henley. "Is his stall ready?"

"Aye, my lord. We've had it ready for several days now."

The sun glinted off the black of the horse's coat and the black of Alex's hair as he took the rope that had tied the horse to the carriage, turned him and began to lead him toward the barn.

Diana followed.

Once Bart had been established in his stall with a bucket of fresh water and a pile of hay, Alex turned away from the door and for the first time seemed to notice Diana's presence.

"So you like him, Dee?" he asked.

"Very much." She began to walk out of the barn with him. "Have you decided what horses you are bringing to London with you?"

They had left the stable yard and followed the path back to the house. "I will have the carriage horses, of course, and I will bring horses for you and Sally to ride. And I'll bring Bart for me."

"Do you think you could bring Monty for me?" Diana asked a little breathlessly. "Annie is basically retired. She's lame more often than she's not."

He frowned. "Monty's all right in the country, but can you trust him in the city, with all the traffic? He's never been in a city in his life."

"I'm sure he'll be all right," Diana said.

"Perhaps we would be better off buying you a horse accustomed to London. I can always go to Tattersalls and pick you up a good riding horse."

"I'd rather have Monty," Diana insisted. "I have grown very fond of him since you left. I ride him almost every day."

He stopped and regarded her with lifted black brows. "So you took over my horse, eh?"

"You left him," she said, her beautiful lips set into a grim line. "You didn't care what happened to him."

He kept looking at her, then he turned and began to walk again. "I left him in my father's stable, where no horse has ever been neglected. I had no worry that he would be mistreated. Moreover, I knew from Sally that you were riding him."

It was stupid to alienate him, she thought. Not when she wanted this favor from him. "He's like my own horse," she said in a softer voice. "Please, Alex, if you're not going to bring him for yourself, bring him for me. I'm looking forward to going to London, but if I can't ride I shall be miserable."

"Very well," he said abruptly. "I'll take Monty."

She drew in her breath audibly. "Thank you," she said.

He nodded and they continued their walk. After a minute of silence, he said, "You don't have to go to London to find a husband, you know. You can marry me."

She had spent her whole girlhood thinking she would marry Alex. But that was all changed now. "That's good of you," she said expressionlessly, "but it's too late, Alex."

"You're only twenty and I'm twenty-two! How can it be too late?"

All of the anger and pain and feelings of abandonment bubbled up inside her and this time she couldn't push them back down. She turned on him passionately. "It was too late the day you made your decision to go into the army," she said angrily. "That was the day you killed whatever it was that I felt for you."

He caught her arm and held her facing him. "I can't believe that's true."

She stared down at his hand and slowly he opened his fingers and let her go.

"Believe it," she said, as she turned and walked away. "Because it's the truth."

Three

It was several days since the shock of seeing Alex again had caused Diana to jump and her breath to accelerate. When he had called her *Dee*...no one else in this world had ever called her Dee. It was a symbol of the bond between them, that name.

But as the time passed, and the unexpectedness of seeing him began to wear off, she found herself more able to steel herself when she was in his presence. He was busy about the estate and she often didn't see him until dinnertime. There, surrounded by the rest of the family, it was easier to be cool and composed, to let herself pretend that she was indifferent to him.

She *wanted* to be indifferent to him. Whatever had been between them had been irrevocably severed three years ago, when he had chosen to leave her. She believed that firmly. What she had felt then, and what had happened to her after his departure, was a chasm between them that could never be bridged.

He showed me how unimportant I was to him, she told herself. *Now that he is home he thinks he can pick up right where he left off. Well, he can't. I don't need him. I don't need to marry a wealthy earl. I need to marry a steady sort of man with a comfortable income, someone who I can rely on, someone who will be a good father to my children. Someone who will be there when I need him. Not like Alex.*

Diana was very aware that she and her mother lived on the edge of poverty. If it had not been for Lady Standish providing them with a home and some social standing, she would have grown up in rented rooms in a city like Bath. Her father had been the younger son of a squire and the only money he had was his army pay. After he died, the Sherwoods had lived on a tiny pension, supplemented by the piano lessons that Mrs. Sherwood gave to local children. It was only because of Louisa Sherwood's connection to Lady Standish that Diana had had the opportunity to ride horses and go to parties.

This opportunity to make a come-out in London was a godsend to her. She knew she had to marry. The thought of spending the rest of her life hanging on Alex's generosity made her shudder. She knew a good marriage wasn't going to be easy for a penniless girl like her. But she was aware of her beauty and she thought that in all of London there must be at least one good man who would find her beautiful enough, and personable enough, to want to marry her.

Sally would attract earls and viscounts; Diana was not foolish enough to expect that kind of attention. What she wanted was a nice, solid man, a house in the country, with dogs and horses and children. Surely that was not too much to hope for.

She only wished that Alex was not coming with them.

A few weeks after Alex's return, an invitation arrived from Viscountess Alston asking the Devizes and the Sherwoods to a small party she was having at Reeve House. The Alstons lived some seven miles away from Standish Court and were the nearest neighbors of their own social standing. Alex's father had been friends with Viscount Alston and when the earl was alive the two families had often socialized. Lady Standish accepted the invitation for herself and the Sherwoods.

"I'm sure they want to see you, Alex," Lady Standish said as they discussed the invitation over dinner that night. Instead of eating in the huge formal dining room, the family usually dined in the smaller family eating room that was much cozier than the elegant perfection that Adam had created in the main room.

"Is it to be just us and the Alstons?" he asked.

"I gather from Phoebe's note that she has asked a few other people from the neighborhood. You know we have never stood on ceremony in the country, Alex. I'm sure Dr. Lawrence will be there, and probably the squire. And Sir Burton Nable, as well."

"I hope Ned comes," Alex said. "I've been meaning to go and see him."

Sir Burton's son Ned had been a good friend of Alex's when the boys were young. Ned had also gone to the Peninsula, but he had not been as lucky as Alex. He had been in an infantry regiment and had lost the lower part of his left leg at Salamanca.

"I would be surprised if Ned were not there," Mrs. Sherwood said. "He is engaged to be married, Alex. Do you remember Lizzie Carruthers?"

"Yes. Good heavens, is Lizzie old enough to be married?"

"She's eighteen, the same age as I am," Sally said.

"It's strange, but when you're away you picture people staying the way they were when last you saw them," Alex said, his eyes on Diana. "You don't picture them as changing at all."

"Everybody changes," Diana replied. "And three years is a long time. I'm certainly not the same person at twenty that I was at seventeen, when you went away."

"I've noticed that," he said.

When dinner was ended they all retired upstairs to the music room, where Sally entertained them on the piano. She was very good and the others sat quietly and listened with pleasure to the strains of Mozart. Alex watched Diana, who was seated on a sofa next to her mother.

The curve of her cheekbones held great sweetness and the large, dark eyes in that fair-skinned face were marvelously arresting. Her mouth was perfect. Not too thin, not too full—just perfect.

She had a right to be angry with him. He knew that. He had had to choose between staying home for her or fulfilling his lifelong dream of being a soldier. He had chosen the latter. At nineteen, the dream had exerted a more powerful fascination than she had.

If he had known then what he knew now about war, he wondered if he would have made the same choice.

As if she had felt his gaze, she turned her head to look at him. For the briefest of moments something powerful flared between them. Then she frowned, looked down to smooth her skirt and returned her gaze to Sally.

She's not indifferent to me, Alex thought over his thudding heart. *No matter what she might say, something's still left of what was once between us. I'm sure of it. Perhaps I haven't lost her after all. If I'm just patient enough…*

The music stopped and Lady Standish said to her daughter, "That was lovely, dear."

Sally turned around on the piano seat and smiled at her audience. Everyone clapped.

Lady Standish said, "Let's move into the Yellow Drawing Room for tea."

On the night of the Alston's party, Lady Standish decreed that they should all ride in the Standish coach.

"There is no reason for you to have to freeze

driving an open carriage, Alex," she said to her son. "You can squeeze in with Sally and Diana. After all, we aren't going far."

Alex, who liked the idea of squeezing in with Diana, did not argue with his mother's pronouncement.

So it was that the five people assembled on the drive in front of the house to get into the elegant, well-sprung Standish carriage. Lady Standish and Mrs. Sherwood got in first, sitting on one side of the carriage, then Lady Standish beckoned to her son to follow her.

Alex climbed in and seated himself by the far window opposite to his mother and Mrs. Sherwood. Outside he heard Sally say, "Would you mind if I had the window seat, Diana? You know I am prone to motion sickness."

There was a distinct pause, then Diana said, "Of course, Sally."

Alex watched as Diana climbed into the carriage and sat beside him. She left a good amount of space between the two of them, but when Sally joined them she was forced to move closer.

Alex put his arm along the back of the seat, as if to make more room. It was dark inside the carriage, but he could feel the closeness of her body with every cell in his own. His body stirred. He hadn't been this close to her since he had been home.

"There now, that's not too bad, is it?" Lady Standish said cheerfully.

"It's fine, Mama," Sally said.

Diana was silent.

After a moment, the carriage started forward.

"I'm glad it's a nice clear night," Lady Standish said. "I dislike driving at night in the rain. I'm always afraid William will drive us off the road. He's getting old and I don't think he sees that well in the dark."

"Good heavens, Mama," Alex said. "Why on earth are you employing a coachman who can't see in the dark?"

"Your father was going to retire him, but I just couldn't bring myself to tell him. He's been with us for so many years…"

"Well, he can't keep his job if he can't see," Alex said reasonably. "There's an empty cottage next to where Nanny lives. I'll give him a nice pension. They can be retired together."

Lady Standish sighed. "You're right, of course. I suppose I just didn't want any more changes after your father died."

"Poor William," Diana said mournfully. "What will he do with himself if he can't drive the coach?"

"He can fish," Alex said. "He always went fishing on his day off. He taught me a thing or two about catching fish when I was small."

"I didn't know William fished," Sally said.

"Fancy that," Lady Standish said.

"We'll find someone younger to replace him, Mama," Alex said. "You'll be more comfortable with a man you're not afraid is going to put you in a ditch."

"Thank you, Alex," Lady Standish said.

"Poor William," Diana repeated softly.

"William will be fine," Alex said firmly, "and his job can be filled by one of the men who are coming home from the war. There are many ex-soldiers in need of a job and there will be many more once Napoleon is deposed. There are not nearly enough jobs to accommodate the numbers that will be thrown on the economy. I foresee hard times for many good men and their families."

Silence fell on the coach until they drew up at the front door of Reeve House. All the windows were lit and a footman was there to assist the occupants out of the carriage.

Alex followed the ladies into the front hall where their wraps and coats were taken by another footman. Then they were escorted upstairs to the large formal drawing room where a group of people had already gathered.

A woman dressed in a green evening gown and a man wearing the same formal clothes as Alex—a black tail coat, buff pantaloons, silk stockings and black pumps—came to greet them. "Amelia, my dear. How lovely to see you," Lady Alston said. "And Louisa, too. And your girls."

The ladies responded appropriately, then Lady Standish said to Lord and Lady Alston, "And here is Alex, newly returned from the Peninsula."

"We have prayed for your safety," Lady Alston said, taking Alex's hand and holding it tightly.

"Thank you, ma'am. I appreciate that," Alex said. Lord Alston took Alex's hand from his wife and shook it hard. "Good to see you, my boy," he said. "Your father was very proud of you."

"Thank you, sir," Alex said. "I am only sorry that I didn't have a chance to see him before he died."

"He understood. He followed the campaign closely, you know. We both did. And he appreciated your letters."

"Well, come along in, and meet our other guests," Lady Alston said gaily. "It is something to celebrate, having you home again."

Alex knew most of the people at the party. He was particularly pleased to see his friend Ned Nable there and the two young men went into a corner to talk. Their sober expressions were in contrast to the gaiety of the rest of the room.

Alex came back to awareness of the party when he heard the piano. For the first time he noticed that the rug had been rolled back. Evidently there was going to be dancing.

It was immediately obvious to Alex that every man in the room wanted to dance with Diana. The doctor moved the fastest and the two of them held hands to join in the circle for a Scottish reel.

"Dance with Lizzie, would you?" Ned said. "The poor girl doesn't get many dances with an amputee for a fiancé."

"I would be delighted to dance with Lizzie," Alex said, and took the hand of Ned's future wife.

In the course of the dance he managed to touch hands with Diana once or twice, which was as close as he got to her for most of the evening. He danced with his mother, with his hostess, even with Sally, but every time he tried to approach Diana she was giving her hand to another man.

He finally grabbed her when she was coming out of the ladies' retiring room. "It will look strange if you don't dance with me," he said. "Everyone here knows we used to be good friends. Do you want to start gossip?"

She glared up at him, her dark eyes stormy. Tonight she was wearing her hair high on the back of her head, with little tendrils falling down her neck. "Oh, all right," she huffed. "Let's get it over with."

She marched into the drawing room and gave him her hand without looking at him. He closed his hand around hers, feeling the long elegant fingers that were so gentle on the mouth of a horse. He held her hand more tightly than was necessary and she shot him a look but didn't say anything. The music started and the circle they were part of began to move.

It was frustrating, to be so close to her yet feel that she was so far away. When the dance finished he went back to join Ned, who was sitting on a sofa with Lizzie.

"Don't tell me you're tired?" Lizzie teased.

He smiled at her. "No. I'm just resting after the triumph of finally having won a dance with Miss Sherwood."

"She's had a proposal from every unattached man in this room," Lizzie said cheerfully. "But I hear she's going to London. She'll probably make a much better match there."

She's refused all of these men, Alex thought. *Surely that's a good sign.*

His eyes rested on his sister. He didn't have to ask whether or not Sally had received any offers. There was no chance in the world that an earl's daughter would marry the country doctor.

The music had stopped and servants were coming in with a tea tray. Alex went to get his cup and looked forward to the ride home, when he would be sitting close beside Diana.

Four

Despite feeling tired when she got into bed after the party, Diana couldn't fall asleep. Her mind was on Alex and, as she lay there on her back, her arm across her forehead, her mind drifted back to the day that they first had met.

She was seven years old when she came to live in the cottage on the grounds of Standish Court. She had come in June and Alex had been home from Eton. She remembered the confusion of the move, the anguished realization that her father was going far away and the pain of separation from the pony she had been riding at their last house. He had belonged to the local squire, who had allowed Diana to ride him as his son had outgrown him.

She had been immensely intimidated by the move. What was going to happen to her in such a place? At her old home she had had her father, her dog, her mother and her pony. Here, at Standish, there was only Mama, as her dog had died a few months previously. And Mama kept telling her how nice she must be to Lord and Lady Standish for letting them stay in this cottage.

It was a nice cottage, much larger and airier than their last house, but just down the road was the immenseness of Standish Court, where lived this aristocratic family to whom she had to be so grateful.

She remembered the first afternoon they were invited to take tea at Standish. Mama had dressed her in her best dress and they had waited for the trap that the countess was sending to pick them up. They were driven to the palace—for that is what it looked like to Diana—and taken through fabulous rooms hung with mirrors and paintings and decorated with classical statues, to a large sitting room where Lady Standish waited for them, with her five-year-old daughter at her side.

Diana had watched as Mama and Lady Standish exchanged hugs and kisses. Then Lady Standish had bent to her. "And this is Diana," she said. "What a pretty girl you are. I am your mother's cousin, Amelia. Would you like to give me a kiss?"

Obediently, Diana kissed the soft cheek of her mother's cousin.

"And this is your cousin, Sally."

Sally was a blue-eyed, blond-haired cherub. She smiled at Diana. "Hello," she said.

"Hello," Diana replied.

Everyone settled down. The tea tray was brought, and lemonade for Sally and Diana.

Lady Standish said apologetically, "Alex was supposed to be here. I can't imagine what is keeping him."

On that note, the door opened and a boy dressed in riding clothes came in. He had black hair and sky-blue eyes and he said politely to his mother, "I'm sorry I'm late, Mama. I got delayed in the stable."

Lady Standish sighed. "You're always in the stable, Alex. Can't you find something else to do?"

"Nothing that I like as much," he said.

Diana was immediately drawn to the boy. "Do you have a lot of horses in your stable?" she asked him.

He looked at her. "Yes," he said.

How wonderful, she thought.

"If you need any help exercising them, I'd be happy to help," she said. "I used to exercise the squire's son's pony when we lived at home."

He looked her up and down. "How old are you?"

"I'm almost eight. And I can ride anything."

The boy's black eyebrows shot up. "I doubt that."

"I can!" she shot back. "The squire used to say that I was the best natural rider he'd ever seen!"

"Diana," her mother chided gently. "Don't brag, darling. It's not becoming."

"It's not bragging, it's true," she insisted. "He did say that, Mama. Truly he did."

The boy's blue eyes narrowed. "Well, we'll see about that," he said.

"You can ride my pony, Diana," Sally said. "He is very sweet."

Diana gave Sally a radiant smile. "Thank you."

After that the two ladies talked and the children drank their lemonade and ate cake from the tea tray. Then a big man with graying black hair and ordinary blue eyes came into the room.

That must be the earl, Diana thought.

"My lord," Lady Standish said with pleasure. "I wasn't sure you would be able to join us."

He smiled. "Of course I wanted to be here to greet Mrs. Sherwood and her daughter. We are very glad to have you at Standish, ma'am."

Diana's mother's cheeks were flushed. "Thank you, my lord. I cannot tell you how much we appreciate your generosity."

"Not at all," he said. "The cottage was just lying there empty. Happy to have it used."

Diana looked at the earl curiously. When it came her turn to be introduced, she curtseyed and smiled at the large man who was suddenly so important in her life. He smiled back and called her a very pretty little girl. People had been calling Diana a very pretty little girl ever since she could remember, so it made little impression on her. She looked from the earl to his son. Alex looked like his father, except for his extraordinary eye color.

Diana was conscious of Alex looking at her and she looked boldly back. She had every intention of pushing him to allow her to ride Sally's pony.

When the tea was over, and the Sherwoods stood to leave, Diana went over to Alex and asked, "When can I come to ride the pony?"

He stared down at her. "Come tomorrow morning. We'll go for a ride together so I can see how *brilliant* you are." There was a definite sarcastic note in his voice.

The following morning Diana rose early and dressed in her riding habit, which consisted of a brown divided skirt and an old brown jacket. She fastened her hair at the nape of her neck and set off for Standish on foot. It was only a little under two miles and she walked it in good time. When she reached the stable yard Alex was just coming in riding a solid-looking chestnut gelding. Diana's face fell.

"I thought you said we would go riding together today!" she accused him.

"How did you get here?" he asked.

"I walked."

He looked at her feet. "In your boots?"

"Yes."

He looked her up and down, taking in her divided skirt. "Do you ride astride?"

"Yes. The squire's groom who taught me said it would be safer for me to learn that way."

"All right," he said briskly. "We'll give you a chance." He turned to one of the grooms. "Danny, bring out Lady Sarah's pony. And don't put a side-saddle on him."

Diana could feel her heart begin to beat harder. She had to impress this boy so he would allow her to ride his horses. Her heart fell when a very small, thick-bodied pony was led out of the stable. "He's so little," she said involuntarily.

"Sally is little," Alex said.

Diana bit her lip and didn't say anything else. She didn't think it was going to be much fun riding Sally's pony.

"His name is Moses," Alex said. "Come along over to the riding ring so I can judge your riding style."

Diana followed him beyond the stable to an enclosed ring with a smooth dirt surface. Alex opened the gate and led the pony in. Diana followed.

"Do you need help getting into the saddle?" he asked.

She cast him a scornful look. "No." She put her foot in the stirrup and swung up. There wasn't very far to go. The squire's pony had been a full hand taller than Moses.

"Just ride him around the rail and let me see how you do," Alex said. She cast him a disgusted look. How was she supposed to show her riding skills on a pony that was much too small for her?

She put the pony on the rail and closed her legs to send him forward. He ambled off. Diana frowned and pressed her legs harder. He went from an amble into a walk. They went around the enclosure once and Diana said to Alex, "I need a whip."

He got her one. She squeezed her legs again and applied the whip smartly behind her leg. The pony broke into a trot. She pushed him some more. After two more rounds she had him trotting forward. In another round she had him going before her leg.

"Stop!" Alex called.

Obediently, she halted, then walked over to where he was standing outside the fence. He was grinning. "I've never seen that pony move so fast."

"He certainly doesn't want to move," Diana returned. "The squire's pony was a speed demon compared with this one."

"Sally likes him. He's a good beginner pony. He will just follow along when we go out on the trails and she never has to worry about him doing something stupid."

"Doing something stupid would take too much energy," Diana said scornfully.

"You're a good rider," Alex said. "But you're too small to ride our horses. You'd be like a fly on top of them. You have no body or legs to hold them."

Diana's heart sank. She wasn't going to be able to ride. She looked at him, her eyes tragic.

"There's my old pony," he offered. "I talked Papa into keeping him for Sally to grow into, but he's been doing nothing ever since I got my new horse. He might be a bit of a handful."

Her eyes sparkled. "I won't mind that. I'll straighten him out."

"Let me ride him for a few days, to get the kinks out of him. Then we'll try you on him."

"What's his name?" Diana asked eagerly.

"Jonathan. He's a grand pony. I was sorry when I outgrew him."

Diana smiled. "Thank you, Alex. If I couldn't ride I think I would just wither away and die."

He looked back at her. "It means that much to you?"

"Yes."

He smiled. "You're a great girl, Diana. I think we're going to get along just fine."

Diana flung her arm off her forehead and rolled over on her side. What was the point of going over old times? The past was the past. It was true that she and Alex had become companions, riding out together every morning. He had friends in the neighborhood, but he didn't despise her company when he had nothing else to do.

She had adored him. He was two years older than she, and a boy. She'd looked up to him and admired him and felt honored whenever he sought out her company. Sally, at five, was too young for her. She'd dreaded the day when he would be going back to school.

I fell in love with him when I was seven years old, she thought now as she lay restless in her bed. *It wasn't fair. He was the only friend I had. I didn't have a chance.*

Well my eyes are opened now. I might have loved him, but he didn't love me. Not really. If he had truly loved me he never would have left me to go into the army.

She curled up into a ball and finally she fell asleep.

The next two weeks were busy as Lady Standish made ready to move her household to London. True to his word, Alex retired William, who was not at all adverse to the idea of being the master of his own time in a snug little cottage close to a good fishing stream, and Alex found a younger replacement, an ex-soldier who had been wounded and retired from the Peninsula army. Thomas lacked the smooth, finished manners of their old coachman, but he was an excellent driver.

The butler, Henrys, would be coming with them to London, as would the cook, Lady Standish's personal maid, the young maid who helped to look after Sally, and Alex's valet, who had come back from the Peninsula with him. As Alex was bringing three riding horses as well as the carriage horses, several grooms would be accompanying them as well. Margaret and Maria were staying at home with their governess, Lady Standish not wanting the children underfoot while she was so preoccupied.

The Sherwoods had far fewer encumbrances than did the Devizes. In fact, they had only one trunk that was filled with all their clothes.

On the morning that they started out for London, there were five carriages—two for the family plus three hired vehicles to carry the servants and the luggage. Alex drove his father's phaeton, an open, high-wheeled carriage with room for two or three people on the front seat. He had asked Diana if she would like to ride with him, but she had told him to take Sally.

"She gets sick if she travels for too long inside a carriage. She will do better in the phaeton," she said. "I, on the other hand, prefer to ride in the comfort of the carriage."

He had acquiesced and so had the chance to spend several hours in the sole company of his sister. She had written to him faithfully during the three years that he was in the Peninsula and had been his chief source of information about Diana. He thought he would use this chance to pump her for as much information as he could get about her best friend.

"Is Mama footing the bill for Dee's come-out?" he asked bluntly after they had finished driving through the village.

"Of course," Sally said. "There is no way Cousin Louisa could afford such a thing herself. Papa wouldn't have done it. He liked Diana, but he felt he was doing enough by housing her and her mother. But Mama and Cousin Louisa are very close—and have become even closer since Papa died."

"So it was Mama's idea to bring Diana out with you."

"Actually it was my idea," Sally said. She tied her bonnet a little more tightly against the wind. "It will be much more fun for me if Diana is with me—she has a way of making the world around her seem brighter, more exciting. And she's not a bit shy—like I am."

"It was nice of you, Sal," he said soberly. "Not every girl would want to be compared to Diana." He turned his head and smiled at her. "But you have turned into a very beautiful girl, yourself."

Sally blushed. "Thank you, Alex. My only real

worry is that Mama said that Diana's lack of money would limit the number of men who would ask for her."

Alex felt a little relieved by this assessment. The fewer rivals he had, the better.

Sally shook her head. "I don't agree with Mama, though. I think Diana has a very good chance of catching a rich man who won't need her money. She is so very beautiful, you know. And besides that, she's *fun*."

Alex frowned.

"You used to be such good friends," Sally continued. "Then you went off to war and she hardly mentioned your name the whole time you were gone. And now that you're home, you still don't talk."

"She was angry with me for joining the army," Alex said stiffly. He was staring straight ahead, over his horses' backs. "I hardly think I should be punished for serving my country."

"I think it's because of her father," Sally mused. "She never forgave him for going away and leaving her and her mother. Life hasn't been easy for them, Alex. If it wasn't for Mama, I don't know what would have become of them."

"He was a soldier," Alex said. "He had to follow orders."

"Yes. That's precisely why Diana doesn't like soldiers." She put a brief hand on his knee. "Give her time, Alex. She'll get over her anger once she gets used to having you around again."

"Hmmph," Alex said.

"I have to confess that I'm a little nervous about this come-out business," Sally said.

They were crossing over a wooden bridge and the horses' hooves thudded hollowly on the boards. "Why?" he said with surprise. "You'll be one of the belles of the season, Sal. You're so pretty and you're the daughter—well, I suppose you're now the sister—of the Earl of Standish. The Devizes are one of the best families in the country. Men will be lining up to marry you."

"But what if I don't love anybody, Alex? I don't want to get married just for the sake of getting married. I want to marry a man I love!"

He tapped one of the horses lightly on the flank to encourage him to move up. "There's nothing wrong with that," he said. "No one will try to push you into a marriage you don't like, Sal. If you don't meet anybody this season, then you can come back next year and try again."

She gave him a smile of relief. "I'm glad to hear you say that," she said. "Mama sounds so determined to push me off…"

"All mothers want brilliant matches for their daughters. But if you want to hold out for love, you do that, Sal."

She straightened her shoulders. "I will," she said.

Five

Diana had never been to London, and she stared out the window as the carriage rolled along the busy streets of the nation's capital. There was so much traffic! And noise! And dirt! She was used to her quiet little corner of Berkshire; London was a big change.

The Devizes' London residence was a solid, substantial house made of brown brick and red dressing, like many of the other houses on the fashionable Grosvenor Square. The family and servants piled out of the coaches and phaeton and Diana stretched her legs and her back as she stood on the pavement outside the front door of the house. She was not accustomed to sitting still for such a long period of time and she felt like taking a nice brisk walk to loosen up her muscles. But the rest of the family was already moving toward the front door, and she followed.

Alex, Lady Standish, Sally, Mrs. Sherwood and Diana all trooped into the green marble entrance hall. The housekeeper came running to welcome Lady Standish and while the two women were talking, Diana peered into a small anteroom set off by round columns that opened off the right side of the entrance hall. The floor of the anteroom was done in black and white squares of marble and there was a portrait of a man in a white wig hung over the alabaster fireplace.

Henrys now came in the front door and Lady Standish presented the butler to Mrs. Daughtry, the housekeeper, as if she was presenting royalty. Henrys was followed by the cook, Monsieur Lapierre, who was presented as if he were God.

Mrs. Daughtry volunteered to show Henrys and Lapierre to their respective domains but Lady Standish said that the family would establish themselves without assistance.

"Let us all go to our bedrooms first," Lady Standish said. "I think we need to freshen up."

"Good idea, Mama," Alex said, and Diana found herself following everyone down the passage to the great curving staircase. The staircase was painted white, with a polished wood railing, and in the roof above the third story was a large window, which allowed for natural illumination during the day.

The bedrooms were on the third floor, except for the master bedroom suite. When they had reached the second floor, Lady Standish said, "Alex, you should have the earl's bedroom now."

He looked a little uncomfortable. "It is not necessary for you to vacate it, Mama," he said. "I don't want to push you out of your room."

"No, I want you to have it," she insisted. "It is the right thing to do and I shall be perfectly happy in the yellow bedroom. It has a dressing room attached and is exceedingly comfortable."

He stood for a moment looking at her and frowning.

"I mean it," Lady Standish said firmly. "You must take your proper place both in the family and in society. The master bedroom is yours."

"Well…" Alex said slowly. "If you are sure."

"I am very sure."

Alex nodded and went off through the second-floor drawing room while the rest of them climbed the stairs to the third floor. Lady Standish opened the first door that was on their left and said to Diana, "This will be your room, dear. Servants will be coming shortly with water for you to wash up."

"Thank you, Cousin Amelia," Diana said, and walked into the largest bedroom she had ever occupied. It had blue-painted walls, a white stucco fireplace and a blue Turkish rug on the floor. The bed was large and hung with blue draperies, and a comfortable-looking upholstered chair was pulled up in front of the fireplace. There were two windows set high in the walls so they could let light in over the top of the building next door.

Diana thought of her closet-size bedroom at home. My goodness, but she had come up in the world!

She was still staring around her when a knock came at the door and her mother came in. "I am right next door," she said. "Aren't these beautiful rooms?"

"They're wonderful," Diana said. "This one even has its own watercloset!"

"So does mine," Mrs. Sherwood said with a smile.

Diana sat on the bed. "This almost seems too good to be true. Cousin Amelia is like a fairy godmother, doing this for me."

Mrs. Sherwood went over to look at a pretty china statue of a shepherdess that reposed on a table along the wall. "It is amazingly generous of her," she agreed. "But then she has always been so good to us."

"She's never spent so much money on us before." Diana looked at her mother, who was still examining the delicate figurine. "It's really Alex's money she's using, isn't it?" she said abruptly. "If the earl was alive, she wouldn't be doing this."

Mrs. Sherwood turned to face her daughter. "I don't know where the money is coming from, my love. But if it is Alex's, he certainly has put forward no objections."

Diana's jaw set. "I hate to be beholden to Alex."

Mrs. Sherwood's pretty face became suddenly somber. "Perhaps he thinks he owes you something, darling," she said. "And perhaps he does."

Diana's eyes flashed and color stained the porcelain skin over her cheekbones. "If I was starving, I wouldn't take a scrap of bread from Alex," she declared.

Mrs. Sherwood came over to sit next to her daughter on the bed. "Don't be foolish, darling. This come-out is a godsend for you. Particularly since you turned down all the nice men who offered for you at home."

Diana scowled. "I didn't love any of them, Mama."

"Diana…" Mrs. Sherwood put her hand up and turned her daughter's face toward her. "I hope you are not still setting your heart on Alex."

Diana pulled her face away and jumped up from the bed. She whirled to face her mother. "Didn't you just hear me, Mama? I wouldn't take Alex if he were the last man left alive on this earth. Believe me, I have no desire to become the Countess of Standish."

"I am glad to hear that," Mrs. Sherwood said quietly. "But if he is financing our trip to London, then it behooves us both to be nice to him. I want you to make a good marriage, darling. I don't want you to have to spend your life hanging on the sleeve of a generous relative. I want to see you with your husband and children at your side. I don't want you to be alone in life. I want you to be happy."

"Oh Mama." Diana came back to the bed and hugged her mother, pressing her cheek against her mother's hair. "You have had so little in your life. Papa left us when I was so young—why you have practically been a widow for all your life."

Mrs. Sherwood's arms came up to hold Diana. "He had no choice, darling. He had to go where he could get advancement. We had no money beyond his officer's salary."

The two women stayed like that for a few moments, and then Diana stepped back. Diana said, "And now we have no money beyond his pension."

Mrs. Sherwood looked up at her daughter. "You have been given a wonderful opportunity to make a good match, darling. Don't alienate Alex and throw it away. Please."

Diana drew a deep breath. "All right, Mama. I promise I will be nice to Alex."

"Thank you, dear."

Diana sat on the bed, staring into space long after her mother had left the room.

It had been late in the afternoon when the Standish party arrived, and after dinner everyone stayed at home except Alex. "Papa was a member of Brooks, and I thought I'd have a look in and see what I have to do to establish my credentials," he said. Brooks was the club most often patronized by the aristocrats of the Whig party, and the Standishes had always been Whigs.

Lady Standish frowned. "A great deal of gambling goes on at Brooks," she warned her son. "Several men have lost their entire fortunes at play there."

He smiled at her. "Don't worry, Mama. I am not stupid enough to do that."

"I know you aren't, Alex. But be careful, please."

Alex knew that his grandfather had almost beggared his family with gambling and consequently Lady Standish had a deep-rooted fear of gaming of any kind.

"I'll be careful," he promised. "And my presence will spread the word that you ladies are in town. You want invitations, don't you?"

Lady Standish agreed that they did, and Alex went off.

Diana was so excited to be in London that she didn't expect to sleep well, but she went right off. When she woke the sun was shining in her window. A young maid came in with a cup of hot chocolate for her to drink while she was getting dressed.

"Thank you," Diana said. The girl reminded her of a kitten, her brow was wide and her face tapered to a small, pointed chin. "What is your name?"

"Nancy, miss," the young girl replied.

"It is nice to meet you, Nancy," Diana said. "Are you one of the new hires?"

"Yes, miss. I'm just come to Lunnon from Derbyshire."

"This must be a big change for you. I know it's a big change for me to come from the country to the city."

"That it is, miss," the girl agreed.

"Well, I wish you good fortune in your new life," Diana said.

"Thank you, miss." The maid gave a big smile, which showed pretty white teeth.

She left and Diana got on with the business of dressing for the day.

* * *

The Standish women spent the entire day shopping. Diana had a wonderful time. She was fitted for morning dresses, driving dresses, a riding habit and evening gowns. Lady Standish ordered her a new pelisse, as the weather was still chilly in April. Sally got a similar wardrobe, and they both picked out dresses to be altered by the afternoon, so they could go driving in the park.

Diana had a moment of unease when she realized the amount of Alex's money that Lady Standish had just spent on her, but she pushed the thought aside firmly. *I am going to have fun,* she told herself. *I'm not going to spoil things for myself by worrying about Alex's money.* So when the time came to dress for their ride in the park, her spirits were high and her thoughts were eager.

Hyde Park was *the* place to be at about five o'clock in the afternoon during the Season. Most of the ton regularly turned out in their best riding and driving gear and took the path along the Serpentine to see and to be seen. Alex had volunteered to drive Diana and Sally and they both proudly wore the dresses they had purchased that morning. Diana's was rust-colored, with a short cape and buttons all down the front. Over her coppery curls she wore a small brown hat, which tilted to one side, almost over her eye and on her feet she wore low leather boots. When her cousin knocked at her door to see if she was ready, Sally was a vision in blue, with a matching bonnet tied under her chin.

The girls complimented each other and together went downstairs to meet Alex. He was wearing a caped driving coat that made his shoulders look very wide. Diana noticed that his hair had been cut. His neck looked tanned and strong.

He glanced from his sister to Diana and said, "You ladies look beautiful."

He was speaking to them both, but looking at her. Diana said a little self-consciously, "It must be our new clothes."

"They are very becoming," he said.

For the briefest of moments their eyes met and held, then Diana looked away. "Is the carriage ready?" she asked.

"Yes, it is right outside," Alex responded and they all turned toward the front door. The park was filled with fashionable carriages and well-turned-out men and women on horseback. The horses were sleek and shiny and all of the carriages sparkled with cleanliness. Everyone was dressed in the height of elegance: the men wore immaculate buff breeches and polished riding boots with black or brown riding or driving coats; the women's outfits were more varied: from curricle dresses and pelisses, to the kind of full-skirted riding habits that Lady Standish had ordered for Diana and Sally earlier that day.

It was an incomparably rich-looking scene, very different from the one in Berkshire that Diana was accustomed to. Certainly none of her suitors from home could match the immaculate and fashionable gentlemen who were gathered in the park today.

She glanced at Alex out of the corner of her eye. He was the handsomest man she had seen so far.

He fits in here, she thought. *And so does Sally. But me? I'm not in the same class with these people.*

A feeling of unease swept through her as she looked at the brilliant scene around her. Had she done the right thing in coming to London? At home everyone knew her situation and was comfortable with it. But what would all of these elegant people think if they knew that her bedroom was the size of a closet and that if it wasn't for the generosity of her mother's cousin they probably wouldn't have meat on their table more than once a week.

She was a little more silent than usual as they drove along the path, letting Sally and Alex do most of the talking. A curricle pulled up next to them and saluted Alex. He stopped.

"See you are taking the ladies for a spin, eh Standish?" the fashionable gentleman driving the curricle said.

"Yes, I am," Alex replied courteously. "Lord and Lady Sudbury, allow me to introduce my sister, Lady Sarah, and my cousin, Miss Diana Sherwood."

"So lovely to meet you," the lady said in nasal, aristocratic tones. "We knew your father well," she said to Sally. "How is your dear mother doing?"

"She is well," Sally said. "She is back at Standish House now, resting."

The lady's small, curious eyes turned to Diana. "I do not believe I know the Sherwoods," she said.

Alex answered before Diana could speak, "Mrs. Sherwood is my mother's first cousin, and the two of them are as close as sisters, as are Sally and Diana. We all grew up together at Standish Court, you know."

"How cozy." Lady Sudbury's gaze raked Diana from her head to her feet. "Is this your first visit to London, Miss Sherwood?"

"Yes," Diana replied in a composed voice.

"Diana and I are here to make our come-outs," Sally said pleasantly. "Mama is planning to hold a big ball in a few weeks. I'm sure you will be getting invitations."

"How lovely." Lady Sudbury's eyes returned to Diana. "And I suppose I shall see you girls at Almack's?"

"I certainly hope so," Sally said brightly.

Lord Sudbury spoke for the first time, "Let's get going Clarissa. I don't like to keep the horses standing for long."

"Of course." Lady Sudbury shared a restrained smile among the three of them. *"Au revoir,"* she said.

There was a little silence as they once more drove along the crowded pathway. Diana had gotten a distinct impression that her cousins had been trying to protect her, and it made her uneasy. Alex had definitely implied that she lived at Standish Court. All of her worry about not being accepted came rushing back.

"I didn't particularly care for Lady Sudbury," Sally, who was usually so kind to everyone, said.

"He's something in the government, I believe," Alex said.

"She seemed—cold, somehow."

"This isn't the country, Sal," Alex said. "You and Dee are going to have to get accustomed to the fact that not everyone in London is warm and friendly, the way they are at home. People here are always jockeying for position in society. For example, perhaps Mama was not planning to invite the Sudburys to her ball. Now you have forced her into it."

Sally protested. "She made it sound as if she and Mama and Papa were great friends."

Alex deftly steered them past another carriage. "Perhaps they were, perhaps they weren't," he said.

"How do you know so much about London society?" Diana suddenly demanded.

He gave her a quick look. "I may never have been to London for the Season, but remember I went to Eton with the sons of all these people—and I served on Wellington's staff with a number of others. I know how they tick."

His words made Diana even more nervous. If position was what was important to these high-fashion people, then what kind of a reception was she going to get? She knew she was attractive enough, and she knew that her beauty had been responsible for all of the marriage offers she had received at home. But would beauty be enough in a society like this one?

She said as much to her mother that evening, when she went into her bedroom to say good-night.

"Perhaps this venture was a mistake, Mama," she said. "Perhaps we should have stayed at home. What if no one asks me to dance at any of these balls? I shall be humiliated."

"That won't happen," Mrs. Sherwood said definitely. "When the young men get a look at you, you will have partners. Don't worry about that, my love."

"Well…perhaps I will have partners, but will anyone want to marry me? I am only an army officer's daughter. I have no money, no status…"

"Stop worrying, Diana," her mother chided. "You are a very beautiful young woman. You will find a husband, I'm certain of it." She kissed Diana's cheek. "Now get some sleep. I will see you in the morning."

Diana gave her mother a shadowy smile and went on back to her own room. She wasn't sure she was going to like London at all.

Six

The following morning Lady Standish took Sally, Diana and Mrs. Sherwood to visit Lady Jersey, an old friend from childhood with whom she had maintained a correspondence over the years. Lady Jersey was one of the patronesses of Almack's—the assembly rooms where young ladies went in search of husbands. Not to be admitted to Almack's was a social blot that was almost insurmountable.

Diana was very nervous about the visit. There was no doubt that Sally would be admitted to Almack's, but she was not so sure about herself.

Diana had grown up in a small society where she had liked everybody and everybody had liked her. She had had an intense relationship with Alex when she was very young and after he had left she had never paid very close attention to any of the other men who would have liked to marry her. She was still consumed with Alex—only this time her emotion was anger, not love.

Now she was in London, a world where for the first time she sensed the vulnerability of her social status. No one at home had minded that she and her mother had little money. They were part of the Standish family, and that was enough. She had blithely thought that things would be the same in London, but their short drive in the park yesterday had left her in doubt.

So it was with some trepidation that she followed Lady Standish and Sally into the drawing room of Lady Jersey, one of the most influential women in all of London society.

Diana was dressed correctly, in a pretty green muslin dress, with a square-cut neck and empire waistline. Sally was dressed in similar fashion, although her dress was blue. Diana knew she looked all right, she just didn't feel that way.

Lady Jersey rose to greet Lady Standish and the two women embraced. After they had exchanged a few words, Lady Standish presented Mrs. Sherwood and the two girls.

"My word," Lady Jersey said, "you have two beauties here, Amelia."

Lady Standish smiled. "Thank you, Sally," she said.

"Please, be seated," Lady Jersey said, gesturing them all to the chairs that were gathered around the marble fireplace in a room that was decorated in the Chinese style.

It was a morning Diana never forgot. In a politely ruthless manner, Lady Jersey ascertained that Mrs.

Sherwood was the widow of a mere colonel who had been killed in the Peninsula and that she had no money. She also ascertained that Lady Standish was determined to give Diana a Season along with Sally.

"The two girls are like sisters. Sally wants to have Diana as her companion," Lady Standish said.

"Does Diana have a dowry at all?" Lady Jersey asked.

Mrs. Sherwood answered, "Unfortunately, no."

"Hmm." Lady Jersey frowned.

"Perhaps Alex would give some money for a dowry…." Lady Standish said tentatively.

"I don't want anything from Alex," Diana returned quickly. "If I cannot be accepted as myself, then I will just go home."

Lady Jersey looked at her. "You are an extremely beautiful girl, Miss Sherwood. But I am certain that you know that."

Diana didn't reply.

"Please give her a voucher," Lady Standish said. "Diana is gently if not nobly born. She certainly will not disgrace you, Sally."

There was a pause, then Lady Jersey shrugged. "Well, why not? I cannot guarantee that you will get an offer of marriage, Miss Sherwood, but one never knows. Men have been known to make fools of themselves over a pretty face before. And being brought up at Standish Court is certainly a recommendation."

Diana had not exactly been brought up at Standish Court, but no one corrected her.

"So you will give the Sherwoods vouchers to Almack's, Sally?" Lady Standish asked.

"I could hardly refuse you, Amelia, now could I? We have been friends for too long. Yes, I will give the Sherwoods vouchers for Almack's."

Lady Standish was jubilant as they got into the coach outside Lady Jersey's house. "You probably don't appreciate how important this is, Diana, but it is *tremendously* important. Once you have been given the approval of the patronesses of Almack's, then all of society is open to you."

"It will be such fun, Diana," Sally enthused.

"Yes," Diana said. "I'm sure it will be." But she wasn't sure at all anymore.

The ladies stopped at Hookam's Library to pick up some books to read before they returned to Grosvenor Square. Diana immediately went up to her room, looked around for her dog and remembered that he had been left at home. She went to the chair by the fireplace, sat down and cried.

"Oh, Freddie, how could I have left you at home? I miss you so much." Diana's spaniel had been the runt of the litter, and the earl had given him to her when nobody else wanted him.

But everyone had told her that he would be better in the country, that there was no place for him to run free in London, that she would be too busy to even miss him.

But she did miss him. She needed him now, needed his unconditional, adoring love. "No one will ever love me like you do, Freddie," she sniffled into her handkerchief.

I wish we were all young again. I wish it was like it was before Alex left to go into the army. I was so happy then. Will I ever be happy like that again?

It seemed to her that she had never truly been happy since Alex had left; but now that he was back, she felt even worse, knowing that she could never be that way with him again.

I have to put Alex behind me, she thought. *I have to look ahead. Surely there is some man who can make me happy, who will be able to give me the stable home that I need so badly.*

A knock came upon her door. "Diana?" Sally's voice called. "May I come in?"

"Just a moment," Diana said, as she scrubbed at the tears on her face. She took a deep breath before she bade her friend to enter her room.

At dinner that evening, Alex said, "Would you like to take the horses for a gallop in the park tomorrow morning, Dee?"

Her whole face lit up. "I should love to."

"What horse will you be riding?" Mrs. Sherwood asked a little nervously.

"Monty," Diana said.

Mrs. Sherwood looked at Alex. "Has Monty ever been out of the country? You have to walk through the streets of London before you get to the park."

"I'll look after Dee, Cousin Louisa," Alex said.

"How about Bart?" Diana asked. "Is he accustomed to traffic?"

"Bart's accustomed to bullets firing all around him," Alex returned. "I think he can handle the London streets."

Mrs. Sherwood looked worried, but she didn't say anything else.

It was seven in the morning when Diana, dressed in her old riding habit, went out to the stables to meet Alex. He was wearing a russet-colored riding coat and brown leather breeches—country clothes. The air was cool, with a slight wind blowing. Their two horses were standing on the cobblestones of the stable yard, all saddled and ready to go.

Diana felt as if a weight had lifted from her chest. She was going to ride again. Everything always looked better to her from the back of a horse. She actually grinned at Alex. "I hope you know how to get to the park, because I certainly don't."

"I drove you there the other day, remember?"

"Oh, that's right. Well, shall we get started?"

"I'll give you a leg up," he said, cupping his hands so she could put her foot into his gloved brace. In a moment she was in the sidesaddle, crooking her leg around the horn and gathering the reins into her competent hands.

It was a short walk from Grosvenor Square to the Cumberland Gate entrance to Hyde Park, but London was amazingly busy for such an early hour.

Wagons piled high with fruits and vegetables lumbered through town on their way to the Covent

Garden market; fishmongers carried their purchases from the wharves to their various shops; and haunches of freshly slaughtered animals bled through the bottoms of wicker baskets as they were driven by cart to the butcher shops. The large number of people who lived in London had to be fed, and this was the hour at which their food was moved.

Monty sidled a little at all the traffic and threw his head about, but Diana spoke soothingly to him. He had been on the roads at home, of course, but not very frequently. Mostly Diana had ridden him through the many wide and well-kept rides that cut through Standish Park.

As they crossed the main street to get into the park, a particularly noisy wagon came along and Monty bucked in protest.

"Are you all right?" Alex asked as Diana urged Monty forward, away from the noise.

"We're fine," she answered calmly. "He's just a bit worried by these new surroundings."

They entered into the welcome greenness of the park and when they reached the path along the lake, Diana was delighted to see that it was empty.

"Marvelous," she said. "No one's here."

"How about a good gallop to wake them up?" Alex asked.

She was gone before he finished his question.

He caught her up in a moment, and the two horses thundered along, side-by-side, under the greening oaks. To Diana, it felt glorious. The feel of Monty under her was so familiar, and it was familiar, too, to look out of the side of her eye and see Alex galloping beside her. They had always ridden out early; both of them liked the fresh morning air.

When Diana felt Monty start to slow, she sat back a little and let him come down to a canter. Alex did the same. From the canter they dropped to a trot, then to a walk. They looked at each other and smiled.

"That felt grand," Diana said.

He nodded. "It's been a long time since we rode together, Dee."

Some of her good mood vanished. Whose fault was that? she thought.

Alex patted the neck of his big black horse. "Damn, but I love this horse," he said.

Diana regarded Bart. "He's splendid," she agreed. "I imagine a cavalryman becomes very attached to his horse."

"They can be the difference between life and death to a man sometimes." His black hair had tumbled forward over his forehead and his light blue eyes were serious.

He looked the same as when he left, yet he also looked different. He was bigger now; his shoulders were wider, his chest broader and there were strong muscles under the tight-fitting riding breeches that he wore. He had gone away a boy and come back a man.

She heard herself saying, "I'm nervous about being introduced into London society."

"You shouldn't be," he replied. "You're under

the wing of my mother. Everything should go very smoothly for you."

She confided her deepest fear. "We're going to Almack's tonight. What if no one dances with me?"

"Don't worry about that," he assured her. "Haven't men wanted to dance with you all your life?"

"But that was in the country, where people knew me."

"Believe me, I don't think you'll have any problem, but if you do I'll round up some men to dance with you. Don't worry, you won't be left sitting with the chaperones."

She gave him a smile. "Thank you, Alex. It's just…I never expected to feel so out of my depth." Tears stung behind her eyes. "And I miss Freddie. I should never have left him home."

"I can send for him if it's that important to you."

Her face lit to radiance. "Can you? Would that not be too much trouble?"

"Not at all. I'll send the curricle for him. We'll have him here in London for you in no time."

"It won't be too confining for him, will it? I can walk him in the park every day."

"He'll be fine. The horses are more cooped up than they're accustomed to as well. That's why it's good for us to get them out in the morning for a gallop."

She nodded.

His voice deepened. "For how many years have the two of us ridden together in the morning, Dee?"

"Ever since we were children." Her voice hardened. "Until you went away."

They were walking side-by-side on a loose rein, the horses' heads swinging comfortably as they went along. A slight breeze ruffled the hair on Alex's forehead. "I had to go, Dee," he said earnestly. "I know you don't understand, and I know I can't really expect you to forgive me, but it was just something in me that I couldn't deny. I *needed* to go. I had wanted to be a soldier for all of my life, and then my father finally agreed…I just couldn't pass up the chance."

"Yes," she said tightly. "You made your choice, Alex. I understood that very well."

"I didn't mean to leave you forever. I told you I would come back when the war was over. I told you I would marry you."

She stared straight ahead, between Monty's small, pointed ears. "You could have come back in a wooden box, like my father. What good would that have been to me?"

"I wouldn't have been much good to you with my heart always someplace else. You knew that. That's why you told me to go."

She turned to look at him. "Was it as glorious as you thought it was going to be, Alex? Did you love being a soldier?"

She thought she saw a shadow pass over his face. "I wouldn't exactly call it glorious," he said. She could hear that he was trying to speak lightly. "It was a pretty dirty job at times. But it was a good cause, and we were successful. What happened in the Peninsula had a lot to do with Napoleon's downfall."

It sounded to Diana as if Alex had not been as thrilled with life as a soldier as he had expected to be. Perversely, this made her glad.

"I expect being in a battle wasn't much fun," she said.

"No." His voice was clipped.

They walked in silence for a while. Then Alex turned to her. "Dee, is it really too late for us? Can't we start over again? I know you have a right to be angry with me. But I love you. I have always loved you. I don't want you to marry another man, I want you to marry *me*. Will you at least consider that?"

She returned his look, her brown eyes grave in her exquisite face. "It's too late," she said. "The feelings I had for you are gone."

His mouth set in a grim line. "I don't believe that. I can't believe it."

A bird flew close to Monty's head and he sidled a little. "It's true," she lied. "Something in me died when you left, Alex. For a long time I was very angry with you, but now that you're back even my anger is gone. We're finished. That's all there is to it. I'm sorry."

He said, "Get off that horse and kiss me, Dee, and then tell me you have no feelings left for me."

She raised her chin and stared ahead. "I have no intention of kissing you! You lost your rights to my kisses a long time ago." She fought to compose herself. "We might start to trot. The horses have caught their breath."

She started Monty going briskly forward, eager to end their conversation. After a moment, Alex followed.

Seven

Diana parted with Alex in the stable yard and went up to the house. Her mother, Lady Standish and Sally were at breakfast and she joined them. Their conversation revolved around what they would do today and about the coming evening at Almack's. Shortly after, Alex came in. Diana ate her breakfast and never looked at him.

After breakfast, Diana went up to her room to change out of her riding clothes. She was upset about her discussion with Alex and after she took off her boots and her habit, she put on a wrapper and went to lie on the bed, staring up at the blue draperies that surrounded her.

He wanted to marry her. In so many ways, that would be the perfect solution to her future. To live at Standish Court which she loved so much…to raise her children there…

But she couldn't marry him. She carried too

much pain. Her mind shied away at the thought of that pain and what had caused it. *Better not to dwell on it,* she told herself. *Better to try to put Alex behind me and go on with my life.*

But the past intruded upon her well intentioned plan and, against her will, her mind traveled back in time to when she was fifteen years old and she and Alex had been riding their horses in the park in the early morning. They had dismounted by the lake to give the horses a chance to drink and as they stood there a deer came down to the other side of the lake. It had been summer, and the air was soft and gentle. At the sight of the lovely animal, Diana had felt something stir inside of her, and, instinctively, she had turned to Alex.

He was looking at her. "You are so beautiful, Dee," he said. His light eyes had darkened slightly and his voice was a little unsteady. Slowly his head bent toward hers and she had lifted her face. For the first time, their lips had met.

They had kissed gently, tentatively, then Alex's mouth had hardened and he had put his arms around her. She had leaned against him and kissed him back. When finally he raised his head, they both were breathing quickly.

"Oh, Dee," he said shakily. "Oh, Dee."

She didn't know what to say. They had been friends for so many years. But this was something new.

"What does this mean?" she asked.

"I think it means we love each other," he had returned.

She thought for a moment, and then she had nodded. "Yes," she had said. "I think it means that, too."

She lay now on her bed, her eyes closed, and remembered that first kiss. She would remember it for as long as she lived. She would remember the look in Alex's eyes, she would remember how his hard, young body had felt against hers.

She shut her eyes very tightly and willed the memory to go away. It was futile to dwell on the past. Alex hadn't really loved her—or he hadn't loved her enough. That was what she had to remember.

I am starting a new life tonight, she thought. *That is what I must concentrate on.*

That evening Diana, her mother and the rest of the Standishes prepared to leave Standish House to go to the famous Almack's Assembly Rooms on King Street. Alex was waiting at the foot of the stairs as Diana and Sally came down, and Diana thought he looked splendid in the evening dress that was demanded for entrance to the club: knee breeches, a white neck cloth and black dress coat with long tails. Diana herself wore a white gown over a sea green slip. Her glorious red-gold hair was caught behind her ears with pearl-studded combs and her jewelry was a simple pearl necklace and matching earrings.

Sally was similarly attired in her usual blue, with a diamond around her throat and diamond studs in her ears. She looked utterly sweet and lovely.

The two older women wore silk gowns, Mrs.

Sherwood in a smoky gray and Lady Standish in dark gold.

They all got into the Standish coach, with the earl's coat of arms painted on its door, and the horses began their route through the city streets. Diana didn't know what she had been expecting but it was certainly something grander than the simple building with undistinguished brickwork that the carriage drew up before. Everyone got out and Alex escorted his mother and Mrs. Sherwood to the front door, with the girls bringing up the rear. At the door they presented their vouchers and were admitted into the inner sanctum of society's self-described "marriage mart."

"It looks terribly plain," Sally whispered to Diana as they went up the stairs to the main floor. There was no architectural interest about the ballroom at all. It was just a big room with a bad floor, but it was crowded with the highest members of London society, all dressed in their finest clothes. The scent of mingling perfumes rose to Diana's nostrils as she stood there, her chest feeling tight under her lovely gown.

Music was playing and the dance floor was filled with dancers. Alex steered his mother and Mrs. Sherwood around the edges of the floor, and Diana saw that he was heading toward Lady Jersey, who was enthroned amidst the rest of the patronesses as they kept an eagle eye on what was transpiring before them.

The patronesses shifted their gaze to the Standish

party and sat silently as Lady Jersey greeted them
and then turned to introduce them. Of the six other
patronesses of Almack's, only Lady Castlereagh,
Lady Cowper and Mrs. Drummond Burrell were
present that evening and they smiled warmly upon
Alex, Lady Standish and Sally. The smiles were
less warm as they greeted Mrs. Sherwood and
Diana.

The music stopped and the dancers began to
stream off the floor. Lady Jersey motioned to a tall,
willowy young man, who obediently came to her
side and was presented to them as Viscount Althorpe. Lady Jersey said, "I thought you might enjoy
a dance with Lady Sarah Standish, Althorpe. She is
newly come to town and doesn't know anyone yet."

The young man beamed and turned to Sally with
alacrity. The dancers were forming up for the next
dance and the two of them moved off together.
Diana felt a moment of panic, but then she felt Alex
taking her hand. "Come along, Dee. You've come
here to dance, after all."

Lady Standish and Mrs. Sherwood moved off to
join the rows of chaperones and Diana went with
Alex. As they walked away she heard the cool, aristocratic tones of Mrs. Drummond Burrell say to
Lady Jersey, "Really, Sally, whatever possessed you
to give vouchers to the Sherwoods?"

Diana stiffened.

Alex said, "Nasty old cat. Don't pay any mind to
her, Dee. You fit in here just fine."

Diana and Alex took their places in the line and

the dance started. It was a country dance, which involved the ladies being passed from partner to partner, and Diana forced herself to smile and look as if she was having a good time. At the end of the dance she and Alex were back together again, and he walked her off the floor.

A young man approached them.

"I say, Standish," he said. "I haven't seen you since Salamanca. Back home for good, I see?"

Alex replied and the young man, who was broad-chested and broad-faced, said, "Aren't you going to introduce me?"

Alex presented Lord Butler to Diana, who immediately asked her to dance. She accepted, thrilled that someone besides Alex wanted to dance with her. Together they went out onto the floor.

That was the way the evening went. Both Diana and Sally danced every dance.

Diana was radiant. Forgotten was the hurtful comment of Mrs. Drummond Burrell. She wasn't going to be shunned. She could attract men in London just the way she had at home. Her London Season was going to be all right.

Alex watched Diana's progress with mixed emotions. He certainly hadn't wanted her to fail, but it hurt to watch her with other men. It hurt bitterly. He wanted to rush onto the floor, drag her away from her partner and claim her as his own.

No matter what she might say about never forgiving him, he wasn't going to give up. He *couldn't* give up. There was too much between them—there had always been too much between them—for him to believe that she could turn her back on him so easily.

Perhaps she wouldn't get another marriage offer. Men liked to dance with a pretty girl, but marriage to a dowerless country girl was another thing altogether. If she had nobody else to marry, perhaps she would think differently about him. If she changed her mind out of necessity, that would be all right. He would take Dee any way he could get her.

He had missed her so much. He had missed her achingly. He had known she was hurt and angry when she hadn't answered his letters, but in his heart he had always thought that he could make everything right when he came home.

He looked at her glowing smile as she danced with her tall, handsome partner, and his stomach clenched.

The following morning a variety of bouquets were delivered to Standish House for the girls. Most were for Sally, but there were a few for Diana, as well. Along with the flowers came invitations to drive in the park. The young men who had sent the flowers all turned up at Standish House at eleven o'clock, the official hour for making morning calls, and they all sat in the downstairs drawing room making conversation, attended by Lady Standish and Mrs. Sherwood.

Diana agreed to drive out with a lively young man

who was the younger son of a baron. His name was Matthew Dunster and Diana found him very entertaining. He also was mad about horses, which immediately gave them something in common to talk about.

Sally chose a more matrimonially advantageous escort, the eldest son of an earl. Lady Standish was pleased to express her approval of both girls' plans, and arrangements were made for them to be picked up at five o'clock that afternoon.

"We have a musicale to go to after lunch," Lady Standish announced to the girls after their suitors had left. "It's at the Countess of Morham's. A very popular pianist is going to be there."

Sally was thrilled. She was a very good musician herself and she loved music. Diana was less excited. She would have preferred to spend the afternoon outdoors.

"Is Alex coming?" she heard herself ask.

"No, I believe he is going to Tattersall's to look at horses," Lady Standish replied.

Horses! This sounded so much better than being cooped up inside all afternoon listening to music. "I believe I'll go with Alex," Diana said.

"You most certainly will not," Lady Standish returned. "Ladies do not go to Tattersall's. You would ruin your reputation were you to do such a thing."

Diana stuck out her lip, just the way she had done when she was a child and was thwarted from doing something she wanted to do. "That's ridiculous," she said. "Why can't I go to look at horses?"

"Tattersall's is strictly a male domain," Lady

Standish explained. "Alex will tell you the same thing. Besides, it will look good for you to be seen at the musicale with us. Lady Morham is an important figure in society."

So Diana dragged herself off to the musicale with Lady Standish, her mother and Sally. It wasn't that she disliked music; she enjoyed listening to Sally play in the evening. But she would so much rather have been at Tattersall's with Alex.

The next two weeks—the weeks before Lady Standish was due to have her official come-out ball for Sally and Diana—were crammed with activities. They went to balls, routs, Venetian breakfasts, musicales and drove in Hyde Park. Alex had been true to his word and sent for Diana's dog, Freddie, to be sent to London. Diana walked her dog in Green Park twice every day. She and Sally had exactly the same schedule, except that Sally's escorts were all highly born and had money, while Diana's escorts tended to be younger sons with few prospects. They were all obviously smitten by Diana, but none could possibly be serious husband material. None of them had the money to marry a penniless girl like her.

One of Sally's suitors was the heir to the Marquess of Norton. Sally was driving with Lord Morple in the area of Pall Mall, a neighborhood which, like so many good neighborhoods in London, bordered on a slum. As Sally's carriage passed in front of Marlborough House, she saw an old cart pulled to the side of the road, with a man and a boy standing beside it. The boy looked to be about five and was dressed in filthy rags. As Sally watched in horror, the man raised his horse whip and laid it across the boy's back.

"Disgusting," Sally's escort said, looking down his nose. "These people shouldn't be allowed in this part of town."

"Stop!" Sally shouted, reaching for the reins. She halted the horses, and Lord Morple looked at her in astonishment as she swung herself down from the carriage.

"Here, Lady Sarah! You can't do that! Come back here!"

Sally ignored him and ran toward the man who had once more raised his whip and it hit the boy again. "Stop that!" she commanded.

Sally had a very soft voice and the man ignored her, raising his whip yet again. "Ye wretched little cur," he said. "I'll have ye obey me or else."

At that, Sally dashed in to throw her arms protectively around the child and the whip came down upon her own shoulder. She flinched but didn't cry out. The man cursed.

"How dare you beat this child?" she said fiercely, the boy gathered safely to her breast. "What has he done to deserve such barbaric treatment?"

"It's none o' yer business, young miss," the man replied. "But he's one of my climbing boys and he refused to go up the chimney in yon house. I'm beatin' some sense into him, that's wot I'm doin'."

"You wretched man," Sally said passionately.

High color stained her cheeks. "Would you send a frightened child up a chimney? What kind of monster are you?"

The boy whimpered and pressed closer to Sally.

"Don't worry, my dear," she said to him. "You are safe with me."

"Here, that's *my* boy," the man said loudly, and he began to advance upon Sally, evidently with the idea of ripping the boy from her arms.

A deep, resonant voice said, "Desist, you worm. Lay one hand on the lady and I shall be forced to kill you."

For a brief moment, Sally thought her escort had come to her rescue but then she realized that the voice was different. She looked up to see a tall, blond man dressed in a many-caped riding coat standing next to the chimney sweeper. "You cannot beat your poor unfortunate boys on the city streets," the blond man said. "At least you can't while there is a lady of mercy in the vicinity. I suggest you go about your business before I have you arrested for vicious conduct."

"That boy's mine," the man said indignantly. "You can't just take him from me! He's worth money!"

"Slavery is outlawed in England," Sally said. "If this boy chooses to leave you of his own free will, there is nothing you can do about it." She looked down at the filthy head that was pressed against her breast. "Do you wish to leave this man, my dear?"

"Yes," came the breathless reply.

"Then I think you have had your answer," the tall stranger said. "Take yourself off before I am tempted to knock you down for attacking helpless children."

His voice was cool and utterly authoritative. After a moment, the chimney man got back into his wagon and started up his poor, skinny horse.

Sally looked up at the man who had come to her rescue. Her escort was still sitting in his phaeton, staring at her. "Thank you, sir," she said. "You came just in time."

For the first time she noticed that the man's eyes were a very unusual shade of green.

"Let's have a look at the lad," he said.

Sally put her hands on the boy's thin shoulders and held him away from her. The front of her pelisse was filthy, from coal dirt and tears and the boy's runny nose. She appeared not to notice.

"What is your name?" she asked gently.

"Jem," came the reply.

"How long have you been a climbing boy?" the man asked.

"Just a few months. But I don't like it. I'm afraid of getting caught in the chimney. But my pa said he couldna feed me, that I'd have to do it."

"How old are you?"

"Eight."

He was small enough to look five. He snuffled. Sally looked at her rescuer and said, "Do you have a handkerchief, sir?"

The thick blond brows rose, but the man reached

into the pocket of his greatcoat and produced the article requested.

"Here," Sally said, handing over the pristine handkerchief. "Blow your nose, Jem, and wipe your face."

The two adults stood in silence and watched as the boy did as he was requested. When he was finished he attempted to hand the handkerchief back to its owner, who shook his head sharply and said, "No, no, you keep it, boy."

Belatedly, they were joined by Sally's stiff and proper escort, Lord Morple. "May I ask what you think you are doing, Lady Sarah?" he asked in chilly tones.

Sally looked at him steadily. "That man was trying to force this boy to climb chimneys to clean them. My cousin and I have been reading about this practice. It is barbaric!"

Lord Morple looked with distaste at the dirty child. "Nevertheless, it is legal. You had no right to interfere and remove him from his employer. You have made yourself filthy from embracing this vermin."

Sally blue eyes flashed. "You are disgusting," she said forthrightly. "Didn't you see him beating this child?"

"It is deplorable, I agree, but it is none of our business," her aggravated escort returned.

"Well, I am glad that someone came along who thinks differently about these matters," Sally said. She turned to her green-eyed rescuer. He was regarding her with an expressionless face and narrowed eyes. "I am Lady Sarah Standish, sir, and I thank you for your assistance."

He bowed. "It was my pleasure, ma'am. You were hit by that whip yourself. You must have it seen to when you get home."

Sally shrugged. "Oh, I am fine. My pelisse is thick enough. It is Jem who is the victim here, not I."

"Er...now that you have him, what do you plan to do with him?" her rescuer asked curiously.

Sally answered immediately, "I will take him home, of course, and clean him up. I am sure my brother will have someone on his estates who will be willing to take him in."

"Do you expect to put that disgusting brat into my phaeton?" her escort asked.

Sally gave him a steady look. "Yes, I do."

"I will be happy to give you a ride home, Lady Sarah," her rescuer said. "Just keep the boy on the outside of the seat. Your clothes are already ruined, mine are not."

Sally gave him a grateful smile. "Thank you, sir. But I don't know your name."

"It's Sinclair," the man said. "I am the Duke of Sinclair."

"Well, this is very kind of you, Your Grace," she said, not showing any sign of recognizing one of the most notorious names in London. She looked down to the child and took his dirty hand into her expensively gloved one.

"You are coming home with me, Jem. This gentleman will take us in his carriage. Don't worry anymore, you will be safe. I won't let that dreadful man get you into his clutches again."

They walked toward the duke's elegant, high-perch phaeton. Sinclair put his hands around Sally's waist and lifted her to the seat as if she weighed nothing. Next came Jem. Then he went around to the other side and climbed easily into the high seat by himself. He picked up his reins and the horses moved off, leaving the marquess' heir behind them, staring with a mixture of astonishment and disgust.

Jem said in a small voice, "Where are we goin', my lady?"

"Don't worry,' she returned soothingly. "We are going to my house, where you will have a bath and a good meal. Then I will find a family for you to live with in the country, where you will have plenty of fresh air and good food. How does that sound, Jem?"

"I ain't never bin out o' the city," the lad replied.

"You will like the country very much. It is green and pretty and there will be no one to hit you or force you to climb chimneys."

"I like that," Jem said fervently.

Sally turned to her driver. "Can't something be done about these climbing boys, Your Grace? My cousin and I have been following the debate in parliament and it seems impossible to us that such a custom should be allowed to continue."

"I agree with you, Lady Sarah," the deep even

voice returned. "But I fear that there are not enough votes to pass the law."

"That's disgraceful!" Sally said hotly.

He shrugged and did not reply.

It was not long before they pulled up before Standish House in Grosvenor Square. The duke got down and came around to first lift the boy and then Sally to the ground. His hand upon her waist caused a strange chill to go up Sally's back.

"I cannot thank you enough, Your Grace," she said. "If you hadn't come along I don't know what I would have done." Her voice took on a tinge of bitterness. "Lord Morple certainly wasn't going to help me."

The duke shrugged. He was as tall as Alex. His green eyes were truly remarkable.

Sally found herself wondering if he was married.

He bowed. "Good day to you, Lady Sarah," he said, and turned to go back to his carriage. Sally stood watching him for a moment before she herself turned and, putting an arm around Jem's shoulders, led him into the house.

Eight

Diana was in the hall and she immediately came to Sally's side when she saw her companion.

"Poor child," she said sympathetically when she had heard the story. "This practice of sending boys up chimneys to clean them must be stopped!"

"Henrys," Sally said to the butler, "please have the bath filled in my room. And send out to the shops immediately to find some clothes that will fit Jem."

The butler, who had been looking with horror at Sally's dirty pelisse, now said, "You're not going to bathe this beggar yourself, Lady Sarah?"

"I certainly am," she replied. "He knows me and won't be so afraid."

"I'll help if you like," Diana said.

Sally gave her a smile. "Thank you."

The water was brought, the tub was filled, and a reluctant Jem was plunked into it. It was the first bath the boy had ever had in his life and he wasn't at all sure that he liked it. He was quite sure he didn't like his hair being washed.

"You won't drown," Sally said, ruthlessly plunging his head under water to wet it, "and you'll feel so much better when you're clean."

Indeed, he did look like a different boy, with his mud-colored hair restored to its natural sandy color and his skin pink and clean. Henrys had managed to procure clothes and once he was dressed in simple nakeen trousers and a white shirt and jacket, he looked perfectly respectable.

Sally let him look in the mirror in her room and he couldn't believe what he saw.

"That's me?" he kept asking.

"That's you," Sally and Diana assured him.

"Now I have to ask Alex if he can make arrangements to take care of Jem," Sally said. She looked anxiously at Diana. "He will help, won't he?"

Diana answered immediately. "Of course he will. He's not in the house just now, but perhaps he will be back for luncheon."

But Alex didn't show up for lunch and Sally was forced to tell her mother and Mrs. Sherwood about her morning's venture without her brother's assurance that he would take care of young Jem.

"Oh, Sally, that's just like you," moaned Lady Standish when she heard how Sally had jumped out of the carriage and run to clasp the boy in her arms. "What must Lord Morple have thought?"

"I don't care one jot what he thought, Mother,"

Sally replied vigorously. "I don't want to have anything else to do with him. He was prepared to drive on by and leave that poor little boy to get a whipping."

"My dear, you can't right the wrongs of the world all by yourself," Lady Standish said gently.

"No, but you can certainly make a difference in one child's life," Diana said forcefully. "Sally had the opportunity to save a little boy from a life of horror and she took it. I'm proud of her."

The two cousins looked at each other.

"I don't know what Alex is going to say," Lady Standish said. "He will have to pay someone to take him. Most of our tenants are amply supplied with children of their own."

"I've been thinking," Diana said. "Perhaps Jem could live with Henley and his wife." Henley was the chief groom at Standish Court and he was childless. "I'm sure he would be glad to have a son to whom he could teach his trade. And Henley is so gentle with the horses, he would be gentle with a boy as well."

"That's a wonderful idea, Diana," Sally said enthusiastically. "I don't know why I didn't think of it myself."

"Alex will have to take Jem to Standish Court himself," Diana said. "Henley will listen to him."

"What will Henley have to listen to me about?" a voice enquired from the door and everyone turned to see Alex coming into the room. He was dressed in morning clothes, a blue jacket with pale yellow pantaloons and gleaming Hessian boots. His hair, which had started the day brushed into perfect order, had fallen forward over his forehead in a tumble of black curls. Many men in London would have killed for those curls, but Alex hated them and tried religiously to brush them back from his forehead. He was rarely successful for any length of time.

He sat at the table and the servants scrambled to bring him a plate of cold meat and some bread. Once more Sally related her encounter of the morning.

Diana said, "I thought Henley would be the perfect person to take Jem. I am sure he would like to have a son."

"Oh you are, are you?" Alex replied.

"Yes. I got to know Henley quite well this last year, since your father died and I rather ran the stables. I think their childlessness has been a bitter blow to them both. I think they will take Jem."

"If you know Henley so well, then you had better come with me," Alex said to Diana. "Such a suggestion would be better coming from you than from me."

"Alex is right," Sally said. "You know Henley much better than he does. Would you mind, Diana?"

"No, of course not," Diana said, sensing her cousin's eagerness to put her alone with Alex.

"I don't know if Diana and Alex should go together," Mrs. Sherwood said. "How would it look?"

Lady Standish looked surprised. "They are like brother and sister," she said. "I don't see a problem."

Mrs. Sherwood didn't answer, but turned her worried gaze to Diana.

"It will be all right, Mama," Diana said. "We will just be gone overnight."

"I think Sally should go too," Mrs. Sherwood said.

"I would be happy to go," Sally said.

"My love," Lady Standish said, "don't you remember that you are to play at the musicale tomorrow afternoon?"

"There is no need for Sally to chaperone me and Alex," Diana said firmly. "We will go to Standish Court, talk to Henley, leave off Jem—I hope—and be back the following day. No one will even know that we are gone." She looked at her mother. "I really do feel that I should be the one to talk to Henley."

After a moment, Mrs. Sherwood nodded. But she still did not look happy.

"Who was the man who rescued you?" Mrs. Sherwood asked Sally. "Did you get his name?"

"I did," Sally said. "He is the Duke of Sinclair. Can you imagine that?"

Lady Standish went pale. Alex's hand, which had been in the process of buttering a piece of bread, went still.

"*Who* did you say?" Lady Standish asked.

"He told me he was the Duke of Sinclair." Sally had not missed the reaction of her mother and her brother and her chin rose slightly. "I thought it was very chivalrous of him to come to my assistance."

"*Chivalry* is not something that one associates with Sinclair," Lady Standish said sharply. "In fact, he is a man I would prefer you to stay away from, Sally. And you too, Diana, dear."

"What is wrong with him?" Diana asked practically.

"He has a bad reputation," Alex said shortly. "I haven't been in town for very long, but I have heard all about him."

"What has he done?" Sally asked.

Alex put down his butter knife. "His father was a very dissolute man and Sinclair grew up in a household that more often than not contained his father's latest mistress. He himself has had a bad reputation with women ever since his school days. He's a duke, of course, and immensely wealthy, but he's not the type of man you should associate with, Sally. To put it bluntly, he's an immoral rake. Don't go making a hero of him."

Sally's gently rounded chin lifted. "I am not saying he is a hero, but he certainly came to my rescue today." She turned to her mother. "Is he invited to our ball, Mama?"

"Of course not!" Lady Standish replied.

"Well, I want him to be invited. He was very kind to me. That wretched Lord Morple would have left me standing there by myself, with that awful slave driver and his whip."

Lady Standish shook her head and frowned.

Mrs. Sherwood said gently, "It appears that he was very kind to Sally, Amelia. Is he so beyond the pale of good company that it would be impossible to invite him?"

"No, he's not," Lady Standish replied reluctantly. "One sees him at balls occasionally, but not at the come-out balls of young girls."

"Perhaps we can make an exception," Mrs. Sherwood said.

Lady Standish turned to her son. "What do you think, Alex?"

Alex was looking at his sister. "I don't think it can hurt to invite him," he said slowly. "Sally is bound to meet him at other affairs, and I suppose we should show our appreciation for his rescue of her and that wretched boy. Besides, he probably won't come. I doubt that come-out balls are quite his métier."

Silence reigned at the table. "All right," Lady Standish finally sighed. "I will send an invitation off this afternoon."

Diana and Alex left the following morning in Alex's phaeton to take Jem to Standish Court. He thought the open-air carriage might be too chilly for her, but she dismissed his concern. "I shall wear warm clothes and we can put a blanket in with us in case we need it," she said. "And we can wrap Jem up in my old melton wool riding jacket. That will keep him warm."

So it was that they started out from Grosvenor Square at eight in the morning, driving through the busy London streets with the little boy between them on the front seat.

"Have you ever been around horses, Jem?" Diana asked cheerfully.

"I was nearly knocked over by one a few times," he replied.

"How about dogs?" she asked.

"I was bit by a dog once," came the lugubrious reply.

Over Jem's head, Diana's eyes met Alex's. He smiled. "It's going to be an adjustment for the lad," he said. "But I bet if we find him a puppy, it would help. There's nothing like a dog's love to make one feel at home."

Diana's face lit. "What a good idea, Alex! There has to be a puppy somewhere we can find for him."

"I'm sure there is."

Silence fell as the horse trotted down the London street.

"How many other boys were there working for your master?" Diana asked gently.

"Six," the boy replied.

"And were they afraid like you?"

"Yes, but they was more afraid of old Coborn than they was of going up the chimney."

"It's shocking, Alex," Diana said soberly. "How can a civilized society allow such things?"

A muscle jumped in his jaw. "I don't know, Dee, but when I take my place in the House of Lords I will work against it, I promise you."

"It's strange to think of you in the House of Lords," she said. "But if you can help to stop such disgraceful things, you will be doing a great deal of good."

He chirruped to one of the horses, then said, looking straight ahead, "The government has asked me to work at the Horse Guards to help coordinate the coming coalition occupation of Paris."

Diana's head jerked up. She had thought he was finished with the military, that he was going to settle down at Standish Court and be a landowner. "But you're a Whig!" she exclaimed. "How can you work with a Tory government?"

"In a time of war, we are all just Englishmen," he said. "If I am asked to do my part, then I will do it."

"You've already done your part! You were even wounded. I think they have a nerve to ask you to do more."

"I did very little, Dee," he replied soberly. "The ones who did the most are the ones who did not come back. They are the ones who gave their all, not I."

There was a long silence. Then Diana said expressionlessly, "You just can't let it go, can you Alex? The fighting is over, but you have to hold on to the life one way or another."

"You're being ridiculous," he said angrily. "I am no longer in the army. I am a civilian, working from the comfort of my own home, here in London. I am even escorting you and Sally to the various events on your social schedule. My work for the army is in no way interfering with my leading a normal life."

Part of Diana recognized that she was being unfair, but she couldn't seem to help it. She hated the army. The army had deprived her of a father, and then it had taken Alex away. Every time the army was mentioned, she felt all churned up inside.

Alex changed the subject. "What if Henley doesn't want the boy? Do you have any other candidates in mind?"

Jem stirred at these words and looked up anxiously at Diana. She put a comforting arm around him and frowned at Alex. "Never fear, dear," she said to the boy, "Henley, and more importantly, Mrs. Henley, will be delighted to have you. You will be the son they never had."

Alex said in French, "I don't think it's such a good idea to get his hopes up. Let's wait to see what transpires with the Henleys first, eh?"

"I'm sure I'm right," she replied in the same language.

"I hope you are, otherwise we're going to have to find someone else." He glanced at her. "And that might not be so easy."

"What is that funny language you're talking?" Jem asked.

"It's French, my dear," Diana replied. "How are you doing? Are you warm enough?"

"Oh, yes," came the confident reply. "I am very warm."

Before long they pulled up to an inn for luncheon.

Alex lifted Jem down from the high seat then came around the carriage to Diana. His hands encircled her waist and he lifted her close to him, so that her body slid along his as he set her on the ground.

A sharp pang of desire shot through Diana at the touch of his hands and his body. She suddenly remembered vividly how it had felt to want those hands to touch her, how that body had felt crushed up against hers as they had kissed passionately. She felt her knees buckle a little as he set her on her feet and she leaned against him for moment in weakness.

Before he could take further advantage, however, her spine stiffened and she pulled away. But there was heat in her cheeks as she shepherded Jem into the hotel to get some food.

Alex had felt that moment of softening, that moment when she had leaned against him. Her almost instantaneous stiffening did not fool him. Her body had told him what her voice had consistently denied; she was not indifferent to him. The old feelings were still there. If only he could get her to admit to them!

Surely there was a way for him to make it up to her. Surely there was a way to make her understand that because he chose the army did not mean he didn't love her. He had loved her then and he loved her now. He had always loved her.

How to make her understand that?

How to make her forgive him for his desertion?

There has to be a way, he thought. *I can't give up. There has to be a way.*

They pulled into Standish Court in the late afternoon, and Henley came into the stable yard himself to see to the care of the horses. He was surprised to find that Alex had driven the phaeton down to the stables himself, and that he was accompanied by Diana and a small boy.

"Henley, this is Jem," Diana said when they were all standing together in the yard. "He has come to live at Standish Court."

Henley looked a little puzzled but he said pleasantly, "Welcome, Master Jem."

Jem looked up at the stocky head groom. "Thank you," he replied in the accents of the streets of London.

Henley glanced from Diana to Alex and didn't say anything.

All of a sudden, Diana wasn't so sure she had done the right thing. How was she to tell Henley that they hoped he would take Jem into his home?"

She said a little nervously, "I would like to introduce Jem to Mrs. Henley, if that would be all right."

Henley looked even more puzzled. "Certainly," he said. "Shall I fetch her?"

"No, we will come with you," Diana said.

Alex shot a look at Diana but didn't say anything.

All of them started toward the cottage that lay between the stables and the grassy, fenced-in paddocks that stretched behind it.

"I believe she's cooking dinner," Henley said, and indeed the aroma of cooking food assailed

Diana's nostrils as soon as she walked in the door. In all the time she had been at Standish Court she had never been inside Henley's home and she looked quickly around at the solid furniture and the clean windows and thought that it would be a perfect place for a small boy.

Mrs. Henley appeared from the kitchen wrapped in a large apron.

"Lord Standish" she said in surprise. "Miss Sherwood!" She clearly didn't know what else to say.

"Mrs. Henley, I wanted to introduce you to Jem," Diana said. "We have brought him from London so he can live at Standish Court." To Jem she said, "Go ahead and shake hands with Mrs. Henley."

Jem approached, his brown eyes so huge they almost engulfed the rest of his thin face. "Hello," he said shyly.

"I am very pleased to make your acquaintance, Jem," Mrs. Henley said warmly.

"Lady Sarah found Jem in London," Diana said. She was gaining more confidence as she talked. Mrs. Henley looked so motherly in her apron. "He was being brutally beaten because he would not climb a chimney. She brought him back to Standish House and we cleaned him up. He is a very nice little boy, and when he has put a little weight on those skeletal bones, he will be handsome as well."

"He's handsome already," Mrs. Henley said, smiling at Jem.

Tentatively, the little boy smiled back.

Diana got to the point. "Our problem, Mrs. Henley, is that we need a family for him to live with. I was wondering if you and Henley might consider taking him in. He thinks he is eight, even though he looks younger. He is hungry for love—his own father sold him to the chimney sweep!—and I think he would fill an empty space in your own lives." There was a pause and she added recklessly, "I'm sure Lord Standish would be happy to help with his expenses."

Silence fell as the Henleys looked at each other. Diana couldn't read anything from their faces. Then Henley said, "We need to talk this over by ourselves."

"By all means," Diana said heartily. "But think how nice it would be to have someone to whom you could pass down all of your vast knowledge of horses."

"Has the lad ever worked around horses?"

"No, but he is eager to try," Diana said with slight exaggeration. She felt Jem slip his hand into hers, and she squeezed it encouragingly.

Henley nodded slowly. "We'll let you know tomorrow, if that's all right."

"That will be fine, Henley," Alex said firmly, as Diana showed signs of talking some more. He turned to her. "Come along, we should go up to the house. We have to find Jem a room to sleep in tonight."

"All right," Diana said. She looked pleadingly at the head groom. "He really is the nicest little boy."

"I'm sure he is," Henley said.

Diana put a protective arm around Jem's shoulders and steered him from the room.

Nine

Diana was surprised to find that Maria and Margaret, Alex's two young sisters, were not in residence at Standish Hall.

"The young ladies and Miss Pendleton went on a visit to Lady Maria's godmother, and they are staying overnight," Spears the underbutler, who was filling in for Henrys, told them.

"I see," Diana replied. "Well, if you can make up a bedroom for me, I would appreciate it Spears. And put a trundle bed in it for Jem."

"Certainly, Miss Sherwood. Shall I have tea served for you and his lordship?"

"Tea sounds wonderful," Diana said. She glanced down at the rail-thin little boy who was standing so close to her. "And perhaps some sandwiches."

"Bring a bottle of port for me, Spears," Alex said.

By the time they had all washed up from the journey, the food and drink had been laid out in the

Yellow Drawing Room. As soon as Jem saw the sandwiches, he stuffed one into his mouth.

"Take smaller bites, Jem," Diana advised. "You don't want to choke yourself." She looked at Alex. He was sitting on the opposite sofa, his long legs stretched out in front of him, a glass of port in his hand.

"Might I have a taste of that wine?" she asked.

He reached forward and handed the glass to her. She took a little sip.

"Mmm," she said, and took another sip.

"Do you like it?" he asked.

"Yes, I do. I've never had port before. Actually, I've never had much wine at all. But I've always liked what I had."

Alex rang the bell and when a footman answered he requested a second glass.

When the glass was delivered, Alex poured the wine into it and handed it to her. She gave him a conspiratorial grin. "Thank you."

"You're twenty," he said. "I think you can handle a glass of wine."

She sipped it and closed her eyes. "It's *very* good," she said. She opened her eyes. "It's nice to be treated as an adult for a change. I've never had so many rules to follow in my life! You won't believe, Alex, what a young girl cannot do in London. Like going to Tattersall's. I adore looking at horses, but your mother was horrified at the thought of my going there with you. In the country I can go anywhere I want to look at a horse."

"There were a lot of common men at Tattersall's, bookmakers and the like. Not the sort of company I imagine ladies usually keep," he said.

"I'm not going to wilt away if I am in company with common men! If I was with you I would be perfectly safe."

"True. There do seem to be a lot of rules in London society—but there are definitely more for girls than there are for men."

"I know," she said moodily, and sipped some more of her wine.

He said, "Do you know what I'd like to do while we're here? I'd like to go and visit Nero's grave."

She looked up from her wine at the mention of Alex's dog. "Have you been there since you got home?"

He shook his head. "No. But I had a dream about him the other night. He was running toward me, his ears pricked, with that stupid grin on his face—you remember. It was so real. I woke up and I missed him almost as badly as I did when he first died."

"He was a wonderful dog," Diana said softly. "He loved you so much."

He nodded. Nero had been Alex's dog since before he had gone away to school and he had died of old age the year before Alex went off to war. Diana and Alex had buried him in the Home Woods, with a stone to mark the site of his grave.

"We'll go tomorrow before we leave," she said.

"I hope his grave isn't grown over," Alex said.

She shook her head. "I make sure the stone is clear."

He smiled at her. "Thank you, Dee."

He looked around the room as if he were seeing it for the first time. "One of these days, when I'm settled, I'll get another dog."

She thought his expression was very strange, but she didn't comment. "And remember, we were going to get a puppy for Jem."

Jem was so involved with his sandwiches that he didn't notice what she had said.

Diana's head was buzzing a little when she rose to go upstairs to the bedroom that had been prepared for her. Jem went with her, holding on to her hand. Once they were inside the room, Diana sat in one of the chairs that was pulled up in front of the fireplace and blinked a few times.

"Are ye all right, miss?" Jem asked anxiously.

"Yes." Diana yawned suddenly. "Do you know, I believe I will take a nap before dinner, Jem. You should do the same. It was a tiring drive."

"I'm not tired," Jem said.

Diana was usually never tired either, but right now she felt quite sleepy. *It must be the wine,* she thought.

She took off her shoes and went over to the bed. *I'll just lie down for a few minutes,* she thought.

The next thing she knew, one of the housemaids was calling her name. She opened her eyes and for a moment was totally disoriented. Then she remembered where she was and sat up abruptly.

"Where is Jem?"

"He's in the kitchen, Miss Sherwood. His lordship thought you would like to know that dinner is in half an hour."

"Thank you," Diana said. She swung her feet to the floor. "I had better change my clothes."

"Shall I help you, miss?"

"Yes, thank you," Diana replied.

Within twenty minutes she had changed out of her driving dress and into a simple white muslin morning dress. Neither she nor Alex had brought evening clothes with them.

He was waiting for her in the sitting room on the first floor. Diana went in and immediately said, "I'm so sorry, Alex, but I actually fell asleep. I can't imagine what happened. I don't ever sleep in the middle of the day."

He grinned at her. "You don't usually imbibe port in the middle of the day either, Dee. It was my fault. I shouldn't have let you drink so much."

"It was good, though," she said.

"Jem is eating in the kitchen," he told her. "I think he'll be more comfortable there than in the dining room. Shall we go in?"

Two places had been set at the table, Alex at the end with Diana placed at his right hand. The roast beef was not quite up to the standards of Lapierre, but it was good enough for Diana and Alex to eat heartily. Alex had four glasses of wine.

Diana had been thinking, and now that Jem wasn't present she mentioned a few families who she thought might be willing to take him if they were reimbursed for his expenses.

"You would know better than I," Alex said soberly. "I was in the army for three years, and before that I was away most of the time at school. My mother seems to think that I just naturally will know everything about running the estate, but in truth I know very little. I did go around and introduce myself to all of the tenants, but it will be a while before I feel I have a grip on things here."

"It was your choice to go away," Diana reminded him.

"I know that," he replied shortly.

After dinner they went upstairs to the Yellow Drawing Room. He sat beside her on the sofa.

The power of his physical presence exerted a frighteningly magnetic pull on her. She moved farther away from him. He turned to look at her. His hair had fallen forward across his forehead.

He said huskily, "I thought about you all the time I was away. Why didn't you read my letters?"

Her heart was beating too fast and she swallowed so that when she spoke her voice would be clear. "I didn't come here to give you an opportunity to harass me." She was staring straight ahead. "I came to help get Jem settled. I don't want to talk about us, Alex. There is no 'us' anymore."

"I don't believe that," he said in the same husky voice.

"It's true." She gave him a defiant look. "I am going to marry a different kind of man from you, settle down and raise a family. I don't love you anymore, Alex."

"But I still love you," he said, and bent his head to kiss her.

At the last moment, Diana turned her face away. She felt his lips on her cheek, the weight of his body against hers, his arms encircling her. She could smell the wine on his breath. Her whole instinct was to give into him, to yield, to kiss him back. She ached for him with an intensity that was almost impossible to resist.

But she did resist.

I can't let Alex do this to me, she thought hazily, as she leaned against him, inhaling his familiar scent. *He can't just throw me away and then think he can have me back when it's convenient for him.*

She stiffened her back—one of the hardest things she had ever done in her life—and pulled away from him.

"I trusted you to act like a gentleman," she said breathlessly. "I would never have come with you if I had thought you would try this."

Her heart was slamming so hard in her chest that she was sure he must hear it. She was upset and angry with herself. She had not expected to react so strongly to him.

He reached out and touched her hair and she pulled away from him forcefully. "Don't!"

She heard him inhale deeply. "You're right. I apologize," he said in a grim voice. She saw a muscle jump in his jaw. "But if you ever change your mind, Dee, remember that I'll be waiting."

She gripped her hands tightly together in her lap.

"Don't wait," she forced herself to say. "Find someone else."

The muscle twitched again and he didn't answer.

The door opened and a footman came in with the tea tray. After he had left, Diana started talking about settling Jem and Alex drank his tea and listened without making any reply.

Alex awoke at two in the morning, shaking all over and covered in sweat. He stared around him in the dark, not knowing where he was. His heart was pounding. The screams of wounded men and horses still sounded in his ears.

"Christ," he said out loud.

A glimmer of moonlight shone through the curtains he had left open. He didn't like sleeping in the dark anymore. He looked around again and recognized the bedroom. He was at Standish Court, not in the Peninsula.

He lay there, struggling for breath, waiting for his heartbeat to slow. He was familiar with this nightmare. He had lived with it ever since Salamanca. But it had been growing worse since he came home.

It's all right, he told himself. *You're all right. Stop being such a fool. Get hold of yourself.*

Slowly his heart began to return to its normal rhythm. The sweat dried on his skin, leaving him feeling chilled. He got out of bed and put on his robe. He went to the window and looked out.

The moonlight shone on the vast expanse of lawn

that fronted the house, making the drive look like a ribbon of black velvet. It was a beautiful sight.

Standish Court, Alex thought. *My home.*

But somehow he could not feel connected to it. Ever since he had returned home, he had gone through the motions of what everyone expected of him. He had toured the estate, gone over the books, tried to pay attention to the myriad details that his estate agent had discussed with him. But he felt distanced from it all, as if he were watching himself do all of these things, as if he were not really present.

It was the same in London. Even his work for the Horse Guards had not fully engaged his attention.

What is the matter with me? he thought despairingly. *I didn't want to stay with the army anymore. I thought I would be happy to be at home. But I can't seem to…connect…somehow. And these nightmares…*

The only time he felt like his old self was when he was with Dee. If he could hold her, kiss her, be with her, then maybe some of this strangeness would go away.

But he had forfeited that right. For the first time he contemplated the possibility that she wouldn't change her mind, that she wanted another kind of man from him. He knew he couldn't really blame her, but he wondered with some despair what would become of him if he lost Dee.

He looked around for his slippers. He would go down to the library and find a book. He knew from experience that his sleep for the night was over.

He lit the lamp in the library and was pulling a copy of *Xenophon* from the shelves, when he heard Dee say, "Alex? What are you doing here this time of night?"

His head jerked around. She was standing in the doorway, wearing a voluminous white nightgown. Her hair fell in a glorious mass of coppery curls around her shoulders.

"I couldn't sleep," he said. "What are you doing here?"

"Jem woke up with a nightmare. I'm going to get him some warm milk from the kitchen."

Poor little boy, Alex thought. *What a hell of a life he must have led.*

"That's a good idea," he said. He stepped away from the floor-to-ceiling mahogany bookcase, his copy of *Xenophon* in his hand.

"Why couldn't you sleep?" she said. "You certainly had enough wine at dinner to make you sleepy."

He had drunk the wine in the hopes that it would do just that.

"I don't know," he answered as lightly as he could. He certainly wasn't going to tell Dee that he had nightmares. "Sometimes one has nights like that."

"True." She sounded as if she understood what he was talking about.

"Go back to bed," he said. "It's cold and you don't have a robe on. I'll get the lad his milk."

"Are you sure?"

"Yes. I'll bring it along in a few minutes. Go back upstairs and get into bed."

She disappeared from his view and he went downstairs to the kitchen, where he located the milk. It took him a bit longer to figure out how to warm it up, but he finally managed it. He climbed the stairs again, coming to a halt in front of the bedroom Diana was using. The door was partially open.

"Dee?" he called.

"Come in," she said softly.

The lamp was on and he walked into the room. Jem was not in the trundle bed, he was sitting up in the big bed next to Diana. Alex walked across the room and sat down on the bed next to him.

"Here you go, laddie," he said. "Drink it up and it will help you go back to sleep."

The boy accepted the glass from his hands. There was a shadowy look around his big brown eyes.

"He had a dream about being forced to climb chimneys," Diana said.

They exchanged a look of sympathy over Jem's head. "Poor child," Alex said sincerely. "Nightmares are horrible things."

Diana nodded.

Alex ran gentle fingers through the boy's mop of hair. "You're going to be all right, Jem," he said. "I am a very important lord, you know, and I am going to make certain that you are all right. No one will ever make you climb chimneys again. We are going to find you a good family where you can grow up to be a happy, healthy boy."

Jem looked up at Alex. "What if I don't like this family?" His voice trembled. "What if they're mean to me?"

Alex looked directly into his eyes. "If you're not being well treated, you will tell me and I will fix it."

There was a moment of silence as the two of them looked at each other. Then the boy said, "What will you do?"

"You can come and live with me," Alex said.

Jem's big eyes got bigger. "Do you mean that?"

"Yes," Alex said.

The boy smiled. Then he drank his milk.

Alex looked at Dee. She had tears in her eyes.

"Thank you," she mouthed to him.

He nodded and got up from the bed. "I'll say good night to you both," he said. "We'll meet again at breakfast."

Ten

Diana lay in bed, wide-awake, with Jem asleep beside her. It was that nap she had had this afternoon, she thought. That was why she couldn't sleep.

Alex had meant it when he had said he would let Jem live with him, she thought. They had almost totally disarmed her, those words of his. For a moment it was as if she had the old Alex back.

She turned on her side, trying to get comfortable, and a memory swam slowly to the surface of her mind. She had been sixteen years old and she and Alex had gone to the lake, ostensibly to fish. Instead they had sat on the grassy bank, his head in her lap, the sun warm on their faces. They had been quiet, content just to be alone together. She could almost feel the weight of his head, could almost smell the faint scent of his sun-warmed skin. Nero had slept at a little distance from them, wuffling a little now and then as he dreamed.

How peaceful she had felt with Alex. How secure in the bond that held them together. She had never once worried that he would be a great earl while she was a mere commoner. He was Alex and she was Dee. That was all that mattered. She trusted him.

What had been amazing was that no one in the family seemed to notice that something unusual was going on between Alex and Diana. She had been like a sister to Sally; everyone thought that she was like a sister to Alex, as well. They had not had to work very hard at covering their tracks. They had been companions for years.

And they didn't want anyone to know. It was their secret, this precious love that had bloomed between them. Eventually Diana knew it would have to come out, but during those halcyon summers when Alex was home from school, they didn't want anyone intruding into the intense privacy of their feelings.

Of course she knew that Alex had dreamed of being a soldier, but she also knew that his father was against it. He was the heir and the earl wanted him to stay at home and learn to shoulder the responsibilities of his position. And at Standish Court, and in his family, the earl's word had been law. He had always intimidated Diana and she had never really been comfortable with him. He had given shelter to her and her mother, but he didn't really care about them, the way Alex's mother did. He had never been a substitute father to her.

She had grown up without the comfort and protection that a father provided to his child. She had seen how difficult it was for her mother to be a woman alone. If Cousin Amelia hadn't taken them in, God knows what would have happened to them.

Diana deeply resented her father for dying in battle and leaving his family to fend for themselves. She thought that he should never have left them to advance his career in the army. He had turned his back on his responsibilities to his wife and child and she would never forgive him for that.

It had truly not occurred to her that Alex would do the same thing to her. As she sat there on that perfect July day, with the sun reflecting off the gray water of the lake, and Alex's head in her lap, she had not had a thought in the world that anyone could come between them. She had certainly never dreamed that the one to destroy her idyll would be Alex himself.

Lying in her bed beside the sleeping Jem, tears came to her eyes. She dashed them away with her hand.

Stupid, she told herself. *There's no use pining over what used to be. You have to go forward with your life, you can't be looking back.*

She couldn't marry Alex and hold his desertion over his head for the rest of their lives. And she couldn't let it go. Once again her mind shied away from thinking too closely about why she blamed him so bitterly.

Please God, she thought. *Let me find a good man to marry.*

* * *

The following morning, Diana and Alex left Jem with one of the maids and went down to the stables to talk to the Henleys. They gathered in the small sitting room of the Henley cottage.

"It's a big undertaking, to take in a strange boy," Henley said. "What if he doesn't work out?"

"If he doesn't work out, we'll take him back," Diana said. "But I think love will make him blossom, Henley. Do you know the terrible lives climbing boys have in London? Well, his own father sold him into that life."

"That's terrible," Henley said gruffly.

Mrs. Henley looked at Alex. "We'll take him, my lord," she said. She turned to her husband. "We discussed this last night. God has not seen fit to give us children of our own. Perhaps it is His will that we take this one into our hearts and into our home."

Very slowly, Henley nodded his agreement.

Alex said, "I will be glad to pay you a stipend for his care."

"No," Henley said decisively. "If he is to be my son, I will take care of him. Your lordship pays me a good enough salary already."

Diana smiled radiantly. "I don't think either of you will regret doing this."

"I hope not, Miss Sherwood," Henley said a little emphatically.

"We said we would take him back if he didn't work out, and I mean that," Alex said. "I can always find a place for him in my household. But I think he will be much better off with a mother and a father."

"I think you're right, my lord," Mrs. Henley said. Her plump face looked very serious.

"We were thinking of getting him a puppy," Diana said. "Would that be a problem for you? I must warn you that Jem has nightmares, and I think a dog to sleep on his bed would be a big help to him."

Henley looked at his wife. "It's up to you, Alice."

"It will be a nuisance, but I think it's a good idea," she replied. "Poor little lad. So he has nightmares?"

"He had one last night. He told me he was dreaming that someone was forcing him to climb a chimney."

Tears stood out in Mrs. Henley's eyes. "The Martins had a litter of puppies about a month ago. I'll see about getting him one of them."

"That would be wonderful," Diana said fervently.

Alex said, "He has no clothes. You will have to take him into town and outfit him." He reached into his pocket and took out a wad of bills. "At least let me pay for his first wardrobe."

After a moment, Henley reached out and accepted the money.

After Alex and Diana had brought Jem down to the Henley's cottage, they went out to the paddock to visit Alex's old hunter, who was retired along with his father's old hack.

"When I get back home for good, I'll have to get a few new hunters," Alex said. "I hunted Bart when I was in Portugal, but I'd rather keep him for a hack and get something else to hunt."

"I haven't hunted since you left," Diana said wistfully.

He turned to her in surprise. The April breeze was blowing his black hair. "Why not?"

"I didn't have a horse," she said. "Your father was very good to let me ride Monty around the estate to exercise him, but I certainly wasn't going to ask to hunt him. And it's been a long time since Annie was fit enough to hunt."

There was a little silence. Then he said, "That's too bad. You loved to hunt."

She shrugged and didn't answer.

The two horses had been standing in front of them, eating the carrots that Diana had brought. Now that there were no more treats, the horses turned around and began to cross the field together. Diana watched the sun reflect off their thinning winter coats.

"If we start back immediately, we can be in London in time for dinner," Diana said.

"I'd like to visit Nero first."

She nodded. "Let's get going, then."

Alex stood by the grave of his dog and had to fight to keep back tears.

This is stupid, he told himself. *Nero has been dead for years. There's no reason for you to behave like a child.*

But the memory of his dog brought back other memories, happy memories that were not scarred by the haze of blood and the screams of the injured and the dying.

If I had to do it all again, would I make the same choice? he wondered.

He looked at Diana, who was standing beside him.

I lost Dee and I got nightmares, he thought bitterly. He looked at Nero's gray stone and after a moment he consciously straightened his shoulders. *But I served my country and helped to rid the world of a tyrant. I can't regret doing that. I can't.*

Diana turned from the grave and began to walk back in the direction from which they had come. He looked away from Nero's stone, to the thick woods, then up to the clear blue sky. *I just wish I knew where I fit in. There's no place in the army for me anymore. My job there is done. But I don't feel as if I fit in here anymore, either.*

Diana stopped and looked back at him. "Are you coming?" she said.

He blinked quickly, so she wouldn't see the tears in his eyes. "Yes," he said. "I'm coming."

The ride back home was quiet. They talked for a little bit about Jem, and how he would fit in with the Henleys.

"I think Mrs. Henley will be very good to him," Diana said.

Alex murmured his agreement.

Silence fell as the horses trotted along the highway, occasionally passing other carriages going in the opposite direction.

"Does your mother know about us?" he asked abruptly.

She gave him a startled look.

"What makes you ask that?"

"The way she's behaved toward me since I got home. She's been polite, but scarcely warm. And she most definitely did not want you to accompany me on this errand."

Diana studied his profile for a moment in silence, knowing well why her mother might have no love for him. "I think you're imagining things," she said stiffly. "Mama has always been very fond of you."

"She used to be," he replied. He turned his eyes her way and for a moment she looked into their crystalline depths. "But she doesn't act very fond of me anymore."

"You're imagining things," Diana repeated, turning away from those questioning eyes. "Just because Mama isn't fawning all over you, like your own mother is doing, doesn't mean she doesn't like you."

"All right," he said after a moment. "If you say so."

Silence fell again, the only sound the horses' hooves as they struck against the road.

At last he said, "I'll buy you a hunter for this coming season, if you like."

"That is nice of you," she said tightly, "but I am hoping by then to have a husband."

The telltale muscle twitched in his jaw. "So you are really serious about getting married?"

"Of course I'm serious. That's why I came to London."

"None of your suitors at home were rich enough, eh?" he said a little nastily. "Certainly none of them could afford to buy you expensive hunters."

"That's a rotten thing to say," she flashed. "I didn't love any of them, that's why I didn't marry them."

"So you're looking for love, not money?"

"That's right," she said defiantly.

He snorted, as if he didn't believe her.

"If I just wanted money, I would marry you," she shot at him. "You're the biggest catch on the marriage mart this Season, did you know that? But I want more than money. I want a man I can love and *trust*. That's what I'm looking for. And I resent your insinuations that I'm nothing but a gold digger."

They were passing a stagecoach and the men packed on the roof looked down curiously at the privileged aristocrats driving by them. Once they were in the clear again, Alex said quietly, "I'm sorry, Dee. I shouldn't have said that."

"No, you shouldn't." Her cheeks were already red from the chilly air, but they had gotten a little redder in the past minute. "You have no idea what it's like to be alone and unprotected. No man does. If a woman doesn't have a man she can rely on, she is completely vulnerable—unless she has money, which Mama and I don't."

"My parents took care of you and your mother!" Alex protested.

"Yes, and I thank God for that. But how do you think Mama felt, having to be grateful for every bite of food she put in her mouth?"

"My parents never made her feel that way!"

"Your mother didn't. But your father definitely saw us as dependents. Oh, he was always very nice to us—to me—but I was always conscious of my place when I was with him. And I know Mama was, too."

He scowled, his black brows drawing together. "I never knew you felt like this."

"I don't think he would have let you marry me, Alex. I never thought about it at the time—I was too much in love with you—but I've thought about it since. He would have wanted you to make a much grander marriage than to a penniless, dependent cousin."

"It wouldn't have mattered what he thought. If he refused his consent, I would have married you the minute I turned twenty-one."

"When you turned twenty-one, you were in the Peninsula," she pointed out.

He didn't reply.

She said, "And now Cousin Amelia has given me this wonderful opportunity to have a Season and meet some eligible men. This is my one chance, Alex, and I'm going to take it. I'm going to find a suitable man who can take care of me and Mama and get married."

He couldn't stop himself from saying, "I can take care of you and your mother better than anyone."

"But I don't want *you*," she said brutally.

He wanted to stop the horses, to reach out and pull her into his arms. He wanted to feel whole again, he wanted to feel the way only she could make him feel. He wanted her so desperately.

And he couldn't have her. The more time he spent with her, the clearer that became. She would never forgive him. He was going to have to learn to live his life without her.

The only problem was, he didn't know if he could.

Eleven

The following morning, Diana woke up in her bed in Standish House on Grosvenor Square. She went down to breakfast and found Sally at the table. She had told Sally the previous night all about Jem and the Henleys, so this morning their conversation was mostly about their upcoming ball and what they were going to do during the day.

"Mama wants us to help her address invitations," Sally said. "I'm glad she is inviting the Duke of Sinclair. If it wasn't for him, Jem might not now be living with the Henleys."

Diana stirred some sugar into her tea. "You would have managed without him, Sally. If necessary, you would have bullied your reluctant escort into driving the both of you home."

"I don't know about that," Sally laughed. "The way Lord Morple was acting, we might have ended up walking."

"What a swine Lord Morple is," Diana said.

"Yes," Sally agreed wholeheartedly.

Mrs. Sherwood walked into the dining room and gave her daughter a long, searching look. Diana had avoided talking privately to her mother since she had got back from Standish Court late the previous day.

Diana gave her mother a sunny smile. "What plans do you have for the day, Mama?"

"I believe we are all spending the afternoon addressing invitations," Mrs. Sherwood said.

"Oh. That's right," Diana returned. She took a piece of toast and very carefully smeared it with marmalade.

Sally stood up. "I have a letter to write. I'll see you later."

After she had gone, and the two Sherwood women were alone together, Mrs. Sherwood asked, "How did it go between you and Alex, darling?"

"Fine," Diana said lightly. "As we told you yesterday, we got Jem settled with the Henleys, and then we came home."

Mrs. Sherwood poured herself some coffee from the pot on the table. "You were alone together for a long time. What did you talk about?"

Diana wiped some marmalade off her fingers. She frowned. "We talked about Jem. And about horses. And we went to visit Nero's grave. Nothing important happened, Mama."

"You didn't tell him?"

Diana put her napkin down and for the first time looked directly at her mother. "No. I'm never going to tell him, Mama. You know that. It's finished. *We're* finished. There's no point in reliving the past."

There was a little silence. Diana took a bite of her toast.

Mrs. Sherwood said, "I know how you feel, darling. And I was as angry at Alex as you were. But…he looks at you, Diana. When you're not watching, he looks at you all the time. He still has feelings for you. I can see it. And now that his father is dead, he can marry whomever he wants. I think you could have him if you wanted him."

"But I don't want him," Diana said passionately. "I don't care if he *is* the bloody Earl of Standish! I don't want him. I thought you were on my side, Mama. How could I marry a man who deserted me like that?"

Mrs. Sherwood had winced at the profanity, but she forebore to protest. "All right, darling," she said softly. "If that's how you feel, then that's fine. I am on your side, you know. I'm always on your side."

Diana bit her lip. "I know, Mama. I'm sorry I yelled at you." She got up and went around the table to bend and kiss her mother's cheek. "I'll find somebody to take care of us. Don't worry. Everything is going to be all right."

Every afternoon when she drove out in the park, Sally looked for the Duke of Sinclair. She also looked for him at all of the social functions she attended. She never saw him.

She remembered him vividly—his tall, wide-shouldered figure, his dark blond hair and striking green eyes. It was hard for her to believe that a man who had been so kind to her and Jem could be as bad as Alex had painted him to be.

I would just like to thank him and to tell him that Jem is settled, she told herself as she addressed his invitation to her ball.

Diana looked up from the invitation she was addressing. "Who is Miss Jessica Longwood?" she asked curiously. "I don't remember meeting someone of that name."

Lady Standish replied. "She's Viscount Longwood's daughter. I don't know if they're going to be in town for the ball, but I thought I'd invite them just in case. Jessica came out last year and, according to Sally Jersey, she's practically engaged to Rumford."

"Who is Rumford?" Diana asked next.

"The Earl of Rumford. He's probably the biggest catch on the marriage mart—after Alex, of course," his mother added.

Sally said, "We haven't seen the Earl of Rumford, have we?"

Lady Standish shook her head. "He hasn't been in town either. But we'll send an invitation to his house on Berkeley Square just in case he arrives before the ball."

"Why is Alex a better catch than Rumford?" Diana asked.

"Well, for one thing, he's younger, which has to be appealing to a young girl," Lady Standish said. "Lord Rumford was married for fifteen years to a sickly woman who didn't give him any children. He has to be forty, at least. And he's looking to marry a young, healthy girl so he can have a family. Not much romance there, I should say."

Sally said, "His wife eventually died, I gather?"

"Yes. I believe her sickliness stemmed from a heart condition."

Sally blotted her invitation. "And Miss Longwood is his choice to be his future countess?"

"Nothing official has been announced, but so Sally Jersey tells me."

Mrs. Sherwood said with amusement, "And Sally Jersey knows all?"

Lady Standish laughed. "She seems to, Louisa." She looked at the next name on her invitation list. "Now here is someone I'd like to see Alex become interested in."

Diana's head shot up. "Who is that?"

"Lady Caroline Wrentham. She's a lovely girl. She made her come-out last year, got a dozen offers and refused them all. She can afford to be picky. Not only is she beautiful, but she comes from one of the best families in the country. The Wrenthams can trace their heritage back to Edward the Third. Her father is the Marquess of Hartly."

"We've seen Lady Caroline," Sally said. "She *is* beautiful." She turned to Diana. "Do you know who I mean?"

"Yes," Diana said. She had seen the tall, slim, blond Lady Caroline dancing with Alex more than once.

Lady Standish said, "She might be your biggest competition for suitors, Sally, dear."

Diana wasn't surprised that she was not included in the same category as Sally and Lady Caroline. She wasn't competition to anyone.

She felt her mother's hand come over hers. Mrs. Sherwood squeezed briefly, then went back to writing invitations.

After the invitations were done, Diana took Freddie for his daily walk in the park. Her mother decided to accompany her in order to get some exercise.

"I did so much walking and gardening at home," she said to Diana as they walked the few blocks that would take them to the park, "that I'm starting to feel like a slug. At least you ride in the morning and dance all night. I do nothing at all!"

Diana looked at her slim, pretty mother. "You're being pampered for the first time in your life, and you're complaining?"

Mrs. Sherwood laughed. "I suppose it does sound like that, but I don't mean it."

"I know, Mama," Diana said, "and I know what you mean. London is grand, but I think that in our hearts we're both country girls."

"I think you're right," Mrs. Sherwood agreed.

They entered the park and followed one of the walking paths that wound in and out through the trees and the shrubbery. Diana bent and took Freddie off his leash so he could run after some squirrels. They had been walking for perhaps twenty minutes when Freddie met up with another spaniel, who was trotting down the path from the opposite direction. The two dogs stopped and began to sniff each other interestedly.

"The dog looks friendly," Diana said, "but we had better catch up with them."

She and her mother reached the dogs at about the same time as the other dog's owner.

"Caleb," the man said in a deep baritone voice. "Here, boy."

"My dog is friendly if yours is," Diana said.

The man looked at her. He had graying brown hair and steady gray eyes. He was of medium height and was strongly built.

"Caleb is very friendly," he said.

Now that the dogs had finished sniffing each other, they decided that a chase was in order. Freddie took off first, with Caleb in hot pursuit.

Diana smiled. "It is good to see Freddie running. I felt so guilty taking him away from the country, but I was so lonely without him."

"I know precisely how you feel," the man returned pleasantly. "We've just come in from the country ourselves and that's why I took Caleb to the park today." He made a slight bow. "Sir Gilbert Merton at your service, ladies."

Mrs. Sherwood said, "I am Louisa Sherwood and this is my daughter, Diana."

"Your dog is very handsome," Sir Gilbert said.

"Thank you. I know he's a little small for his breed, but he has a huge heart."

The dogs came back, panting and frantically wagging their tails.

Mrs. Sherwood laughed. She had a delightful laugh, rich and full and contagious. Diana had inherited it from her. "They look so pleased with themselves," she said.

Sir Gilbert looked at her with a smile in his eyes. "What brings you to London, ma'am?" he inquired. "Are you here for the Season?"

"Yes. My daughter is making her come-out under the aegis of my cousin, Lady Standish," Mrs. Sherwood returned.

Sir Gilbert raised his eyebrows. "My daughter is here for precisely the same reason. I am a widower and she is making her come-out under the aegis of my sister, Lady Mary Barlow. They dragged me along for window dressing."

"I don't believe I have met Miss Merton," Diana said.

"We only arrived in town the other day. She will be making her first appearance at Almack's tonight." He raised his eyebrows. "I cannot believe what a commotion my sister is making about a simple assembly dance. Charlotte has been going to dances in the country ever since she was seventeen."

Diana chuckled. "Almack's is the *sine qua non* of the marriage mart," she said. "We will be going ourselves tonight. Perhaps we will see you there, sir."

He bowed again, his sturdy figure making the motion with surprising grace, his eyes never leaving Mrs. Sherwood. "I will look forward to it."

Twelve

The night of the much-anticipated Standish come-out ball finally arrived. The polished carriages were lined up around the square, waiting to let out their finely dressed passengers, and the great chandelier in the ballroom on the second floor of the house shone on a botanical garden of hothouse flowers that Lady Standish had ordered from the finest florists in London. Almost everyone who had been invited was coming, and the evening was going to be that most successful of all events—a "sad crush."

Diana stood in the receiving line with Alex, Lady Standish, Sally and Mrs. Sherwood. She wore a dress of white sarconet draped over an underslip of green satin. Her hair was knotted high on her head, with tendrils of red-gold curls falling around her long, slender neck. Her large brown eyes sparkled with excitement and a delicate natural pink stained the exquisite curve of her cheekbones.

"You'll be the most beautiful girl in the room to-night," Alex had said to her in a low voice when he had first seen her before dinner.

He stood now at the head of the receiving line, with the rest of the family between them, passing the guests along from one person to the next. Diana couldn't believe how many people she greeted. Most of them she had seen before, but a few were new faces. One new face that she made particular note of was the Earl of Rumford, the man whom Lady Standish had said was the second-best catch on the marriage mart after Alex. She noticed him because of the way he looked at her—as if he were a little dazed. It was a look Diana had seen before on the faces of men, but she had not expected to see it on the face of a sophisticated middle-aged earl. Rumford was a nice-looking man in his early forties, with blue eyes and brown hair that had just begun to gray. He held her hand for a second too long and he blinked, as if to clear his vision.

"How do you do, Miss Sherwood," he said.

"I am so glad you could come this evening, my lord," she responded, giving him a radiant smile.

Her mother spoke, passing along the next person in line, and the earl left her and went into the ballroom.

Finally the family was able to enter the ballroom themselves. Diana looked around at the sea of expensive jewels and colorful gowns and black-and-white clad gentleman, and took a deep breath. A scent of mingled perfumes and flowers drifted to her nostrils.

How kind Cousin Amelia was to include me in this world, she thought. She turned to her mother and flashed her a quick smile. Mrs. Sherwood smiled back.

The orchestra began to play a waltz. Sally was to lead off the ball with Alex, and Diana stood with her mother and watched as the two of them went around the floor. Sally looked lovely in her white gown over a light blue slip. The slip, Diana found herself thinking, was almost the same color as Alex's eyes.

The dancing couple suddenly stopped in front of Lord Dorset, the eldest son and heir of the Earl of Winchester, and one of Sally's chief suitors. Lord Dorset stepped forward gallantly to partner Sally, and Alex strode across the room toward Diana.

"Come along, Dee," he said. "It's your turn."

She hadn't expected this and the pink in her cheeks deepened as she took his hand and followed him onto the floor. His hand encircled her waist and she put her hand on his shoulder. He took her other hand into a firm clasp and they began to dance.

She was so close to him. It felt as if the hand on her waist was burning through her dress. She could feel the strength of his shoulder through the fabric of his evening coat. Their bodies moved as one, in perfect harmony with one another. Neither one of them spoke. For a few perfect moments, it seemed to her as if they were alone together in a timeless bubble. Then other dancers began to join them on the floor.

Diana struggled to say something. "It was kind

of you to dance with me like this," she managed to get out.

"It's your come-out ball as well as Sally's," he said. His face as he looked down at her was grave.

"I am so grateful to your mother for doing this for me," Diana said. She inhaled and went on determinedly. "And I'm grateful to you, too, Alex. I imagine you're the one who's paying the bills."

"I owe you something, Dee," he said. His expression was still grave. "I know that. If there's ever anything I can do for you, please know that I will always be at your service."

She couldn't reply.

The music stopped and everyone on the floor applauded.

"Come," Alex said. "I'll take you back to your mother."

As Sally had stood in the receiving line, she'd kept looking for one particular face, but it never came.

Stop being such an idiot, she told herself, as she danced with a variety of admiring young men and made superficial conversation. Halfway through the evening, she was sitting on one of the chairs along the wall with Lord Dorset, sipping punch during a break in the dancing, when Henrys appeared in the door of the ballroom and announced with impressive dignity, "His Grace, the Duke of Sinclair."

Sally's head jerked around, and there he was, standing in the doorway, his dark blond hair illuminated by the great chandelier. Her heart began to beat faster.

"Now there's a surprise," Lord Dorset said. "One doesn't usually see Sinclair at an affair like this."

Apparently Lord Dorset was not the only one to be surprised. It seemed to Sally as if half the people in the ballroom had turned to stare at the duke.

He appeared superbly unconscious of the attention he was attracting, and moved with smooth grace to greet his hostess, Lady Standish. If she was surprised to see him, she hid it well. She smiled at him and they stood talking for a few moments. Then the music started up again, dancers began to move onto the floor, and the focus of the ballroom shifted away from the notorious duke.

"I wonder what he's up to," Lord Dorset said.

"Perhaps he just came to be sociable," Sally returned a little breathlessly.

Lord Dorset made a sound indicative of disbelief.

Sally knew the exact second that Sinclair saw her. She watched him crossing the room until he was standing in front of her. "Lady Sarah," he said. "How nice to see you again."

Sally hoped she did not look as overwhelmed as she was feeling. "Your Grace. It was good of you to come to our ball."

The duke glanced at Lord Dorset. "You won't mind if Lady Sarah and I have a dance, will you, Dorset?"

Lord Dorset obviously did mind, but there was nothing he could do about it. Sinclair was, after all, a duke. "Or course not," he said tightly.

The dance was a country one, so there was no chance for Sally and the duke to have a conversation. When it had finished, the duke said, "I took you away from your punch, Lady Sarah. Would you like to have another glass?"

"Yes, thank you," Sally replied.

So it was that she found herself sitting along the ballroom wall, with the Duke of Sinclair beside her, each of them sipping champagne punch.

"I am glad to see you, Your Grace," she said. "I wanted to tell you that the climbing boy we rescued is happily settled at Standish Court. Our head groom and his wife, who have no children, have taken him to be their adopted son. I have wanted to thank you for your help that day, Your Grace. If you hadn't come along, I don't know what I would have done."

His green eyes regarded her enigmatically over the rim of his punch glass. "I'm sure you would have prevailed somehow, Lady Sarah. You were very determined to rescue that child."

"Yes, I was. I have done some research on climbing boys since then, and I feel very strongly that it is a practice that must be stopped. In fact, I have joined a society whose purpose is to get Parliament to pass a bill outlawing the use of children to clean chimneys."

"It is certainly a deplorable practice," he said.

"There are no words to describe how hateful it is," Sally said forcefully. Her large blue eyes flashed. "If people would only refuse to employ chimney sweeps who use climbing boys, the practice would stop on its own. It is perfectly feasible to clean a chimney by using a long-handled broom. That is how we always had our chimneys cleaned at Standish Court. I never knew about climbing boys until I found Jem."

"There are a lot of ugly things that happen in London that you didn't see in the country, Lady Sarah," the duke said.

She searched his eyes, but she could not read him. "Yes," she said. "I know. At home, if people are poor, there is always someone to help them…family, neighbors, us. In London, no one seems to be responsible for the poor."

"And does that bother you?"

"Yes. It does."

He put his glass down on the chair next to him. "Let me give you a warning, Lady Sarah. Life is hard for those who care too much. Now, if you have finished your punch, I will take you to your mother."

Alex did his duty, dancing with as many unmarried young ladies as he could and being charming to their mothers. He didn't try to dance again with Diana, but he kept track of her and whom she was dancing with, and he was surprised to see her go out to the floor a second time with the Earl of Rumford. And the second dance was a waltz.

One dance by Rumford with a beautiful girl was not noteworthy, two dances were.

Alex happened to be dancing with Lady Caroline Wrentham. He looked into her cool blue eyes and said, "I thought Rumford was supposed to be engaged to the Longford girl, and there he is, dancing for the second time with my cousin."

"The engagement is not official yet," Lady Caroline said.

"They aren't even betting on it in the clubs, it's considered such a sure thing," Alex said.

Lady Caroline raised two perfectly arched eyebrows. "You men are so disgusting," she said. "You bet on anything."

Alex smiled. "I would never bet on a lady's possible marriage, Lady Caroline, I promise you."

"But you know about the bets."

"In this case, it's the lack of bets. And I know everything about all the eligible bachelors in the ton. My mother hounded me to get the information. She doesn't want my sister to waste her time on someone who isn't suitable."

Lady Caroline nodded her golden head in agreement. She was a very elegant-looking girl, tall and reed slim. She and Alex made a striking couple.

"I was at the house party last fall where Miss Longwood and Lord Rumford met," she said. "It was his first social outing after his mourning period was finished. She was *very* nice to him and apparently the relationship flourished. But as far as I know, he hasn't come up to scratch, yet. At least nothing has been published in the papers."

Alex looked at Diana circling in the arms of Lord Rumford, who was gazing at her as if she were a goddess.

Alex scowled. "Miss Longwood isn't here tonight, is she?"

"No, I don't believe she is."

There was a noise at the door and a streak of brown-and-white came racing into the room, followed by a footman in hot pursuit.

"Oh my God," Alex groaned, "it's Freddie." He stopped dancing.

Lady Caroline looked at the spaniel who was running wild among the dancers, trailing his leash. "Is that your dog, my lord?"

"No."

Everyone stopped dancing and the music came to a halt.

"Freddie!" Diana's voice was clear above the murmur of many voices. "Here I am, boy! How did you get in here?"

The frightened dog spotted her and raced in her direction. Diana dropped down to pet him reassuringly. His tail began to beat back and forth and he barked twice.

Alex took Lady Caroline's hand and towed her along until they reached Diana's side. The footman reached her at the same time.

"Thomas," Alex said sternly. "How did the dog get in here?"

"I'm that sorry, my lord," the young man replied miserably. "I was taking him up the stairs to Miss Sherwood's room after his nightly outing, and when we reached this landing he just pulled the leash out of my hand and ran in here."

"He heard the music," Diana said. "Freddie loves music."

Sally arrived at their side. She was laughing as she bent to pet Freddie. "Now everyone will remember our ball, Diana," she said. "It will be 'the ball where the dog got loose.'"

The two girls smiled at each other.

"Get him out of here," Alex said to the footman.

"Yes, my lord," the footman said. He bent and picked up Freddie's leash. "I'm sorry," he said again.

"He seems to be a very sweet dog," Lady Caroline said to Diana as Freddie was led away.

"He is," Diana returned. She looked at Lady Caroline's hand and for the first time Alex realized that he was still holding it. He dropped it hastily.

Lord Rumford said, "You appear to love animals, Miss Sherwood." He looked as if he thought that this was a miraculous trait.

"Oh, Diana is a regular Saint Francis," Sally said cheerfully. "You should see her with horses. She's magic."

Her dancing partner, one of the many young men who had been squiring her around over the past few weeks, said, "I don't believe I've ever seen that happen before, a dog getting loose in a ballroom."

Alex raised his voice and said to the people who were watching them, "Hopefully Freddie has been put to bed." He looked at the orchestra. "You can resume playing, thank you."

The orchestra picked up the music smoothly and the couples on the floor turned to each other once again and began to dance.

A few days prior to the ball, as they were sitting at dinner, Diana had asked Lady Standish that a last-minute invitation be dispatched to Miss Charlotte Merton, her father and her aunt, Lady Mary Barlow. She and Mrs. Sherwood had twice more met Sir Gilbert walking his dog in the park, and Diana heartily approved of a man who took care of his own animal and did not hand off the job to servants. She had also met his daughter at Almack's and Miss Merton had seemed to be a very nice young lady. Diana thought that the Mertons would appreciate an invitation to one of the premiere social events of the Season, and so she had suggested the invitation.

Lady Standish did not know either the Mertons or Lady Mary Barlow, however, and she had demurred. "We haven't seen them at any of the affairs that we have attended," she said. "They can't be among the best people."

"They have just arrived from the country and they were at Almack's this week," Diana had said. "If they have the entrée into Almack's, surely they are socially acceptable."

Lady Standish had looked a little exasperated, which was unusual for her. She had been finding the preparations for the ball rather stressful. "We have a huge crowd coming as it is, Diana. I don't want to send out any more invitations."

Diana had flushed. "I'm sorry, Cousin Amelia. I didn't mean to annoy you. I am fully cognizant of how kind you have been to me. Forget I mentioned the Mertons."

"I knew a Lieutenant Albert Merton in the army," Alex said quietly. "He was in my unit when I first arrived in the Peninsula. He was killed at Salamanca. Before the battle he asked me to write a letter to his family in Sussex if he should die."

Mrs. Sherwood said softly, "Sir Gilbert is from Sussex."

There was no expression on Alex's face. "That was the name of Albert's father," he said. "Sir Gilbert Merton."

A little silence fell on the room. Alex looked at the tablecloth, his face still unreadable.

"Did you write the letter?" Lady Standish asked.

"Yes," Alex said, his voice barely audible.

Lady Standish signaled for the next course to be served. "Well then," she had said briskly, "we shall certainly invite the Mertons. If you will give me their direction, Diana, I will send a card off tomorrow morning."

Diana dragged her eyes away from Alex's face. "Thank you, Cousin Amelia," she had said.

So it was that Sir Gilbert Merton was present at the ball and came up to greet Mrs. Sherwood after Freddie had been dragged out of the room.

"Freddie certainly made his presence felt tonight, didn't he ma'am?" he asked with a chuckle.

Mrs. Sherwood smiled back. "It's a good thing he didn't knock anybody over. Then we would have been in real trouble."

Diana's mother had been standing by herself, watching her daughter dance with Lord Rumford. She was dressed in a gold silk gown and her unfashionably long brown hair was caught in a chignon on the nape of her neck. Sir Gilbert said, "Would you care for a glass of punch, ma'am? Hanging around these balls watching the young ones dance is thirsty work."

"Why, thank you," Mrs. Sherwood replied. "I would like a glass of punch very much."

Once the punch had been fetched, the two of them went to sit on the uncomfortable, straight-backed chairs that lined the ballroom walls.

"Is your husband here, ma'am?" he asked, scanning the floor as if he could conjure the man up.

Mrs. Sherwood shook her head. "My husband was killed at the Battle of Coruña, Sir Gilbert." She took a sip of her punch. The wedding ring she still wore glinted a little as her hand moved.

There was a short silence. Then Sir Gilbert said gruffly, "I lost a son at Salamanca."

"I know," Mrs. Sherwood said gently. "Lord Standish mentioned him the other night. I believe your son had asked him to write you a letter."

"He wrote me a very kind letter," Sir Gilbert

said. He stared down at the punch in his hand. "It was very good of him to do so."

"It is a terrible thing to lose a child," Mrs. Sherwood said.

"Yes." Finally Sir Gilbert took a sip of punch. His gray eyes looked bleak. "If my wife hadn't been dead already, I think the news would have killed her."

Out on the floor the music stopped and the gentlemen who had the next dance on the girls' dance cards moved in the direction of their new partners.

"Your daughter is very beautiful," Sir Gilbert said, changing the subject. "I've been watching her. She has danced every single dance."

"I've noticed that your daughter has been busy, as well," Mrs. Sherwood said.

"Lord Standish has seen to that," Sir Gilbert said. "He must have introduced a dozen young men to Charlotte. My sister is in heaven."

They both looked toward Lady Mary Barlow, who was sitting among the chaperones beaming like the sun.

"Your daughter is a pretty girl," Mrs. Sherwood said. "I'm sure most young men are happy to dance with her."

"Frankly, I wasn't much in favor of this London come-out business," Sir Gilbert said. "But Charlotte wanted it, and my sister offered to sponsor her if I would pay the bills. The money is not the issue. I have more than enough of that to pay for a Season. But Charlotte's the only child I have left, and

I don't want to lose her to some man who will take her to live far away from me. I'd much rather her marry one of the men from home."

"There's only so much influence a parent can have, Sir Gilbert," Mrs. Sherwood said resignedly. "In the end, the young will go their own way. We don't live in the eighteenth century any more, when parents could dictate whom their children would marry."

He looked into her face. "You have the same fears about your daughter, eh?"

She smiled slightly and nodded.

They sat in silence for a few moments, then Mrs. Sherwood said, "How long do you plan to remain in London, Sir Gilbert?"

"I was only planning to stay for a few weeks," he replied. "Charlotte and Mary really don't need me, but Charlotte wanted me to come. So here I am, but I'd really much rather be at home."

"Tell me about your home," Mrs. Sherwood said.

Sir Gilbert obliged, and talked comfortably for two more dances. Then Charlotte came over and he and Mrs. Sherwood went their separate ways.

Thirteen

The day after the ball, the Earl of Rumford came to call on Diana and asked her to go driving in the park with him that afternoon. Diana, who had been amazed to see him, accepted.

"I thought he was supposed to be engaged to Viscount Longwood's daughter," Mrs. Sherwood said when the earl had left.

"It isn't official until it's in the papers," Lady Standish pointed out. "And it hasn't been in the papers."

"I think he saw you last night and was smitten," Sally said to Diana. "He danced with you twice, didn't he?"

Diana nodded.

Lady Standish smiled triumphantly. "Wouldn't it be something if Diana took him right out from under Miss Longwood's nose?"

"She isn't in London," Diana said. "Perhaps he is merely amusing himself until she arrives."

Lady Standish shook her head. "I think Sally is right. He's smitten."

"He's old, though," Sally said.

"If he's not too old for Jessica Longwood, then he shouldn't be too old for Diana," Lady Standish said. She clapped her hands. "He has a great estate in Oxfordshire as well as other properties all over the country. He's a *huge* catch, Diana. Oh, this is almost too good to be true!"

Diana clasped her hands very tightly in her lap. "He seems very nice," she offered.

"I have never heard anything against him," Lady Standish said. "Actually, I've never heard very much about him at all. He didn't go about much in society—he was apparently devoted to his sickly wife."

Mrs. Sherwood spoke for the first time. "Well, I suppose it won't hurt for you to go driving with him this afternoon, darling."

"It certainly won't," Lady Standish shot back. "Take advantage of your opportunity, my dear. It's not too often that a tremendously wealthy earl comes onto the marketplace."

Diana felt a little breathless. She twisted her hands in her lap. *This is what I wanted isn't it?* she demanded of her quickly beating heart. *It's stupid to become all flustered because a possible suitor has come along.* She drew a deep, steadying breath, looked at Lady Standish and said, "What shall I wear?"

"Let's go and look at your clothes," Lady Standish returned, and all the women went upstairs to help pick out Diana's wardrobe.

* * *

Lord Rumford arrived promptly at five where Diana awaited him garbed in a light velvet tan pelisse with a small Spanish hat of the same color. She accompanied him to his slightly old-fashioned phaeton, which was parked in front of the house. He helped her up into the seat and then went around to the driver's side. They started off toward the park.

The earl didn't say much at first—his attention was on the traffic on the street. Diana was silent also, but instead of facing forward she was turned a little, so that she could observe her escort as he drove.

Lord Rumford was a nice-looking man, with brown hair, even features and blue-gray eyes. There were some lines at the corners of his eyes and around his mouth that indicated his age, but his figure was slim and upright under his caped driving coat. His hair showed only a little gray at the temples. Diana thought it made him look distinguished.

When they had reached the park and were rolling along beneath the trees, he relaxed his vigilance and turned to her. "You were very kind to come out with me, Miss Sherwood," he said. "I'm sure you have many younger men who were clamoring for your company."

"I was happy to come driving with you, my lord," she replied simply. "And I am even happier now that I see what lovely horses you have. They are an exceptionally handsome pair."

He smiled at her. *He has a nice smile,* she thought. It looked kind. "Thank you. I am very particular about my horseflesh," he said. "I bred this pair myself."

Diana's whole face lit up. "You did? Where? On your estate?"

His eyes crinkled at the corners in a way she found charming. "Yes. I have a small breeding operation at Aston Castle, my home in Oxfordshire. I have two stallions and eight mares and I breed all my own horses—carriage horses and riding horses, as well."

Diana clapped her gloved hands in delight. "How marvelous. You must know that I am mad about horses. I think breeding your own horses must be one of the most satisfying things in all the world."

"That's right," he said. "I remember that your cousin said last night that you were magic with horses."

Diana laughed. "I don't know if magic is the right word, but I most certainly do love them. A day that I don't ride is a day lost, as far as I am concerned."

A couple trotted past them on the path and Lord Rumford said, "Perhaps I should have invited you to ride with me, instead of driving."

"Oh, I rode this morning," Diana said blithely. "My cousin, Lord Standish, and I go out every morning at about seven and give the horses a good gallop. Riding in this mix of traffic wouldn't be much fun."

"I couldn't agree more," Lord Rumford said, looking around the crowded path. A young man driving a dangerously high phaeton was coming to-

ward them and the earl deftly moved his horses farther to the left. "Dare I ask if you hunt, Miss Sherwood?"

The driver of the phaeton was a young man who
had frequently danced with Diana and he called out,
"Good day, Miss Sherwood," as he went by at too
fast a clip.

Diana nodded to him and said to her escort, "I
have hunted. I adore the hunt. But I haven't had a
horse to hunt in years, I'm afraid."

He gave her a curious look. "Why not?"

"Mama and I don't have much money, Lord
Rumford," Diana said, determined to be honest. "I
was riding Lord Standish's horse while he was in the
Peninsula, and he has been good enough to allow me
to continue to ride Monty since he came home. But
I haven't hunted since my mare, Annie, became too
old and lame."

"I understand your mother is a widow?" he said.

"Yes." She looked at the trees that lined the walking path that flanked the carriage path. "My father
was killed at Coruña."

He didn't say anything and Diana looked back at
him. His blue-gray eyes looked attentive. She found
herself saying, "Mama was really a widow long before Coruña. My father went to India with Lord
Wellington and we never saw him after that."

"That must have been hard on you," he said
quietly.

"Yes," Diana said. "It was. But Lady Standish
was very kind to us and invited us to live at Stan-

dish Park. And now she has been so incredibly kind as to give me this Season."

"And are you enjoying it?"

"Yes. Of course. It's wonderful."

He smiled at her. He really did have a very kind smile, she thought. "Perhaps the lady doth protest too much?"

She laughed. "Well…riding in Hyde Park isn't the same as riding through the woods in the country. And I feel sorry for the animals—the horses cooped up in the stables, my dog cooped up in the house…"

"I like the country best, too," he said. "But sometimes one must show one's face to the greater world."

"Yes. And I *am* having fun. I have never had so many beautiful clothes in all my life."

"You certainly look very beautiful in them," he said.

Diana, who had been hearing compliments all her life, actually found herself blushing. There was a *gravitas* about this man that was missing in all of her younger swains. She liked it. "Thank you," she said quietly.

"I believe that is your cousin, Lord Standish, coming toward us now," the earl said.

Diana looked ahead and saw first a familiar pair of matched chestnuts and then Alex sitting behind them on the seat of his phaeton. Next to him was Lady Caroline Wrentham.

Alex pulled up and Lord Rumford did so, as well. "How are you Standish?" the earl said pleasantly.

He looked at Lady Caroline and smiled. Clearly he did not know her name.

Lady Caroline looked a little put out at not being recognized, but she managed a polite smile as Alex introduced them. Then he said to Diana, "Enjoying your outing, Dee?"

"Yes," she returned sweetly. "And you?"

"Driving in all of this fashionable traffic is not my favorite activity," he said frankly. "The horses don't like so much stopping and starting."

"Your horses are beautifully behaved, my lord," Lady Caroline protested.

"Lord Standish means that *he* doesn't like so much stopping and starting," Diana said.

Lord Rumford said in his pleasant voice, "Perhaps we could all go on an expedition to Richmond Park one of these days. I understand the trails there are excellent and one can gallop to one's heart's content. It would get us into the country for a day."

Diana gave him a brilliant smile. "What a wonderful idea, my lord!"

Alex pushed his hair off his forehead and didn't say anything.

Lady Caroline said, "It is a good idea, my lord. But we can't go with just the four of us. Miss Sherwood and I will need a chaperone."

"Mama can't come," Diana said. "She rode when she was a child, but she hasn't ridden in twenty years."

"I'm sure I can convince my sister to accompany us," Lord Rumford said. "She and her husband are in town for a few weeks."

"If Lady Moulton would accompany us, that would be perfectly acceptable," Lady Caroline said primly.

Everyone looked at Alex, who hadn't spoken a word. Diana saw him shoot a quick look at Lady Caroline.

He's being pushed into this, she thought. But it would be good for him to get out of the city. She had thought he was looking tired lately, as if he had not been sleeping well. Some fresh country air would benefit him.

"It will be fun, Alex," she said.

He looked from her to Lord Rumford then back to her again. "All right," he said at last.

"When shall we go?" Lady Caroline asked, looking at Lord Rumford.

"I have an engagement tomorrow," Alex said. "I must go to the reception the regent is holding for King Louis. How about the day after that?"

"Excellent," Lord Rumford said. "I'll check with my sister."

"Perhaps Sally will want to come with us," Diana said to Alex. She turned to Lord Rumford. "My cousin, Lady Sarah Devize. She might enjoy a ride to Richmond Park as well."

"Then by all means ask her," the earl said. "I'll speak to my sister and see if the date is suitable for her. Then we can make more definite plans."

Alex nodded. One of his horses began to paw the ground. Diana, who had seen his finger move on the reins, knew that Alex had instigated the action.

"I'm afraid my horses are growing restless," he said. "We'll be in touch, my lord."

Lord Rumford nodded graciously and Alex's phaeton pulled away.

The rest of Diana's drive with Lord Rumford was exceedingly pleasant. He told her all about his horses, which she found fascinating. Then he told her about his home, which he obviously loved. When he dropped her off at Grosvenor Square, he asked her if she was attending the Sefton ball that evening. When she said she was, he said he would see her there.

Lady Standish and Mrs. Sherwood were waiting for Diana, and Lady Standish accosted her almost as soon as she entered the house.

"How did it go?" she demanded, pulling Diana into the drawing room that opened off the marble hallway.

"It was fun," Diana said honestly. "He's a very nice man. I like him."

Lady Standish beamed.

Mrs. Sherwood said hesitantly, "He is a little old for her, Amelia. He must be my age."

"Don't be a fool, Louisa," Lady Standish said briskly. "He's young enough to be a good husband and to give her children. *And* he's an earl. A very wealthy earl. He can give Diana everything she wants. If he was sixty, I would be concerned about the age difference. But forty is still a relatively young man."

"Let's not get ahead of ourselves, Cousin Amelia. He hasn't proposed," Diana said reasonably. "And once Miss Longwood comes to town, he might drop me like a hot potato."

"Did he say anything about seeing you again?" Lady Standish asked.

"He said he would see me at the Sefton's this evening. And Lord Rumford and I and Alex and Lady Caroline Wrentham are going on a riding expedition to Richmond Park."

Lady Standish looked meaningfully at Mrs. Sherwood. "This sounds serious, Louisa."

Mrs. Sherwood said, "You can't go without a chaperone."

"Lord Rumford said he would ask his sister—I forget her name."

"The Countess of Moulton," Lady Standish said. "My goodness—this *is* serious."

The three of them had been standing just inside the door of the drawing room and now Diana went and sat down on one of the red tapestry chairs that made a big circle around the fireplace. She stared at the Persian carpet on the floor.

"Are you all right, darling?" Mrs. Sherwood said. She went to put an arm around her daughter.

"I think I'm a little—overwhelmed," Diana replied. She looked up at her mother. "It's hard to grasp that someone of the stature of the Earl of Rumford might be interested in *me*."

"Lord Rumford doesn't need a wife with money. He has more than enough of his own," Lady Standish said from her place by the door.

"But I'm not nobly born," Diana said, turning to look at her.

"You have the face of an angel, my dear," Lady Standish said. She nodded wisely. "Sometimes—if she's fortunate—that's all a woman needs."

Diana nodded very slowly.

Mrs. Sherwood said, "It would be nice to invite Sally to join your expedition to Richmond Park. Perhaps she might invite Lord Dorset."

"I had planned to ask her," Diana said.

"Speaking of Sally," Lady Standish said. "She came in about fifteen minutes ago and went upstairs to change for dinner. We should be doing the same."

"Yes." Diana stood up. Her knees felt a little weak, but she managed not to wobble.

Mrs. Sherwood linked her arm in Diana's. "Come along, darling, and we'll go upstairs."

Fourteen

The first thing Diana saw when she entered the ballroom at the Seftons that evening was the sight of Lord Rumford waltzing with a young, black-haired girl.

"We haven't seen her before," Sally murmured in her ear. "I wonder if that's the elusive Miss Longwood."

It didn't take long for them to find out. Lord Dorset came immediately to Sally's side and when she asked him who was dancing with Lord Rumford he replied immediately, "Oh, that's Miss Longwood. I believe the family has just come to London."

Diana looked at the girl who might be her rival. Miss Longwood was perhaps a little too plump, but she was vivaciously pretty. She was smiling brilliantly up at Lord Rumford as he said something to her.

"She's attractive, but she's nothing like you," Sally murmured in Diana's ear.

Yes, but she's a viscount's daughter, Diana thought. *In this world, it's birth, not looks, that counts.*

One of the young men who always danced with Diana came up to her now and requested the next dance. She acquiesced gracefully and looked around to see if Lady Caroline Wrentham was present.

She was.

Diana felt a wicked stab of delight. *Poor Lady Caroline,* she thought mendaciously. Alex had decided not to come to Lady Sefton's. Instead he was going out with some of the officers he worked with at the Horse Guards. Then she frowned, as she realized how happy she was at the prospect of Alex's separation from the beautiful Caroline.

I don't care what Alex does, she told herself firmly.

As soon as the dance was over, Lord Rumford came to Diana's side, asking to be put on her dance card. She penciled him in for a waltz and a quadrille. Then he asked her to have supper with him, as well.

She couldn't resist glancing over at Miss Longwood.

He said quietly, "It's all right. I have no obligations in that direction."

"But perhaps you have raised expectations," she said softly in return.

"Believe me, Miss Sherwood, I am my own man," he replied, his voice quite firm.

Could it really be true? Diana thought as she gazed up into the earl's steady eyes. Could he really be seriously interested in her?

Her chest felt tight as a storm of emotion churned within her. This was what she had wanted, but now that it seemed to be happening, she was surprisingly apprehensive.

She drew a deep breath. "Very well, my lord, then I will be happy to have supper with you."

The following morning Diana and Lord Rumford were the talk at all the breakfast tables of those who had been to the Sefton ball. The earl had danced once with Miss Longwood and twice with Diana. And he had taken Diana into supper.

The Longwood breakfast table was not a happy one. The viscount had not been in attendance with his daughter and his wife and when he learned about Rumford's obvious interest in Diana, he cursed.

"Who the hell is this Diana Sherwood?" he demanded of his wife. "I've never heard of the chit."

"Her mother is a cousin of Lady Standish," she replied. "She is making her come-out along with Lady Sarah Devize. She is a nobody, my lord. I asked around last night. Her father was a mere colonel who was killed in the Peninsula and she and her mother have been virtual pensioners of the Standishes for years."

"Then what the bloody hell is her attraction for Rumford?" the viscount demanded.

"She's beautiful, Papa," Jessica Longwood replied. "She's the most beautiful girl I have ever seen."

The viscount slammed his hand down on the

table. "We need this marriage, Jessica! Financially, we have to have it! I thought we had Rumford signed, sealed and delivered."

"I thought so, too, Papa," Jessica replied unhappily. "But he never did actually ask me to marry him, you know. I thought he was going to, at the house party at the Websters'. If he wants to change his affections to Miss Sherwood, I'm afraid he is free to do so."

Lady Longwood said vehemently, "He *does* have obligations to you, Jessica! The entire ton expects him to offer for you. He gave every indication that he would do so! He can't humiliate you now by turning to someone else."

Silence fell as the Longwoods considered these words.

"I have just mortgaged Longwood to pay your brother's gaming debts, Jessica," Lord Longwood said. "I have confined him to the estate, but it's too late to turn back the clock. We desperately need an infusion of cash. Your marriage to Rumford was the perfect solution to our problem. Once the knot was tied, I could have asked him for a substantial loan. He couldn't refuse me, then. He wouldn't want the scandal. And we have to act fast, before the truth becomes known about our financial situation. Then no one will want to marry you."

"I know that, Papa," Jessica cried. "I have done everything I could to attach Lord Rumford. I thought for certain that he would ask me to marry him this Season."

"Damn! We should have come to town sooner. But I had to borrow the money before we could do so."

"Perhaps this is just a brief infatuation of Rumford's," Lady Longwood said. "She *is* a beautiful girl, my lord. But she certainly isn't well born enough to marry an earl. Perhaps Rumford will come to his senses—particularly now that Jessica is here to show him the alternative."

"I hope to God that is so, my lady," Lord Longwood said. "Because if we lose Rumford, I don't know what we are going to do."

That afternoon Alex went to Grillon's Hotel, to a reception that the prince regent was holding for King Louis XVIII before the French king left England to take up his newly restored position in Versailles. A large throne had been put in place for Louis and, as Alex stood with a group of other Peninsula veterans, the king moved slowly toward the chair, rather dragging his large body and weak limbs than walking. The regent shared some of the spotlight by investing Louis with the Order of the Garter, graciously buckling the garter around a leg even fatter than his own.

Captain Thomas Stapleton, an old friend whom Alex hadn't seen since he'd returned home, was standing next to him. Stapleton said, "There was no question that we had to get rid of Napoleon, but I wish I could be more confident about his replacement."

Alex looked at the fat Bourbon king. "We're working hard to make the transition smooth," he said. "Wellington will be in Paris to command the occupation." He sighed. "The transition from war to peace is not as easy as I thought it would be."

Captain Stapleton immediately grasped that Alex was speaking on the personal not the political level. "No," he agreed soberly. "I was glad to see my mother and father again but life at home seems somehow…remote. I was only just out of school when I left; I never had the chance to build an adult life for myself here in England. Life in the army is what is real to me now. Yet I don't want to go back to that, either."

Alex felt a chill go through him as he heard his own feelings spoken out loud.

"Let's get out of here," he said. "We need to find a tavern where we can get very drunk."

It was after two in the morning when Alex staggered into the house. Instead of going upstairs to bed, he made his way down the hall to the library, where he flung himself into a leather chair that was placed comfortably in front of the fireplace.

He didn't want anything else to drink. He and Tom Stapleton had almost drunk each other under the table. But it had been very good to be with someone who was going through the same feeling of displacement as he was.

I can't continue like this, he told himself as he stared with blurred vision into the empty fireplace.

I have to make a new life for myself. I am the Earl of Standish. I have responsibilities.

But he was meeting his responsibilities, he thought. He was here in London, doing the things that a young man in his position was supposed to be doing. Wasn't he?

What do I want? he thought.

The answer came immediately. *I want Dee. She is home to me. She's the only one who can bring me back to my old world. Stapleton doesn't have anyone like that, but I do. I have Dee.*

But he didn't have Dee, of course. He had thrown Dee away when he had gone away to war. He had loved her all his life, and he had left her anyway.

What a fool he had been. And now it was too late. She wouldn't forgive him, and there was nothing he could do about it. He couldn't even blame her. He was the guilty one, not her. She deserved someone better than he.

He heard the night footman open the door and there were voices in the hall. The ladies had returned from whatever ball they had been out to this evening.

Tomorrow he had to ride to Richmond Park with Dee and Lord Rumford. And with Lady Caroline Wrentham, who for some reason appeared to be interested in him.

She seemed to be a nice enough young woman, but he wasn't interested in her. He wasn't interested in anyone except Dee.

What if she married the Earl of Rumford and was lost to him forever? What would he do?

There is so much between us, he thought. *Can she really turn her back on it all and marry a man old enough to be her father?*

She had never really had a father, he thought. Perhaps she was looking for one in Lord Rumford.

When Diana invited Sally to join the expedition to Richmond Park, Sally had been delighted to accept. However, instead of asking Lord Dorset to join her, as everyone thought she would, she sent a note to the home of the Duke of Sinclair inviting him along.

She did it with much trepidation. Sally had always thought of herself as a quiet girl, but she was discovering a boldness that she had not known she possessed. First she had rescued Jem from the chimney sweep, and now she was chasing after one of the most notorious rakes in London.

She couldn't explain it, but there was something about the Duke of Sinclair that spoke to her. There had been a look in his eyes when he had come to her rescue that day. He had not helped her on a whim. He had been as disgusted as she with Jem's situation.

Most of the men she danced with and drove in the park with were quite pleasant and charming. It was impossible not to like a nice young man like Lord Dorset. But she was not certain that he would have rescued Jem as Sinclair had. So she daringly sent a note off to Sinclair House asking the duke to escort her on the trip to Richmond, and he responded several hours later saying that he would.

Fifteen

Diana was riding beside Lord Rumford as they approached the entrance to Richmond Park. The day had started out overcast, but the clouds were burning away as the morning progressed. Diana gave Monty a pat with her gloved hand and looked around her with pleasure. It was nice to get out of the city for a change, she thought.

At that moment, the sun came out.

Lord Rumford said, "You really ought to have your picture painted on horseback, Miss Sherwood. You and Monty make a magnificent pair."

Diana turned to him. "He's grand, isn't he? I'm so glad Alex brought Bart home so that I could continue to ride Monty."

"Standish's horse is very nice, as well," he said. "Is that the horse he rode while he was in the army?"

"Yes. They went through several battles together.

I imagine that's a bonding experience that can't be equaled."

"I should think so," he replied.

Lord Rumford and his horse made a wonderful picture as well, Diana thought. The earl was riding a beautiful bay thoroughbred gelding, whose long legs and aristocratic face proclaimed his excellent breeding. The earl himself completed the picture, in his blue riding coat, tan breeches and highly polished riding boots.

Diana had been very impressed by Rumford's horse and even more impressed when she learned that the earl had bred the horse himself. The thought crossed her mind that it would be splendid to be married to a man who had such fabulous horses.

And Rumford was easy to talk to. She had wondered what they would have to say to each other if they spent the whole day in each other's company, but so far the conversation had flowed very comfortably. She looked forward to getting into the park and having a nice, long gallop with a man who probably could ride almost as well as Alex.

Ahead of Diana, Sally was paired with the Duke of Sinclair. She rode her solid chestnut gelding, who could always be counted on to be sane and reliable. Sally rode well, but she didn't like horses who might do something unexpected. She would never have ridden Monty, who was known to spook sometimes just to amuse himself.

The duke's horse was quite a bit taller than Sally's chestnut, and she had to look up when she spoke to him. As the sun came out, it glinted off his dark gold hair, and his eyes seemed to get greener, and Sally thought he was the most striking man she had ever seen.

His conversation had been polished and amusing. Sally had tried to respond in kind, talking about the people she had met in London and the things she had been doing. He had several funny stories about some of the odd people she mentioned and he had made her laugh.

He was so obviously a man of the world. He was thirty years old, immensely rich, and a duke—the most noble noble of all. Listening to him, watching him, Sally wondered that she had had the temerity to invite him to accompany her. She was just a green girl and, according to Alex, not at all the kind of woman the duke usually associated with.

But he came, she thought, with a flash of triumph.

She had been surprised by that—she really hadn't expected him to accept her invitation. But her surprise had been nothing compared to the surprise of the other people in her party when Sinclair had shown up at their designated meeting spot instead of Lord Dorset.

Alex had given her a look that clearly denoted displeasure and even Lord Rumford had looked startled. The only one who had not been surprised was Diana. When Sally had received the duke's acceptance note, she had confided in her best friend, so Diana had been prepared to give Sinclair a friendly smile and a welcome.

Too bad if Alex doesn't like it, Sally had thought defiantly. *It's my life, not his.*

Now, as they approached the entrance to the park, Lady Moulton, Lord Rumford's sister, rode up beside Sally. Sally knew she had been under her chaperone's observance for the entire ride, and she had done her best to ignore Lady Moulton's penetrating gaze. But she had resented it. What did Lady Moulton think Sinclair would do? Ravish her while they were on the road?

Now Sally turned her head to the newcomer and said pleasantly, "It appears to be turning into a lovely day, Lady Moulton."

"Yes indeed," Lord Rumford's sister replied. She looked across Sally to Sinclair. "Have you been enjoying yourself, Your Grace?"

"Very much," the duke replied smoothly. "It is a pleasure to get out of the city in such lovely weather."

Lady Moulton smiled. She was a handsome woman in her late forties and the resemblance between her and her brother was strong.

"I don't think you'd find a party anywhere that had such a collection of well-bred horses," she said conversationally to the duke. She looked at the duke's tall, handsome gray and then, for a fraction of a second, her eyes alighted on Sally's chestnut. Her eyebrows rose skeptically.

Sally bristled. All of the other horses were thoroughbreds, but Moses was a thoroughbred-pony cross. His body was broader and more solid and his legs were shorter than the pure bred aristocrats that everyone else was riding. She patted him, as if to apologize for Lady Moulton's insulting glance.

Sinclair saw her action and said, "All of the horses have good looks, but I'd wager that the best brain belongs to Lady Sarah's animal. He just looks smart and sensible."

Sally gave him a grateful smile. "He is. Nothing fazes Moses. The thoroughbreds act with their nerves, Moses acts with his head. That's why I love him so much. He never does anything stupid."

"A horse like that is a pearl of great price," the duke said.

The soft breeze blew the veil on Lady Moulton's hat and she pushed it out of her way. She asked Sally, "Have you ever hunted him?"

Sally shook her head. "Galloping over fences was never my idea of a good time. Besides, I had rheumatic fever when I was twelve, and although it doesn't seem to have affected my heart, the doctors said I should avoid strenuous physical activity."

The duke raised his golden eyebrows. "Rheumatic fever," he said. "That is a very serious illness."

For a brief moment, the image of herself, lying in her bedroom and looking yearningly out the window, flashed through Sally's mind. Then she forced her attention back to the present and answered the duke. "Yes. I was kept in bed for six months. But my heart seems to be fine and I'm sure I could hunt if I wanted to. I just choose not to. Alex and Diana used to hunt all the time, and the stories they brought home made my blood run cold."

Lady Moulton said, "I'm sure you hunt, Your Grace."

"Yes," Sinclair replied. "I am a member of several hunts. But very few women are hunt members, Lady Moulton. It can be a dangerous sport. Lady Sarah is probably wise to avoid it."

"I hunt all the time," Lady Moulton said, raising her chin.

"Good for you," Sinclair replied. On the surface his voice was perfectly pleasant, but Sally heard a definite note of sarcasm underneath.

Evidently Lady Moulton heard it, too, for she flushed and her chin went even higher.

Sally, who appreciated his sticking up for her, still couldn't bear to hurt anyone's feelings. She said earnestly, "It's true that not many women hunt. At home, Diana was the only one who always finished the whole course. Most of the other women dropped out after a few fields. You must be a very good rider, Lady Moulton."

"I am," Lady Moulton replied seriously. "It runs in my family." She glanced over her shoulder at Diana and Lord Rumford. "It's interesting that Miss Sherwood is such a neck or nothing rider. My brother is the same."

The three of them chatted for a few more minutes, then Lady Moulton dropped back to join her brother and Diana.

Sally and the duke rode in silence for a few minutes. The sun had come out strongly, making the green beginning to push out on the trees look very bright. Finally the duke said, "That must have been difficult for a twelve-year-old, to be confined to bed for such a long period of time."

"It wasn't fun," Sally replied, shrugging in a replica of the gesture she had picked up from Diana. "It was actually very educational. I read hugely. And my family was very attentive—especially Diana." She smiled reminiscently. "It was like a breath of fresh air every time she walked into my bedroom."

The duke was regarding her with unreadable green eyes. "You two are very close, I gather," he said.

"I couldn't be closer to her if she were my sister," Sally replied. "She was the one who had the idea to place Jem with our head groom. And she and Alex were the ones who took him to Standish Court the day after I found him."

"But you were the one who rescued him," the duke pointed out. "I don't know of another lady in the ton who would have clasped that filthy child to her breast the way you did."

"I can't bear to see children suffering," Sally said simply. "That is why I joined this committee to stop the use of climbing boys."

"Who else is on this committee?" the duke asked.

At that moment, a squirrel dashed across the path in front of them. The duke's horse jumped sideways and spun around, ready to run. Sinclair quieted him and got him turned back in the right direction. Moses gave the elegant thoroughbred a look as if to say, *How can you be so stupid?*

Sally saw the look, patted her horse and said, "You're so smart, Mose."

The chestnut's ears flicked back to listen, then pointed forward once more. Sally turned to the duke to answer his question.

"The committee is composed of three members of the House of Commons, Mr. Eggleston, who owns a bank in the City and provides our financing, several other men from the City, Lady Barnstable, Mrs. Adams, Sir Henry Bartlet and me. Unfortunately, I don't have the power to contribute much, but they all assure me that having an earl's sister on their committee will make us more powerful."

Silence. Then the duke said slowly, "I might be interested in joining such a committee."

Sally's whole face lit up. "Oh, Your Grace! That would be wonderful! If they were happy to get an earl's sister, imagine how ecstatic they will be a get a duke!"

"What exactly does this committee do?" the duke asked.

Sally spent the ten minutes before they reached the park gates telling him about it.

Alex and Lady Caroline had led the party from the time they left their meeting place. At first Lady Caroline had been curious about Sally's escort.

"I've never known Sinclair to spend any time with a young girl," she said. "All of his previous flirts have been women of the world."

"He has a bad reputation," Alex said grimly. "I don't want to see my sister get involved with him."

"Perhaps he's thinking of settling down," Lady Caroline suggested. "It's about time he was setting up his nursery. He's thirty, at least."

"Well, he can set up his nursery with someone else," Alex said. "Sally is a very sensitive girl. If she marries a rake she will be exceedingly unhappy. She's the kind of girl who wants to marry for love, and I don't think Sinclair is the man to give her that."

They rode in silence for a minute or so, then Lady Caroline said, "What do you think of Miss Sherwood and Lord Rumford?"

Alex felt a stabbing pain in the region of his heart.

"He's too old for her," he said shortly.

"Age notwithstanding, he's a tremendous catch. Most mamas of eligible girls would be thrilled to see their daughters married to him."

Alex thought of how happy his own mother was about this possible match for Diana, and said nothing.

Lady Caroline said, "I had a cousin who fought in the Peninsula. Perhaps you knew him? Lieutenant Edward Foster?"

For the first time all morning, Alex really looked at Lady Caroline, really saw her. He had been so preoccupied with Dee and Rumford and Sally and Sinclair, that he had spared little thought for his own companion. Now he looked into her dark blue eyes and replied, "Yes, I knew Ned Foster. He was wounded at Vitoria, wasn't he?"

"Yes. He lost an arm."

"Jesus." Alex took one hand off his reins to rub his eyes. "How is he doing?"

"He's doing about as well as can be expected," she replied. "His mother and my mother are sisters, so I hear about him frequently. But it's hard for a twenty-one-year old man to lose an arm."

"It's terrible," Alex agreed. He thought of his own wounded arm and of how lucky he had been that the wound had not turned putrid, necessitating an amputation.

"It's so wonderful that the war is over," Lady Caroline said. "So many men, killed or wounded. There's not a family that I know of who hasn't lost a friend or a relative."

Her short blond hair peeked out from beneath her stylish hat with gleams of gold, her eyes were darkly blue, her skin was as pure as alabaster. She was utterly lovely, he thought.

But she wasn't Dee.

He said grimly, "War is hell, and if anyone tells you otherwise, he's lying."

She gave him a searching look. Then she said, "Well, it's over, Lord Standish, and Napoleon has been defeated. So I suppose it was worth all the sacrifice after all."

"Yes," Alex said. He turned in his saddle to glance back at Diana. Her coppery hair was hidden under her riding hat so all that could be seen was the pure beauty of her face as she smiled up at Lord Rumford.

Abruptly, Alex turned back to his own partner.

What are we to talk about? he thought a little desperately. *I don't know this girl at all.* He struggled mightily to come up with something to say. *We've talked about Sally and Dee. We've talked about the war. What is left?*

Lady Caroline said smoothly, "Have you been to visit all of your properties since you came home?"

Relief that she had come up with something caused him to be more talkative about his various estates than he would ordinarily have been. Lady Caroline listened intently and asked intelligent questions, and the topic carried them all the way to Richmond Park.

Once they were in the park, they all had a good long gallop. The thoroughbreds were glad of the chance to run and Moses gamely managed to keep the rest of them in sight. The duke soon dropped back to join Sally at the end of the pack. He shortened his horse's stride and rode beside her where the path was wide enough and just before her where it narrowed. When the horses in front slowed down, from gallop to canter to trot to walk, Sally and the duke continued galloping until they caught up with the rest of the party. Then they, too, walked.

Lord Rumford had arranged for a carriage to meet them at the park, carrying a luncheon, and when they reached an open, grass-covered clearing, the carriage was already there and footmen were setting out the food. The servants had also brought blankets for everyone to sit upon and they were spread out on the grass.

"How wonderful," Diana said enthusiastically. "I'm starving."

"I rather thought we might be hungry," Lord Rumford said. "I believe there are cold meats and bread and salads."

The food had been laid out on a folding table, and everyone helped themselves and went back to sit upon the blankets.

The food tasted wonderful, Diana thought. Silence fell as everyone ate hungrily. Diana glanced over at Alex and saw that he had put his sandwich down after only a few bites.

She frowned. She thought he had been looking too thin lately. He needed to eat.

"Don't you care for the sandwich, Alex?" she asked quietly.

He looked at her from the other side of the blanket. "It's delicious. I'm just not very hungry."

"You never seem to be hungry anymore," Sally commented. "You're losing weight. I can see it. Eat the sandwich, Alex." Then, when he did nothing, she added pleadingly, "Please."

He shrugged, but he took another bite. He chewed slowly. Sally and Diana looked at each other.

Something's wrong with Alex, Diana thought. *Sally's right, he isn't eating. And from the looks of him, he isn't sleeping much either.*

Of course, she and Sally weren't getting their accustomed sleep either; they rarely got home before one in the morning. But neither of them had that shadowed, haunted look that Alex was wearing.

Perhaps he's missing the excitement of life in the army, she thought. *London must seem very boring after three years of fighting in the Peninsula.*

Diana watched as Alex put down his sandwich to talk with Lady Caroline. Lady Caroline laughed at Alex's response, and Diana looked appraisingly at the classically beautiful face that was looking up at Alex.

The unattainable Lady Caroline Wrentham appeared to be definitely interested in Alex. *Well, why not?* Diana thought cynically. *He's the best catch on the marriage mart—probably the best catch in years. He's only twenty-two and already he's an earl. Lady Caroline would be a countess immediately. And he certainly has the wherewithal to keep her in the style to which she is accustomed.*

Dimly Diana was aware that she was being unjust. But her feelings outweighed her conscience. She didn't have any real reason to dislike Lady Caroline, but the fact remained that she did not like the girl. *She seems cold,* she thought. *Alex needs a girl with a warm heart, not a beautiful ice maiden.*

Lord Rumford said something to her and she turned to him, grateful to be distracted from her thoughts.

The rest of the afternoon went very smoothly. Diana had wondered how Lord Rumford would fit in with a party made up mostly of young people, but it was the young people who were drawn up to his level, not the other way around. This phenomenon was helped along by the Duke of Sinclair, who was certainly not as young and playful as was Lord Dorset, Sally's usual escort. And Alex, although he was much younger than the other two men, did not have the carefree levity of so many of the young men Diana had met in London.

They talked about the war and its aftermath, both older men listening with great respect to Alex's opinions. Lady Caroline also listened closely, her dark blue eyes fixed intently on Alex's face.

She means to have him, Diana thought grimly and a feeling she did not understand and did not want, twisted in her stomach. She turned hastily to Lord Rumford, who was seated on the blanket next to her. He felt her gaze and turned his head to give her a warm smile, which she returned.

He's such a nice man, she thought. *He didn't run away from his wife when she was sick. He stuck with her. He's the kind of man one can count on.*

For Diana, this was of paramount importance. The two most significant men in her life had deserted her when she needed them most: her father and Alex. She wanted desperately to marry a man she could rely on to be there for her when she needed him.

From what she had seen of Lord Rumford, she was beginning to think that he could be that man. She sensed a stability about him that drew her strongly. If she married a man like him, her future—and her mother's—would be settled. She would never have to feel vulnerable and unprotected again. She would be safe.

On the ride home she listened as he told her about his home.

"It sounds lovely, my lord," she said softly.

"You must come on a visit one of these days, Miss Sherwood," he said seriously.

Diana's heart gave a jerk. "That…that would be nice."

"I'll speak to Standish about it. Perhaps your mother could come, as well."

"Thank you," Diana said a little breathlessly. "We would be honored to visit your home."

It sounds as if he's really serious, she thought, as the horses walked comfortably along. *But I've only known him for a week,* another voice in her brain said. She inhaled deeply, trying to quiet the tumult inside her heart and her head.

He turned his head to look at her. "You seem older than your years, did you know that?"

"Sometimes I feel as if I'm a thousand years old," she replied truthfully.

He chuckled. "Even I am not that old, my dear." He sobered. "But I know what you mean. I think everyone who has suffered knows what it is to feel that way."

Diana said gently, "I heard that your wife was ill for a long time."

"Yes, she was." He looked straight ahead, giving

her a view of his profile. His nose was a little too large, Diana thought, and his eyes were set a little too widely apart. But there was no denying that he was a handsome man.

She said, even more gently than before, "Never mind. I can see it's hard for you to talk about it. Let's speak of something else." She looked around, seeking a distraction. Above them the white cirrus clouds were gathering in various formations. "Look!" she said pointing upward. "Doesn't that look like a bear?"

A little unwillingly, he laughed. "Yes, it does."

Sixteen

That night Diana had a nightmare. She was running and running, with something evil chasing close behind her, and suddenly Alex appeared in front of her. She ran straight into his arms and felt them close around her tightly, and she knew that she was safe. "It's all right, Dee," he said. "I'm here. Nothing can hurt you now."

Am I dreaming? she thought, *Or is this real?*

She forced her eyes to open and, after a moment's confusion as to where she was, realized that she was lying in bed in her room at Standish House. Her heart was thudding in her chest and she was sweating.

It was a dream, she thought. *Just a dream.*

She turned over on her back then lay still, breathing quickly, waiting for her heart to quiet. She had not had this dream for a long time, but she knew where it came from.

Lying there in the silence and the dark, she let herself drift back over the years to the summer she was seventeen, to the day she was searching in the woods for mushrooms for the evening meal her mother was going to prepare. She was wearing the raggedy old dress and ancient boots she usually wore for such an errand and her coppery hair was casually pulled back off her face with a ribbon.

She had filled her basket and was on the bridle path walking toward home when she heard the sound of galloping hooves.

It must be Alex, she thought with pleasure. He had told her he might come over this afternoon.

But the man riding one of Lord Standish's horses was a stranger. Diana knew that the Standishes had visitors, and she supposed this man to be one of them. She stepped off the path to give him room to pass.

But instead of going by her, he pulled the horse up. "Hallo," he said in a deep gravelly voice. "And just who are you, my dear? A wood nymph perhaps?"

She looked up at the man sitting astride Lord Standish's second-best hunter. There was something about the way he was looking at her that made her uneasy. He was a broadly built man of middle years, with cropped brown hair and a strongly curved nose.

"I live in a cottage not far from here," she said. "Are you looking for Standish Court? If you keep following this path, it will take you there."

But the man didn't start his horse up again; in-

NO POSTAGE
NECESSARY
IF MAILED
IN THE
UNITED STATES

BUSINESS REPLY MAIL
FIRST-CLASS MAIL   PERMIT NO. 717-003   BUFFALO, NY

POSTAGE WILL BE PAID BY ADDRESSEE

THE READER SERVICE
3010 WALDEN AVE
PO BOX 1341
BUFFALO NY 14240-8571

The Reader Service — Here's How It Works:

Accepting your 2 free books and gift places you under no obligation to buy anything. You may keep the books and gift and return the shipping statement marked "cancel." If you do not cancel, about a month later we'll send you 3 additional books and bill you just $5.24 each in the U.S., or $5.74 each in Canada, plus 25¢ shipping & handling per book and applicable taxes if any.* That's the complete price, and — compared to cover prices of $5.99 or more each in the U.S. and $6.99 or more each in Canada — it's quite a bargain! You may cancel at any time, but if you choose to continue, every month we'll send you 3 more books, which you may either purchase at the discount price....or return to us and cancel your subscription.

What's your pleasure...

Romance?

Enjoy 2 FREE BOOKS that will fuel your imagination with intensely moving stories about life, love and relationships.

OR

Suspense?

Enjoy 2 FREE BOOKS that will thrill you with a spine-tingling blend of suspense and mystery.

Whichever category you select, your 2 FREE BOOKS have a combined cover price of $11.98 or more in the U.S. and $13.98 or more in Canada.

Simply place the sticker next to your preferred choice of books, complete the poll on the right page and you'll automatically receive 2 FREE BOOKS and a FREE GIFT with no obligation to purchase anything!

We'll send you a wonderful surprise gift, ABSOLUTELY FREE, just for trying our books! Don't miss out — *MAIL THE REPLY CARD TODAY!*

OFFICIAL OPINION POLL

Dear Reader,

Since you are a book enthusiast, we would like to know what you think.

Inside you will find a short Opinion Poll. Please participate in our poll by sharing your opinion on 3 subjects that are very important to all of us.

To thank you for your participation, we would like to send you your choice of **2 FREE BOOKS** and a **FREE GIFT!**

Please enjoy them with our compliments.

Sincerely,

Pam Powers

Editor

P.S. Don't forget to indicate which books you prefer so we can send your FREE gifts today!

stead, he surprised her by dismounting. Diana felt a warning stab of fear and her fingers tightened on the basket of mushrooms she was carrying. She took a step backwards, her eyes still fixed on the man.

"You're a real little beauty," he said, his gravelly voice sounding even deeper. He looped his horse's reins over a bush and started toward her. "But you must know that. I'll wager all the local swains are after you."

"I am a cousin of Lady Standish," Diana said quickly. Her heart had begun to hammer but she managed to keep her voice relatively normal. "You had better get back on your horse and leave me alone."

The man snorted and kept on coming. "Don't tell me lies. No cousin of Lady Standish would be dressed like you are."

Diana looked at his hard face, his narrowed eyes, then spun around to run. He reached out and caught the back of her dress, causing her to fall to her knees. She dropped the basket of mushrooms.

He laughed, a sound that made Diana's blood run cold. "Don't worry, sweetheart," he said. "You'll like it. You'll like it better with me than with all the ignorant locals, I promise you that."

Diana tried to pull away, but her dress held her captive. Then his hand was on her upper arm, holding her so tightly that he would leave bruises. He jerked her to her feet and swung her around to face him. "God," he said, "but you are beautiful. Maybe I'll make you my mistress. It's a sin to keep such beauty hidden in a hovel."

While he was talking Diana had been filling her lungs and now she screamed as loudly as she could.

"This'll shut you up," the man muttered and a second later his mouth was mashing hers back against her teeth. She gasped and his tongue penetrated between her lips. She tried to fight him, flailing at him with her fists, but he continued to hold her. Then he began to push her down to the ground.

Oh God, Diana thought as she fought fruitlessly to keep on her feet, to get away. *This can't be happening. Please, someone, help me. Alex. Where are you, Alex? Don't let this awful thing happen to me.*

Then she was down on the ground, and the man was pawing at her skirt, trying to lift it.

One moment he was on top of her, and the next moment he was flung away. Diana looked up to see Alex, fists clenched, going after the stumbling man.

"Hallo!" the man protested, as he backed away from the oncoming Alex. "Don't get so upset. She wanted it as much as I did."

"Is that why she screamed?" Alex said, and punched the man square in the middle of his face. His nose started to bleed heavily.

Diana scrambled to her feet. Her heart was thudding so loudly she could actually hear it.

"Jesus," the man said, "I'm bleeding." He raised his hand to his nose and brought it away, covered in blood.

"Do you know who this is, Hawley?" Alex demanded from between clenched teeth. "This is my cousin. What the bloody hell did you think you were doing?"

The man, who was shorter than Alex but much bulkier, backed away, blood still gushing from his nose. Diana could feel the waves of Alex's fury in the air. It was scary. "I would like to beat you into a bloody pulp," he said, and there was no mistaking the menace in his voice.

"There's no need for that," the man said. The blood was dripping off his chin and onto his clothes. He outweighed Alex by at least thirty pounds, but he clearly didn't want a fight. He took a few steps toward his horse, sputtering, "I'm sorry. I made a mistake. I thought she was just a local wench."

"And you think it's all right to go around raping innocent women just because they are commoners?" Alex was still talking from between clenched teeth.

The man looked at him warily and didn't reply. He had almost reached his horse.

Alex said, "Pack your bags and be out of my father's house before I get back. I don't care what excuse you give, just get out. And never come back again."

"I'll do that. Calm down. I'll be gone before dinner." He looked at Diana. "Sorry, miss," he said, swung up on his horse and rode away, his nose still pumping out blood.

Alex and Diana watched him go.

When Hawley was out of sight, he turned to her. "Are you all right, Dee? Did he hurt you?" His eyes were still blazing.

She said in a small voice, "My lip is bleeding."

"One moment and let me tie Monty." He did this, then returned and took her into his arms. She began to shake.

"Come on," he said. "You need to sit down."

She let him lead her through the woods to a small stream which had a grassy patch on its bank. Diana sat, drew her knees up and pressed her forehead against them. Alex sat beside her and put his arm around her shoulders.

"Do you feel faint?" he asked.

All of a sudden, she began to cry.

"Oh, Dee," he said, and gathered her to him, so that her face was pressed against his shoulder. "It's all right," he kept saying. "Nothing terrible happened. I got there in time. You're going to be all right, Dee. It's going to be all right."

She tried to stop sobbing and couldn't.

"I should have killed that bastard," Alex said, his lips against her hair.

She shook her head. "N-no. I wouldn't want you to do that."

The coat under her cheek was soaked with her tears. She made another heroic effort and got herself under control. She lifted her head and said shakily, "I've made a mess of your coat, I'm afraid."

"The hell with my coat," he replied. He took a handkerchief out of his pocket and handed it to her.

She mopped her face and blew her nose. "I never cry," she said. "I don't know what got into me."

"You were scared," he said grimly. "And you had

every right to be scared. If I hadn't come along in time, that bloody Hawley would have raped you."

"Oh God. I know." She shuddered. They were sitting close together, their shoulders touching, and she put her hand on his knee. "Thank you, Alex. Thank you for being there when I needed you."

"I was riding to your house to see if you wanted to go fishing," he said.

She drew a deep, steadying breath. "Who was that awful man?"

"Some idiot my father invited because they sit on the same parliamentary committee. But don't worry. Once I tell my father what happened, he won't ever invite him again."

"Don't tell him," Diana said instantly.

He frowned. "Why not? We don't want him ever coming here again."

"Because if your father knows, then he'll tell Mama, and I don't want her worried."

"I'll tell my father to keep it to himself. He needs to know, Dee. I don't want to take a chance that Hawley might return here. Next time I might not be around to rescue you."

She searched his face. "You will ask him not to tell Mama?"

"Yes."

She continued to look up at him. The fury had left his eyes and all that was left was concern for her. Concern and something else...

She picked up his hand and kissed it. "Thank you," she said again. "Thank you for saving me."

He put his hand on her nape, under the cloudy mass of coppery curls. "When I heard you scream… Well, it terrified me."

"How did you know it was me?"

"I just did."

"Yes." He was gently rubbing the back of her neck. "You would."

"Dee…" Then his face was coming down toward hers. She closed her eyes and their lips met. Instantly, passion ignited between them.

They had kissed before. In fact, over the past two summers they had gotten very good at kissing. But this was something different. The earlier threat of violence had stripped away the barrier that social and religious convention had heretofore placed between them, and desire flooded through Diana's veins. When Alex laid her back upon the grass, she went willingly, wanting him to keep kissing her, wanting him to touch her. When he fumbled with the front buttons of her dress, she raised her hands to help him. Then he was kissing her everywhere, kissing her throat and her uncovered breasts. When his mouth touched her nipple, a shock of raw sensation ran from her breast to down between her legs. She buried her hands in his black hair and felt her breath begin to come hard and fast.

"Alex," she gasped. "Alex."

"Dee," he moaned. "I love you so much. So much."

She felt him lifting the light summery material of her dress and then his hand was caressing her bare thigh. Her back arched. Then his fingers touched her between her legs. She felt the strange gush of liquid that greeted his intrusion. He began to move his finger up and down, creating the most incredible sensation. Involuntarily, she spread her legs wider, urging him to continue.

Then he was looming over her.

"All right?"

"Yes," she panted, thinking she would die if he didn't continue.

She felt him entering her.

At first there was pain, a burning pain, and involuntarily she tried to pull away. But as he moved inside of her, all of the intense feeling that had been building up in her loins seemed to gather together and then, just when she felt she could stand it no longer, it exploded. Diana's body shuddered with the power of that explosion and her fingers dug deeply into Alex's coat.

Alex drove one more time and she heard him cry out.

They clung to each other, both of them profoundly shaken by what had just passed between them. Alex's heart was beating like a drum, and it was a long time before it slowed and he was able to lift his head to look down at her.

"We shouldn't have done that," he panted. "*I* shouldn't have done it. But I'm glad we did. I love you so much, Dee. So much."

She looked up into the crystal blue eyes of her lover. "I love you, too," she said. "Alex. I love you, too."

It had been a long time since Diana had let herself remember that scene. It hurt to remember it. She had gone home so happy, thinking that nothing could ever separate them. She had dreamed of marrying Alex, of living with him at Standish Court, of riding horses and having babies. He would always be there to protect her. She would never feel vulnerable and lonely again.

The very next day, Lord Standish had told his son that if he wanted to go into the army so much, then the earl would buy him his colors.

Diana closed her eyes and flung her arm across her eyes. She would never forget that meeting with Alex. It was scalded into her mind, soul and heart.

He had come to the cottage to see her. Diana and her mother had been out in the vegetable garden and Diana had taken Alex into the small parlor when he said he wanted to speak to her. She had smiled at him radiantly, but the smile he gave her in return was not the wholehearted one she had expected.

"Is something the matter?" she asked.

He sat next to her on the old leather sofa. "My father has changed his mind about the army. He told me this morning that he would buy me a commission."

Diana had stared at him, not fully comprehending what this meant. "Did he?" she said.

"It's my dream come true," he continued. "All my life I have wanted to be a soldier. You know that. And now my father will buy me a commission under Wellington." The blue eyes that were looking at her held a mixture of pleading and guilt. "After yesterday, I know my first responsibility is to you. But…"

Diana had felt a chill settle over her. "But what?" she had said.

He had set his jaw. "I'll stay if you want me to stay."

"But you want to go."

A muscle jumped in his jaw. "It wouldn't be forever, Dee. It would only be for a few years. I'm my father's heir. I know I have to come back to Standish Court and learn to take over. I plan on doing that. I want to do that. But our country is at war and, for a little time, I would like to help."

"You mean you prefer the army over me," she accused.

"It's not forever!" he repeated. "I'm only nineteen years old, Dee. You're only seventeen. We can get married when I come home. You will only have to wait a few years. I promise you."

"What if I don't want to wait?"

The muscle jumped in his jaw once more. "Then I'll stay."

"How kind of you," she said.

He reached over and took her hands. "I love you. I will never love any woman but you. You're part of me. We have a whole lifetime to be together. Can't we wait for just a few years?"

"Did it ever occur to you, Alex, that soldiers get killed in war? Do you have some invincible shield that is going to protect you from the enemies' bullets? My father was killed in battle. What makes you think you won't be?"

"I won't be killed," he said confidently. "I won't be killed because I know I have to come home to you."

She had stared at him and seen all her dreams going up in flames. He didn't love her, not the way she loved him. He wanted to leave her, just the way her father had.

She said, "Go, if that's the way you feel. But don't expect me to be waiting when you get home."

"Don't say that!" He looked appalled. "After all we've been to each other, how can you say that, Dee?"

"It's your choice, not mine," she said. "You can't have both. It's the army or me."

A flush of angry color had come into his face. "I may not have a choice," he said. "After yesterday, you may be with child. If that's the case, we'll have to be married right away."

"And you'd stay?"

"Yes." The telltale muscle jumped once more.

"Well, you can stop holding your breath," she said. "I know I'm not with child. It was the wrong time in my cycle."

He couldn't hide the relief in his eyes.

Fury washed over her. "Go, if that's what you want," she said. She stood up. "I certainly don't want to stand in the way of your dream."

"I can't go if you feel like this," he said miserably, standing also.

"I can't help the way I feel, Alex. But one thing I can tell you. I don't want to marry a man who feels he has sacrificed his dream for me. Such a situation would hardly make for a happy marriage, would it?

So if you want to go, then go. I release you from any responsibility you may feel for me. I shall go on perfectly well without you."

He looked down at her. "I have loved you all my life," he said quietly.

"But you love your dream more," she returned. "So follow it."

"It will only be for a few years," he repeated. "Then we can be married."

"Don't count on it," she said cruelly.

He had looked down into her eyes and drawn a deep, steadying breath. "I'll stay," he said. "I can't leave you like this."

"But you want to go," she said. And that, of course, was what she couldn't forgive. "And if you want to go, then I want you to go, as well. Go and fulfill your dream. I will pray for your safety."

Hope had glimmered in the crystalline blue of his eyes. "Do you mean that?"

"Yes, I do."

"And we will be married when I come home. I will be my own man by then. I will be able to marry whoever I want."

They both heard the front door open. Her mother was back from the garden. When she had reached the parlor door, Diana said, "Alex is going into the army, Mama. Lord Standish has offered to buy him a commission."

Mrs. Sherwood raised her eyebrows. "That must have made you very happy, Alex. When are you leaving?"

"I'm to go to London tomorrow. I have to get outfitted for a uniform. Then I will join the army in Portugal."

Mrs. Sherwood came into the room. "Congratulations," she said. "I know this has long been a dream of yours, Alex. I remember how you always loved to listen to all of my husband's letters."

He smiled. "Yes. I remember that, too."

Then Alex had asked Diana to walk out to his horse with him. She had made an excuse and he had left the house alone. That had been her last sight of him before he had come home to Standish Court a month ago.

Diana lay in her bed, her arm across her forehead, tears sliding down her cheeks. Years had passed, yet the heartbreak was as fresh and real as it had been on that day he walked away from her. Every time she looked at him, she remembered that moment. She would never be able to forget. Never.

Seventeen

At the next two balls that Diana attended, Lord Rumford asked her to dance twice and he asked Jessica Longwood only once. The clubs began to take bets as to which girl Rumford would propose to. The odds tended to lean toward Diana.

Then Rumford took Jessica driving in the park, and the odds began to shift back in her favor.

Lord Longwood was very insistent that his daughter attach the Earl of Rumford.

"I am trying the best that I can, Papa!" she cried to her father when he called her into the library of their London town house to question her. "I agree with everything that he says and I smile all the time. I couldn't possibly be more encouraging!"

"Damn this Sherwood girl," he said, scowling heavily. "Everything was going just fine until she arrived on the scene."

"It isn't fair," Jessica sulked. "I had him caught,

Papa. I know I had. And then he came to London and saw *her*. I can't compete with the way she looks. There isn't a girl in London who can. It just isn't fair."

"She may be a good-looker, but she's a nobody. I had someone look into her background for me. She grew up at Standish Court all right, but she didn't live in the house with the family. She and her mother live in a cottage on the estate. They are nothing more than pensioners of the Standishes. The father was a mere colonel who was killed at Corunna. She's trying to pass herself off as a Standish, but she's far from that. Once I circulate this information, I think we might see Rumford come to his senses. He has enough awareness of who he is and what is owed to his position to marry a girl like that."

"Lady Standish *is* sponsoring her, though," Jessica said doubtfully. "And she has the entrée to Almack's. She can't be all that badly born."

"Compared to you, she is. Remind Rumford of that when you get the chance, eh?"

Jessica sighed. "I'll try, Papa. I'll try."

Lady Moulton, Lord Rumford's sister, heard the gossip about Diana and taxed her brother about it.

"They are saying that the Sherwoods are poor relations of Lady Standish and that they live in a cottage at Standish Court. The father was just the younger son of some country squire, although the mother is apparently a cousin of Lady Standish. But *that* family is nothing to boast about. Amelia Standish's father gambled them into ruin."

"Where is all this gossip coming from?" Lord Rumford asked quietly. He and his sister were sitting at Lady Moulton's breakfast table—Rumford had responded to her urgent request to visit him immediately.

"I heard it last night from Maria Lewis," she said. "I don't know who she got it from, but it's all over town.

Lord Rumford had refused breakfast, having already eaten at home, but he had been sipping a cup of coffee. Now he pushed it away. "It seems to me that someone has gone to a lot of trouble to delve into Miss Sherwood's background. She hasn't misrepresented herself as far as I am concerned. All the ton knew that she hadn't any money. And she is obviously a valued member of the Standish family, wherever she may have lived on their estate. Lord Standish would certainly not be paying for her come-out if the case was otherwise. This whole whisper campaign sounds dirty to me."

Lady Moulton frowned as she looked at her brother. "You can marry whoever you want to, Edward. I just don't want to see you bowled over by a pretty face."

"Miss Sherwood is more than a pretty face. She is a well-read young woman and she is extremely knowledgeable about horses. She has the best seat I have ever seen on a woman. I like her, Regina. She's fresh and vibrant and she makes me feel young again. It's a good feeling. I haven't felt that way in a long, long time."

Lady Moulton reached across the table and put her hand over her brother's. "All I want is for you to be happy, Edward. God knows, you deserve some happiness in your life. And if you feel that this girl can make you happy, then I am with you. But take your time. Don't jump too soon. You thought you would probably marry the Longwood girl this winter. This is a very sudden change of heart."

He sighed. "I know. I can't explain it. It's just...when I saw her, every other woman went out of my mind. I feel badly about Miss Longwood. I know I raised expectations in that quarter. But..."

"I think you need some time to get to know Miss Sherwood better. What if I invited the Sherwoods and Standishes to visit me at Chisworth next week for a few days? We can make a small house party of it—invite a few other people, so it doesn't look too obvious that we are singling out Miss Sherwood. What do you think?"

He nodded slowly. "I think that's a very good idea, Regina. I appreciate your thinking of it. It would be nice to have a chance to spend more time with Miss Sherwood than one can cram in at a ball or in a brief drive through the park."

She patted his hand then withdrew her own.

"Good," she said. "I'll send out the invitations."

Alex was furious when he heard the gossip about Diana. He gave the man who inquired about her a blistering set-down, then stood up in the club room at Brooks and announced to everyone there that Diana Sherwood was the cousin of the Earl of Standish and was perfectly entitled by reason of her birth to marry anyone she wished in English society.

He went home fuming and discovered that Lady Standish and Sally and Mrs. Sherwood had gone out and Diana was alone in her bedroom. He took the stairs two at a time and knocked on her closed door with authority.

There was no answer.

"Dee!" he called. "It's me. I'm coming in."

He pushed the door open and saw her curled up in one of the chairs in front of the fireplace with Freddie snuggled against her. She looked very pale and the great brown eyes that met his were filled with distress.

"Damn," he said. "You've heard."

"If you mean I've heard that I'm nothing but a pensioner of yours, then, yes I have," she said. Her voice sounded steady, but he could hear the undertone. He knew her very well.

"It's all nonsense," he said. He crossed the room and sat down in the other chair, facing her. The day was damp and there was a fire in the fireplace. "I told them all at Brooks that you were fit to marry anyone you chose, no matter how high his position may be in society."

"Oh God," she said. "Did you really say that?"

"I did. When that whiney little Staley asked me

about you, I just saw red. Who the hell turned up the information that you lived in a cottage?"

"I don't know. But maybe it's good that it came out, Alex. I know you and Cousin Amelia have been trying to make it sound as if I grew up in the house with you, but that was really misrepresenting me. If someone wants to marry me, he should know the whole truth."

Her eyes looked so large and dark in her pale face. There was a vulnerable look about her mouth that made him want to kiss it. A treacherous thought flickered through his mind. *If no one wants to marry her, perhaps she will marry me.*

He was instantly ashamed of himself. "We only did what we thought would make things easier for you," he said.

"I know. And I appreciate that. Truly I do. But…I'm not of the same station as you and Sally and it's folly to pretend that I am."

"Dee, your father was a gentleman. His family has held the same land in this country since the Domesday Book was written, for God's sake. Your mother is a Parry, just like my mother. You may not be noble, but you are gently born. You are good enough to marry a duke if you want to!" He paused, then added quietly, "At one time you thought you were good enough to marry *me*."

"That was different," she said.

"How so?"

She shook her head. "You and me—we neither of us ever thought about things like birth or money.

We just thought about ourselves. But people in London think about birth and money, Alex. They think about it a lot."

We just thought about ourselves. The words stabbed like a sword in Alex's heart. That's exactly how it had been once, and he desperately wanted it to be that way again. But she was thinking of marrying another man, and here he was, reassuring her that she could.

He said slowly. "Any man who thinks you are not good enough to marry him is a nincompoop and not worthy of you. And that is the truth."

She buried her face in Freddie's fur. There was silence in the room for a minute and then she raised her head. "Thank you, Alex," she said. Her voice trembled slightly.

He smiled at her. "There's no one else like you, Dee. You know that. Don't let yourself be cast down by ugly rumors. You have always been able to throw your heart over a fence. You need to keep on doing that."

She took a deep breath and nodded. "But what if Rumford doesn't ask me to dance tonight, Alex? I will be so humiliated."

"That won't happen," he said positively.

"Why not?"

"Because the man is mad for you," he said crisply and got to his feet. "Surely you know the signs by now. You've had men running after you for years, or so Sally tells me."

She bit her lip. "Yes, but…"

"Don't worry about it," he said. He went to the door. "Rumford will ask you to dance."

He opened the door and went out into the hallway.

Rumford will ask her to dance or I'll pummel him into a coma, he thought as he walked toward the staircase. Despair washed over him suddenly, chasing away all the anger he had felt.

God. How did I come to this? What am I going to do.

The Standishes and Sherwoods went to Almack's that evening for the weekly assembly dance. Lord Rumford was not there when they arrived, and Diana felt her stomach tighten. Had he stayed away because he didn't want to see her?

Lord Dorset came over to greet Sally immediately and ask her to dance. The two of them went out onto the dance floor and for a few horrible moments, Diana was alone with her mother and Lady Standish. Alex had been detained at the door by someone he knew from the Horse Guards, so he wasn't there to rescue her.

Then Mr. Dunster appeared at her side, smiling and asking her to dance.

Thank God, Diana thought. Matthew Dunster had always danced with her, and she had driven out with him once or twice. The earl's younger son needed to marry for money, but that hadn't stopped him from enjoying Diana's company, and she was immensely grateful to him for standing by her now.

As they went out onto the floor, she thought she could feel the eyes of the whole room trained on her.

"Thank you," she said quietly to Mr. Dunster as they stood together waiting for the music to start.

"Someone is spreading nasty rumors about you, Miss Sherwood," he replied.

"So I have heard. I can't imagine why anyone would bother."

He shrugged. "People in this town need gossip like they need air. But I would hate to think that you were upset by it. Don't be. Standish and his mother are standing by you, and that is what will count with the ton."

"I hope so," Diana murmured. "I never tried to misrepresent myself. Everyone knows that I have no money."

He replied with a rueful smile, "That is true. If you had money, I would have asked you to marry me weeks ago."

She returned his smile. "Thank you for the compliment—I think."

The orchestra played the opening bars of the dance tune, and Diana and Mr. Dunster faced each other and prepared to bow.

An hour later, Diana excused herself from Lady Standish's side and went to the ladies' retiring room. There was one other person there, standing in front of a mirror and adjusting her hair. It was Jessica Longwood.

Diana stopped in the doorway. Miss Longwood was intent upon her reflection and didn't notice who had come in. Diana slowly walked all the way into the room.

Miss Longwood turned, and when she saw Diana she jumped.

"My goodness," she said with a forced laugh. "You gave me a start, Miss Sherwood. I didn't know anyone else was here."

"I didn't mean to startle you," Diana said. "I'm sorry."

The two women stared at each other. Jessica was wearing a white dress, which went nicely with her shining black hair. She had a voluptuous figure, which contrasted to Diana's elegant slimness. She was looking at Diana warily, as if she were an animal who couldn't be trusted.

Diana said lightly, "The slip of my dress ripped and I came in here to pin it up. Mr. Westover stepped on it. He is not the most adept of dancers."

"I know," Jessica replied. "I have often had my feet stepped on while I was dancing with him."

"He makes up in enthusiasm what he lacks in skill," Diana said. She took a pin out of her reticule and went to sit in one of the chairs so she could fix her skirt.

Miss Longwood said, "Lord Rumford is not here tonight."

Diana didn't look up from her skirt. "So I noticed."

"Do you know where he is?"

Diana shook her head. She had put the pin in and now she smoothed the dress and let it fall. She glanced up at Miss Longwood and was surprised to see a look of great animosity on the other girl's face. She smoothed it away when she saw Diana looking, but the hostility lingered in her light brown eyes.

Good heavens, Diana thought with a shock of recognition. *I wonder if the Longwoods could be responsible for those ugly rumors.*

She ran her tongue around her lips to moisten them. "Lord Rumford does not confide his every movement to me," she said.

The other girl pressed her lips together. "I heard that you went on an excursion to Richmond Park with him. Is that true?"

"Do you know, I really don't think that what I do is any of your business," Diana said pleasantly. She got to her feet.

"You're nobody," Miss Longwood said fiercely. "Do you hear me? Nobody. If you think that Lord Rumford is going to marry you, you're wrong. He comes from one of the best families in the country. He's hardly going to marry the granddaughter of a country squire."

"Well, that's up to Lord Rumford, isn't it?" Diana said. She walked past the girl at the mirror and over to the door. "It's been interesting talking to you, Miss Longwood," she said, and left the room, closing the door firmly behind her.

She felt herself shaking as she walked down the corridor.

The venom she had seen in Miss Longwood's face! It was scary to think that she could provoke such hatred in another person.

It was the Longwoods who started those rumors, she thought. *It had to have been. They were afraid they were going to lose Rumford, and they tried to discredit me.*

She stopped at the entrance to the ballroom and drew a deep breath, trying to compose herself. She looked around for her mother and saw, out of the side of her eyes, Alex standing talking to Lord Rumford.

Diana could feel herself pale and she surreptitiously pinched her cheeks before she went to join Lady Standish and her mother, both of whom were standing by the punch bowl with Sir Gilbert Merton. Sir Gilbert smiled at her as she came up to them. "I was just telling your mother that Caleb missed Freddie today in the park," he said.

"I know. I feel very badly that he only got out into the garden today. I promise faithfully that I will take him to the park tomorrow."

Sir Gilbert looked at Mrs. Sherwood. "You ladies must have been very busy. You're usually very faithful about walking Freddie."

Mrs. Sherwood replied easily, "I had an engagement, and Diana did not feel well enough to go out."

Everyone looked at Diana.

"Are you all right, dear?" Lady Standish asked. "I didn't know you weren't feeling well this afternoon."

"I'm fine," Diana said.

As she was speaking, Alex and Lord Rumford began to cross the room, which was filled with couples waiting for the next dance to begin. Lord Rumford smiled as he joined their group. "How is everyone this evening?" he asked in his mild, pleasant voice.

"We are all very well," Lady Standish said. She glanced quickly at Diana, then back to Rumford. She was clearly anxious to see what Rumford would do.

"Lord Rumford has been kind enough to invite us all on a visit to his sister's home in Kent," Alex said. "It sounds like a good idea to me. I think it will do us good to get out into the country for a few days."

There was a moment of stunned silence. Then Lady Standish said, "That is very kind of Lady Moulton, Lord Rumford."

"She will be sending you a formal invitation tomorrow, ma'am," the earl said. "I only mentioned it to Standish because I was anxious to know if you would be free."

"When would she want us?" Lady Standish asked.

"Thursday through Saturday was the time mentioned, ma'am. I know you ladies have many things planned here in London, but if you could find the time to come for a visit, my sister would be very pleased." He smiled at her. "The invitation includes your daughter as well as Mrs. and Miss Sherwood. And Standish, of course."

Lady Standish said, "Will there be other guests, Lord Rumford?"

"My sister mentioned inviting a few other people. I don't know who they are."

Lady Standish looked at Diana, then back to Rumford. "I believe my daughter may have an engagement with Lord Dorset on Friday."

"We'll invite Lord Dorset, as well," Lord Rumford responded promptly.

Lady Standish smiled. "When I receive Lady Moulton's invitation, I will be pleased to accept, my lord. It was very kind of her to think of us. My son is right. A few days in the country will be very pleasant."

Rumford looked pleased.

A waltz had been playing for over a minute and now Lord Rumford said to Diana, "Would you give me the pleasure of this dance, Miss Sherwood?"

"Of course," Diana said, and took his arm. She hoped that Miss Longwood was watching.

As soon as they were out of earshot, Lady Standish turned to Mrs. Sherwood, her eyes bright with triumph. "She's got him, Louisa! He wouldn't be having his sister invite her on a visit if he wasn't serious." She snapped her fingers. "*That* is what all those rumors are worth. Precisely nothing. Rumford is well and truly caught."

Mrs. Sherwood was watching her daughter as she danced. "I just wish he was a little younger," she said.

"Nonsense," Lady Standish said forcefully. "A mature and stable man who will be good to her is just what Diana needs. Youthful passion blazes hot and then it dies away. The kind of relationship that Rumford will offer Diana is the kind that makes for a solid, satisfying marriage."

Alex heard what his mother said as he, too, watched Diana circle the floor with the Earl of Rumford. She had a trick of seeming to capture all the light in the room, he thought.

How could he bear it if she actually decided to marry Rumford? He turned away from the dance floor. It was too painful to see her in the arms of another man. He went into the card room, where he spent the remainder of the evening playing whist. When he got home, he went into the library, called for a bottle of port, and got drunk enough that he actually slept through the night.

Eighteen

Lady Moulton's invitation arrived the following morning, and Sally heard about it over the breakfast table. Her mother was jubilant and Diana looked excited, so she was reluctant to tell them that she didn't want to go. In fact, she *couldn't* tell them she didn't want to go. If she said she wanted to stay in London because there was a chance of her seeing the Duke of Sinclair, her mother would probably bundle her up and take her back to Standish Court until she got over her foolish *tendre* for a notorious rake.

She soothed herself with the thought that she would be seeing him that afternoon, at the meeting of the Committee to Save Climbing Boys. He had said he would attend, and the rest of the committee was very excited at the prospect of gaining such a high-born member.

Oh well. If she had to miss the chance of seeing him for a few days in order to further Diana's romance, she would do it. Sinclair hardly ever came to the balls she went to anyhow. She was more likely to see him at the opera, which he appeared to love, as he was there every time she went. Lately Sally had developed a great fondness for the opera. This had not aroused any suspicion in her mother as everyone knew Sally was an excellent musician.

The committee meeting was in a small house off of Oxford Street and the duke picked up Sally and drove her there himself. No one realized she was being escorted by the duke as the family was all out of the house when he arrived.

Sinclair sat quietly for the first part of the meeting, listening as different members spoke to him passionately about their cause. Sally watched his face as stories were told of the horrors climbing boys endured, and he looked grave and concerned, although he said little.

Finally, Mr. Anisman, a member of the House of Commons, said bluntly, "What is your feeling about all of this, Your Grace? You have been kind enough to join us today. Dare we hope that we can count on your support?"

The duke's green eyes slowly scanned the group and came to rest on Sally's face. She looked back, her blue eyes full of hope. Surely he could not have been unmoved by some of these horrible stories.

He said, still looking at her, "I am against the practice of sending small boys into chimneys to clean them. And I admire the zeal which this group evinces in trying to right this grievous wrong. But I hope you realize that it is going to be extremely difficult to get an act banning climbing boys through Parliament."

Sally's heart sank. She glanced at the other members and was surprised to see that they did not look upset by such a statement. She looked back at the duke and said passionately, "How can that be? How is it possible for a civilized society to allow such a practice to continue to exist?"

The duke's perfectly sculpted face did not move, and when he spoke his voice was dispassionate.

"You must understand the temper of the times, Lady Sarah. There is great and growing discontent—political, economic and industrial—in this country, and the government's way of handling it has been to pass a succession of severe Acts of Suppression. The example of the French Revolution still hangs over the rulers of England, from Lord Liverpool, the prime minister, to lords, lieutenants, and commanding officers, to land-owning magnates and magistrates and wealthy employers. The thrust of this government is to discourage protesters and reformers of every sort—and that includes the Committee to Save Climbing Boys."

"Then you're telling us that we're wasting our time," one of the men said in a flat voice.

"No, I am not saying that. I am just warning you that you face an uphill battle in this particular fight."

"It would help if we had a highly placed member of the House of Lords on our side, Your Grace," another man said. "The more people there are to speak up for these unfortunate children, the better our chance of success."

"For what it is worth, you have my support," the duke said. "I have spoken in the past about the situation of climbing boys and I shall continue to do so in the future. In the meanwhile, I think it would behoove us to look into some of these chimney sweep operations. Perhaps we can better conditions for these children while we are waiting to get the practice completely outlawed."

A murmur of interest went around the room.

"How can we better conditions for them if they are still forced to climb chimneys?" Sally said, her voice as passionate as it had been before.

"We can see that they are adequately fed and have proper shelter," the duke replied. He looked at Sally and for the first time there was sympathy in his eyes. "I understand your indignation, Lady Sarah. And I share it. But climbing boys are not going to be outlawed tomorrow. Isn't it better to do what we can even if we cannot have what we want? Not every climbing boy is going to be lucky enough to be plucked out of his miserable life and sent to live at Standish Court. I am not saying that we should not continue to fight for legislation, but I think we should also try to regulate the industry as best we can."

The meeting had gone on around Sally as she brooded about what Sinclair had said. When the meeting was over, and they were finally alone together in his curricle, she said, "I know that you're right about trying to make things better for the children, but I simply cannot fathom how anyone could vote against banning such a devilish practice. It just doesn't make sense. It's not...*human*."

"I will not disagree with you," he said, "but there is a great deal of fear in the government just now. There have been too many social disturbances recently—the Luddites, for example. The government feels itself to be under siege."

"My family have always been Whigs," Sally said defiantly. "We would never support Lord Liverpool and his Tory Acts of Suppression."

The duke turned his horses onto Oxford Street. "My family have always been Tories," he said. "I broke with a long line of Sinclairs when I declared myself a Whig."

She turned to him. "Good for you, Your Grace!"

He shrugged. "It doesn't mean much, I'm afraid. The Whigs are a totally disorganized opposition these days, Lady Sarah. There are factions within factions within factions. I'm afraid we're in no position to mount an attack upon Lord Liverpool's citadel."

They were driving down Oxford Street, and now a single horse and loaded wagon came out from one of the side streets and pulled in front of them. Abruptly, the horse fell to his knees, stopping the wagon. The duke managed to pull his team to a halt just a few feet from the vehicle in front of them.

The fallen horse didn't try to get up and the driver raised his whip and began to beat it, cursing loudly as his arm came down.

"Stop! Stop hitting him!" Sally called frantically, and scooted toward the side of the curricle so she could climb down.

"Stay where you are, Lady Sarah," the duke commanded in a voice that ensured instant obedience. He looked at her, then wrapped his reins, told his horses to stand and jumped down from his side of the carriage. His face wore a look of resignation.

The man stopped beating his horse as the duke approached, glaring at the aristocrat belligerently.

The duke said, "This animal is incapable of pulling a load of so many bricks. There is no point in hitting him for something he clearly cannot do."

"He kin do it," the man replied, scowling. "He's just lazy."

Now that the beating had stopped, the horse scrambled to regain its feet. The duke looked at the animal, which was showing all its ribs as well as its hip bones. "Perhaps if you fed him, he could pull it, but in the condition he is in, he cannot."

"He has to," the man said. "I have t' deliver these here bricks or I don't get paid."

While the men were talking, Sally had climbed down from the curricle. She came up to them now and demanded of the man, "Why are you hitting that poor animal? It's cruel."

The man's narrow jaw set. "He's my horse and I kin do with him what I want ter. You nobs should worry about yer own horses and leave mine alone."

Sally looked pleadingly at the duke. "We can't

leave this animal with such a person. He'll end up killing it. It's already being starved, poor thing."

The duke looked grim. "Neglected and abused horses are killed every day in London, Lady Sarah."

She lifted her chin. "That may be so, but we haven't seen them. We've seen this one, and we have to help."

She was absolutely determined.

"What do you suggest we do?" he asked interestedly.

"I'll buy him," Sally said.

"He ain't fer sale," the man said promptly. "I won't have no livelihood if I don't have a horse."

"You aren't feeding him!" Sally flashed. "How can you expect him to work for you if he isn't fed?"

"I feed him what I can afford," the man returned. "I don't look too fat neither, do I?"

In fact, the man was skeleton-thin under his shabby brown rags.

Sally's brow furrowed with worry. She looked up at the duke, clearly expecting him to do something.

He looked back at her and sighed. Then he turned to the man. "What kind of job do you do?"

"I deliver things for people. I'm supposed to be delivering these here bricks, but the bloody horse keeps fallin' down."

As they were talking, traffic had been building up around them in Oxford Street. The three of them were the object of many curious stares as people veered around the two carriages to get by.

The duke said, "I'll hire a pair of horses for you

to hitch to the wagon so you can deliver your bricks—what is your name?"

"Blake, m' lord. Colin Blake."

"Very well, Colin Blake. The pair of horses will be here in an hour. In the meanwhile, I am going to unhitch this sad animal and take him home with me. You may call upon me tomorrow morning at eleven and we will discuss the conditions under which you may retrieve your horse. I am the Duke of Sinclair and my home is Sinclair House in Berkeley Square. I will leave instructions with my servants that you are to be admitted."

Colin's eyes nearly popped out of his head when he heard these words.

"A dook?" he said.

"Yes. A duke. I'm sure we will be able to work out an arrangement that will be satisfactory to you, Colin. In the meanwhile, you can unhitch your horse for me."

Colin stared suspiciously from the duke to Sally then back again to the duke. "How do I know if yer tellin' me the truth? How do I know yer a dook?"

"He is, Mr. Blake," Sally said earnestly. "You can trust him, truly you can."

Colin looked into Sally's clear blue eyes. The suspicion faded from his face and he nodded. "All right, miss. If you say so."

Colin went to unhitch his horse and Sally went to its head, to rub its face and talk to it. More traffic went by on Oxford Street. When the horse was free, the duke led it around to the back of his curricle and tied it up. Then he said to Colin, "Stay here with your wagon. I will hire you a pair of horses from the nearest livery stable. Deliver your bricks and keep the horses over night. You can bring them with you when you come to see me tomorrow morning."

"Yes, m' lord," Colin replied.

The duke lifted Sally back into the curricle, climbed into the driver's seat himself, and set off in the direction of Grosvenor Square.

"I'll leave you at home and then I'll see about getting a pair of horses sent over to Blake," he said to Sally as he drove down the street, the pitiful nag trailing behind them.

"He was right, you know," she said. "He was as starved-looking as the horse."

"Mmm," he said.

"I wonder if Alex could find a job for Mr. Blake at Standish Court," Sally mused.

"Your poor brother," Sinclair said. "Do you saddle him with every stray you pick up?"

Her spine got straighter. "We have so much. God would say that it is our responsibility to help those who are less fortunate than we."

Silence reigned as he continued to drive down the street. At last Sally said, "You don't have to keep the horse, you can leave it off at my house. My cousin Diana will take care of it. She is better than a horse doctor."

"The horse will do very well in my stable," he said. "My head groom will take as good care of it as Miss Sherwood would."

By now they were entering Grosvenor Square. The duke pulled his curricle up in front of Standish House and Sally turned to him, putting a hand on his arm to keep him from getting down.

"What are you going to do with that poor man tomorrow morning? You can't just send him away with that starved horse! I'll talk to Alex…"

"Have no fear, Lady Sarah," he replied calmly. "You won't have to foist Colin Blake and his nag upon your brother, you have already foisted them upon me. I'm quite sure that a comfortable place can be found on one of my many estates for Colin Blake, his horse and his wife and children should he have any. You need not fear that you will run into them in London again."

Sally's face lit to radiance. "You will do that? Thank you, Your Grace! I cannot tell you how much I appreciate your goodness."

"Goodness is not something I am usually known for," he said. "It makes for a nice change."

He jumped down from the curricle and came around to her side and lifted her down. She was so slim that his hands nearly encircled her waist. He looked down at her, his face sober. There was a moment's silence. "Why are you bothering with me?" he asked slowly.

At first she looked surprised, then her blue eyes grew luminous. "You rescued Jem," she said. "And now you are rescuing Colin Blake and his horse. I haven't met any other men in London who would do that."

"You are the one responsible for those rescues," he said.

She smiled. "We did it together," she said, turned, and went into the house.

Nineteen

It didn't take long for word to reach the Standish household that Sally had been seen on Oxford Street with the Duke of Sinclair and a ragamuffin man with a broken-down horse. Lady Standish heard about it from Sally Jersey, who sent her a note detailing the information she had received from Lady Westover, who had driven past the trio earlier in the afternoon. Alex learned about it at Brooks, from Lord Morple, of all people, the man whom Sally had been with when she first saw Jem.

The subject came up as soon as the family met in the drawing room before dinner.

"What were you doing in company with Sinclair?" Alex demanded. "First you asked him to accompany you to Richmond, and now this. He's not a proper escort for you, Sally. I've told you before— he's a notorious rake."

"He came with me to the Committee on Saving

Climbing Boys," Sally said. "He was interested in helping. He's interested in reform. We need reform in this country. I don't care about his reputation. I like him."

"Good heavens," Lady Standish said. "You like him for *political* reasons?"

"He helped me save Jem, and this afternoon he saved a horse from being beaten to death. And he is going to find a place on his estate for both the horse and the poor starved man who was beating him. I think he's a good man and I don't care about his reputation."

"Sinclair is a member of the reform faction of the Whig party, that's true," Alex said. "I can't quarrel with his politics. But he's not a white knight, Sal. He's not the sort of man an innocent girl should be seeing."

"Your brother is right," Lady Standish said.

Diana looked at her friend's flushed face. "What else do you see in him, Sally?" she asked quietly.

"Oh…" Sally gestured with her hands. "I just feel…I don't think he's had an easy life, somehow. He strikes me as someone who's been…hurt."

"Wonderful," Alex said sarcastically. "The most notorious rake in London and my sister thinks *he's* been hurt."

Lady Standish frowned and looked worried.

Diana said, "Sally has wonderful instincts about people, Alex."

"She's eighteen years old! What can she know about a man like Sinclair?"

"I just know," Sally said. "I can feel it in him, Alex. He's not a hard-hearted rake. He's not."

At this moment, Henrys came to the door and announced that dinner was ready. With the servants present, the topic of conversation necessarily changed to something less personal.

When dinner was finished, the women retired into the drawing room and Alex left to meet an old army friend. Diana and Sally sat together and looked over a book of horse prints that Sally had bought for Diana earlier that morning. Lady Standish turned to her cousin and dear friend.

"Do you think it may be possible?" she asked. "Sally and the Duke of Sinclair?"

"Sally is a special child," Mrs. Sherwood said. "Her illness—almost dying, then having to spend six months in bed—it gave her a dimension that most young girls don't have. If she sees something in the duke, then perhaps there is something there to see."

"My God," Lady Standish said. "Imagine—my daughter a duchess!"

Mrs. Sherwood smiled.

"And your daughter may be a countess! Who would have ever believed that this Season could turn out so brilliantly!"

"They aren't married yet," Mrs. Sherwood said.

"We leave tomorrow to visit the Moultons. I will lay a wager with you that Diana will be engaged by the time that we return to London."

"Perhaps," Mrs. Sherwood said softly. "Perhaps."

* * *

The Standish ladies had stayed home for the night for a change, and everyone went to bed early to catch up on lost sleep. Diana could not sleep, however. Her mind was filled with the coming visit to the Moultons, and what might happen between her and Lord Rumford.

Lady Standish was certain that he was going to make her an offer.

Diana was fond of Lord Rumford. She admired him for being a faithful and devoted husband to a sickly wife. He had not turned his back upon his responsibilities and run away. He had been there for the woman he loved.

He would always be a bulwark she could count upon. She had not had that kind of presence in her life when she was growing up. It would be good to have it now. And he was a nice-looking man, too. Marriage to him would be the answer to everything she wanted.

So why did she feel so uneasy, so…restless?

After two and a half hours of tossing and turning, she decided to give up on sleep and go downstairs to the library to get a book. She put on her velvet robe and slippers and went out into the hallway, which was dimly illuminated by a few sconces.

She was surprised to find a light on in the library, and even more surprised to find Alex there, sprawled on the leather sofa in front of the flickering fire. She remembered finding him in similar circumstances on their brief visit to Standish Court.

Wasn't he sleeping at all?

"Why are you still up?" she asked from the doorway.

His dark head swiveled around. "Dee! I might ask you the same question."

"I couldn't sleep and came down to get a book."

"I only got home a short time ago," he said. "I was having a glass of wine before going upstairs."

His hair was rumpled, his cravat was loosened and his jacket was off. There was just the beginning of a dark stubble under his skin. She felt her stomach tighten.

"You're drinking too much," she said. "Is that a habit you picked up in the army?"

"No," he said.

The house was perfectly quiet. The only sound in the room was the crackling of the fire. She slowly walked across the room and sat down on the sofa beside him. The tie from her velvet robe just brushed his leg. "What's wrong, Alex?" she asked softly.

He took a sip of his wine. "Nothing that time can't fix," he said. "It's a bit of an adjustment, coming home. That's all."

His eyes were shadowed and the curve of his mouth looked bitter.

"Do you wish you were back in the army?" she asked.

"No!" He frowned and shook his head. "No," he repeated more quietly. "I'm finished with the army, Dee. This business I'm doing for the Horse Guards is just political. The army is behind me now." He ran his fingers through his hair, disordering it further. "I want it to be behind me."

She was so close to him she could see the shadow his eyelashes cast on his cheeks. He had always had absurdly long eyelashes. He looked as if he were stretched as tautly as a drawn bow. She knew him so well. Something was wrong with him—something serious. Something had happened to him in the Peninsula that he couldn't throw off.

He had been in battle. He had been wounded, had seen his friends killed.

"It must be hard to forget," she said softly. "The war, I mean."

His head jerked around and he looked her fully in the face for the first time. "God," he said. "Dee." And then he was reaching for her.

Their lips met and she slid her arms around his neck. They kissed passionately, and she ran her fingers through his tousled black hair, cupping the back of his head with her palm. His hand came up to slide under her robe and cover her breast. Her nipple stood up hard. Her senses were filled with him; all thinking had stopped. All she knew was the feel of him, the smell of him, the sensations his mouth and hands were creating in her body.

Then, suddenly, there came a single sharp bark, and a small, furry body was trying to insinuate itself between them.

Alex swore.

Diana struggled to regain her composure. She pulled away from him and Freddie reached up to lick her face.

"Where did that damn dog come from?" Alex said. His voice sounded hoarse.

"My room," she said breathlessly. "I left the door open. He must have followed me."

She clutched Freddie to her, using his warm furry body as a shield between her and Alex, between her and what had almost just happened. She moved farther away on the sofa.

Alex didn't try to stop her, he just stared at her out of shadowed eyes. They looked at each other for what seemed a long time. "I love you, Dee, and I think you still love me."

Her insides were in complete turmoil. She had been telling herself for so long that she no longer loved him. But she couldn't deny what she felt at this moment. She couldn't deny that every inch of her body was longing to go back into his arms.

She panicked. She had to protect herself. She couldn't let him see the devastating effect he had on her. She had to make him understand how impossible it was for them ever to have a future together. Desperately she sought for a weapon, and after a brief, frantic moment, she found it.

She said in a low, trembling voice, "I was never going to tell you this, but now I think I will. Six weeks after you left, I found out that I was pregnant." She held Freddie close, seeking comfort from his warmth. "I didn't know what to do, Alex. You were gone and I was so afraid and alone... At first I was even afraid to tell my mother."

His face was stark with shock. "You told me you were all right! I never would have left if I'd suspected you were with child!"

She buried her lips in Freddie's fur. It was so hard to think about this, to talk about it. "I didn't want you to stay for a baby," she said, her low voice muffled by the dog. "I wanted you to stay for me."

He shut his eyes. Even in the dimness of the room, she could see how white he was. "Oh, Dee. I am so sorry. I am so very, very sorry."

Her chest tightened with pain as the memory of that time washed over her. She rested her cheek against Freddie and stared into the fireplace; she couldn't bear to look at him. "No one ever knew but my mother," she said. "I had a miscarriage. My mother said it was a blessing and I suppose in a way it was." Her eyes turned back to him. "But my baby died, Alex. Our baby died. And you weren't there."

He didn't say anything, just looked at her with that pale face and those shadowed eyes.

Tears began to pour down her cheeks. "You shouldn't have left me," she said, her voice breaking. "After what had been between us, you shouldn't have left me."

"I know," he said. His voice ached with pain. "I knew it then, and I did it anyway. I don't blame you for hating me, Dee. I hate myself for what I did to you. I convinced myself that nothing would be lost by us waiting a few years. I thought it would be like me being away at school. All I could think of was what I wanted. I didn't think of you at all." He reached out and took her hand into the two of his. "I'm sorry."

She let her hand remain within his for a moment, then slowly she withdrew it. Her heart was filled with a tumult of emotions, but primary among them was sadness, sadness for the girl and boy they had been, sadness for the lost little life that would always stand between them. In her rational mind she knew that the baby could well have died even if Alex had stayed home. But deep in her heart and soul, she blamed him. If she hadn't been so frightened, if she hadn't been so distraught…then, perhaps, the baby would have lived.

She smoothed her hand over Freddie's silky head. "I know that there will always be something between you and me. I can't completely erase those years of loving you. But I can't marry you, Alex." Her voice shook. "I just…can't."

There was a long silence. Freddie closed his eyes, reveling in the bliss of her caresses. Finally Alex said, "I failed you. I understand that." He rubbed his eyes as if they were burning. "I want you to be happy, Dee. I want that more than anything else in the world. And if Rumford is the man to do it, then I wish you both well."

He looked so tired, so unhappy. Part of her wanted to comfort him. Part of her wanted to throw herself into his arms and kiss away that strained, sad look. Part of her wanted to comfort herself by bring-

ing back the old Alex and Dee that for so long had
been the touchstone of her life.

But she couldn't do that. Too much had happened.
Too much blame and sorrow lay between them.

Slowly she got up from the sofa, dislodging Freddie from her lap as she did so.

Alex looked up at her, his eyes dark with pain. "I
would give everything I have if I could turn back
time."

Her heart cried out in response, *Oh Alex, so
would I!* But her brain spoke when she returned,
"No one can do that."

He looked at her with those shadowed eyes and
said desolately, "I know."

She looked at the bottle and the empty glass that
reposed on the table next to the sofa. "Don't drink too
much, Alex. It's not the answer to your problems."

He smiled crookedly. "It helps."

"No, it doesn't. Not really." She bent down and
picked up Freddie, who was sniffing at her robe.
"Don't sit here by yourself any longer. Go to bed."

"I will."

"Good night, Alex."

"Good night, Dee."

As soon as she had left the room, he buried his
face in his hands and didn't move for a long, long
time. Finally he turned to look at the bottle of wine
next to him on the table. The minutes ticked by as
the fire died lower in the chimney. At last he got to
his feet and walked out of the room, leaving behind
the half-full bottle on the table.

Twenty

Lady Moulton's home in Kent was only a few hours drive from London. Chisworth Hall was not nearly as impressive a residence as Standish Court, but it was a pretty brick house with a lovely view of meadows and a rushing river. Lady Moulton and Lord Rumford greeted the guests—Lord Moulton was a member of the government and was in Paris at the moment, so Lord Rumford was acting as host.

When the Standish party arrived they found that Lady Caroline Wrentham and her parents, the Earl and Countess of Stowe, were there before them. Alex had not expected them and didn't know how to react. He seemed to have been thrown into company with Lady Caroline more and more often lately and, while he enjoyed her company, he did not want to find his name coupled with hers.

He was in no shape to get involved with any woman right now, he thought. He had to get his life in some kind of order first. He couldn't let Dee see him falling apart. She would worry about him and that would impinge on her happiness. And after all she had been through, she deserved to be happy.

Sally was not pleased to see that Lord Dorset was also a guest. He was a perfectly pleasant young man, and she had no objections to spending some time in his company, but she had no intention of marrying him and she was afraid that that was the way he was tending.

It would have been so nice to be able to spend some uninterrupted time with the Duke of Sinclair.

Alex and Sally solved their problems by sticking together and managing never to be alone with either Lady Caroline or Lord Dorset. They never actually voiced this intention to each other, but whenever either of them was invited to take a turn in the garden, or a walk along the river, they made sure to include the other couple in the outing. Both of them were perfectly aware of what they were doing, and both managed to ignore with aplomb the growing frustration of Lady Caroline and Lord Dorset with the constant foursome.

Diana's situation was quite different. Since Lady Moulton's purpose in inviting her was to give her brother a chance to get to know Diana better, the two often found themselves alone. Diana thoroughly enjoyed the time she spent with Lord Rumford. She loved being out of London and she liked it that Lord Rumford showed himself to be so at home in country surroundings. He talked to her about his horses, his art collection, what he was doing on his estate, and he expressed a desire for her to visit his home in Oxfordshire soon. She liked his quiet authority, his kind attentiveness, and his calm, blue-gray eyes. She and Lord Rumford cantered together along well-manicured rides through the woods, strolled up and down the paths of the garden, and fed the ducks on the river. He had an air of almost paternal protectiveness toward her that made her feel warm and comfortable and safe.

The day before they were to return to London, Diana and Lord Rumford took a last ride. It was a glorious day and they went along the river, with the sun glinting off the water, off the horse's polished coats, and off of Diana's uncovered hair. After a while, at Lord Rumford's suggestion, they dismounted and tied the horses to a tree while they went down to the water to watch two swans that were floating along the opposite bank along with their offspring.

Diana held her face up to the sky. "It's so lovely here," she said. "I hate the thought of going back to London."

"Most young girls having their first Season would never say such a thing," he said.

She smiled at him. "I suppose I'm different, then."

"Yes," he said. "You are."

He put his hands on her shoulders and turned her to face him. "Miss Sherwood," he said. "Diana. You must know how I feel about you. I think I fell in love with you the moment I first saw you in the receiving line at your come-out ball. I know I'm much older than you, but in so many ways I think we suit. You would love Aston Castle, I'm sure of it. You would have everything you want there—horses, dogs, beautiful surroundings. And I would do everything in my power to make you happy."

She looked into his serious blue-gray eyes and felt everything inside her become very still. "Are you making me an offer, my lord?" she asked softly.

"Yes." His hands slipped from her shoulders down to hold her hands. He was not nearly as tall as Alex, and their eyes were more on a level. "Will you marry me, Diana?"

It was as if her heart stopped beating. For the briefest of moments, Alex's face hung before her eyes. She felt frozen, unable to move, unable to think.

"Diana?" Lord Rumford said gently.

His voice banished Alex's picture and once again she saw the man before her. She lifted her chin slightly and said clearly, "I will be honored to marry you, my lord."

His face lit with a joyful smile.

She steeled herself to say what had to be said. "Before we make any announcement, I have to tell you something."

A faint, puzzled line appeared between his brows. "Yes?" he said.

Her nostrils flared slightly as she drew in a breath. Her hands tightened slightly on his as she sought for the right words. She forced herself to keep looking into his eyes. "This is hard for me to say, but you have a right to know. When I was seventeen, I fell in love. And...I behaved unwisely." Her eyes dropped for a moment, but then she lifted them again. "I was young and stupid and I thought we would be married. It didn't happen—he went away to join the army instead. So I am not a virgin, my lord. If that is important to you, than you should know now. It's not something I would want you to find out on your wedding night."

His own eyes had darkened as she was speaking. "He left you?" he said incredulously.

She found she couldn't speak, so she just nodded.

"And you were seventeen and had no father to protect you."

Tears sprung to her eyes. One of them trickled down her cheek. "No," she said. "I had no father."

"My poor girl," he said. He held out his arms. "Well, from now on, you will have me."

Diana stepped into the shelter of his arms and pressed her face into his shoulder. She struggled not to cry. "Thank you, my lord," she said thickly. "You are so good. Thank you."

He stroked her beautiful hair. "I will take good care of you, my dear," he promised. "Nobody will ever harm you again."

The words were like balm to her soul.

"Look at me," he said softly.

She lifted her tear-stained face to his and he bent his head and kissed her.

Diana kissed him back. Behind her she heard the

running water of the river and one of the horses snorted and pawed the ground impatiently. The sun was warm on her head and shoulders. She felt the buttons of his coat pressing into her flesh. At last he raised his head and looked at her.

"You have made me a very happy man, Diana," he said.

She gave him what she hoped was a radiant smile. "Thank you, my lord."

"Edward," he said.

She reached up and laid her fingers on his cheek. He was such a good man. "Edward," she said. And he kissed her again.

Alex thought he had been prepared to hear the news of Diana's engagement, but still it came as a bitter blow. The thought of her marrying another man, of her living in intimacy with another man...his fists clenched and his blood rose at the mere thought of it. How was he to bear it?

I have to bear it, he told himself grimly. *I've already done enough harm to Dee. I have to let her think that I'm happy for her.*

He could only hope that his mother's and Sally's obvious delight would cover up his own more restrained reaction.

Mrs. Sherwood had concerns about her daughter's future marriage. "Are you sure that this is what you want, darling? He's a very nice man, but he is old enough to be your father."

"It's what I want, Mama," Diana said positively. "I really think I will be happy spending the rest of my life with such a man. He's everything I could want in a husband."

Her mother was silent for a moment. Then she asked quietly, "What about Alex?"

They were sitting together in Diana's bedroom, side by side upon the four-poster bed.

Diana stiffened. "Alex and I are finished, Mama. I thought you understood that."

"Are you sure, darling? Alex loves you. And there was so much between you once...."

"It's precisely because of what was between us that I can never marry him," Diana said. She stared down at her sprig muslin skirt. "I told him, Mama. I told him about the baby. So he understands how I feel. He told me that if I could find happiness with Lord Rumford, then he wished me well."

"I see," Mrs. Sherwood said quietly.

"I told Lord Rumford about Alex," Diana said next. At her mother's sharp intake of breath, she added hastily, "Not by name, of course, but I told him I was not a virgin."

She turned to look at her mother, her eyes glittering with unshed tears. "He was so kind, Mama. He said that I had not had a father to take care of me then, but that I was not to worry, that he would take care of me from now on." She blinked away the tears. "He's a wonderful man. I am very lucky to have found someone so caring and so strong."

Mrs. Sherwood looked at Diana for a long moment, then she put her arm around her daughter's shoulders. "He does sound like a fine man, darling. Perhaps this is the right thing for you to do."

"And you will come to live with us, as well. We talked about that, and he expects you to come and live at Aston Castle with me." Diana hugged her mother. "It's all so perfect, Mama. I am very happy."

Mrs. Sherwood put her cheek against her daughter's smooth one. "You deserve happiness, Diana. Life has not been easy for you, I know. I am so happy for you, darling. I am so happy."

Lady Standish sent the notice to the *Morning Post* and by the time the family arrived back in London, the news was all over the ton. All of a sudden, Diana's status was transformed. As the future Countess of Rumford, she now counted in the upper echelons of London society. Matrons who had heretofore ignored her, now went out of their way to be pleasant. She was no longer Diana Sherwood, poverty-stricken hanger-on to the Standishes. Now, she was the future wife of the Earl of Rumford, a title that had stood in English society for centuries. People might privately have thought that Rumford had been caught by a pretty face, but Diana's family was respectable at least, and the match, though surprising, was certainly not unprecedented. High-born nobles long before Lord Rumford had married for beauty. Look at the famous Gunning sisters, everybody said. One of them had actually caught two dukes!

The Longwood family was infuriated. And frightened.

"How could this have happened?" Viscount Longwood raged at the breakfast table as he read the notice in the newspaper. "She's a nobody and Rumford actually is going to marry her?"

Jessica's eyes were red. "I thought he had chosen me, Papa. I really did. But once he saw her, it was as if I didn't exist anymore."

"What are we going to do?" Lady Longwood said. "Once our financial situation becomes known, no one is going to want to marry Jessica. And we have no funds! We're fast going through the money you borrowed to come to London. Once that is gone, we'll have to return home to Longwood, and there isn't even enough to live on there."

"I would like to kill Gerald," Jessica said viciously. "You shouldn't have paid his gaming debts, Papa. You should have let him go to debtor's prison."

"We'll come about," the viscount said. "This isn't the end. I'll think of something."

"I haven't got another suitor," Jessica wailed. "Everyone thought I was going to marry Lord Rumford!"

"What about Standish?" Lady Longwood said. "He's even more wealthy than Rumford. He's danced with you, hasn't he?"

"He's danced with me a few times, but he's only being polite," Jessica said. "He's not interested. He spends more time with Caroline Wrentham than with anyone else."

"The Stowes have plenty of money. They don't need Standish the way we do. Perhaps we can come up with a way to bring you more to Standish's attention," Lady Longwood said hopefully.

"I don't see how. I'm not beautiful, like Lady Caroline," Jessica said mournfully.

"We only have a short window of time," Lord Longford said in a clipped voice. "Jessica has to marry someone with money. It's the only way out of our difficulties. The choices are Rumford, Standish—" here he lifted his eyebrows "—or Sinclair is always a possibility. He has plenty of blunt."

"Sinclair has never shown the slightest interest in young, marriageable girls," Lady Longwood said. "He seems perfectly satisfied with his many mistresses."

"He has to get married some time," Lord Longwood said. "He has the succession to think about, after all."

"I don't like the Duke of Sinclair," Jessica said. "He scares me."

Lady Longwood said, "The best answer to our problem is definitely Standish."

Jessica thrust out her lower lip. "I don't see how I am supposed to coax an offer out of Lord Standish. He's simply not interested in me."

Silence fell as the family stared fixedly into their variously filled coffee cups.

"What about Gerald?" Jessica said. "Can't he marry a rich girl? Perhaps we could find him a Cit who wants a title."

"I've thought about that," Lord Longwood said. "But no rich Cit is going to marry his daughter to an inveterate gambler. They have too much regard for their money."

Lady Longwood said slowly, "What if something should happen to Miss Sherwood? Perhaps then Lord Rumford would look Jessica's way once more."

Her husband and her daughter stared at her.

"What do you mean, Mama?" Jessica asked in a small voice.

"Well…what if she was found compromised with another man? That would certainly put off a prospective husband."

Lord Longwood frowned. "That would be difficult to arrange."

"Yes. I suppose it would be."

"Still…" Lord Longwood tapped his lip. "We have to do something." He folded his hands on the table and looked at them. "Perhaps getting rid of Miss Sherwood is not such a bad idea."

Twenty-One

When Alex got back to London from Lady Moulton's, one of the first things he did was to look up Captain Thomas Stapleton, the young veteran he had encountered at the reception for King Louis. They met for dinner at a small eating place near the Horse Guards that was frequented by military men.

"I have been thinking of establishing a small club for Peninsula veterans," Alex said as they ordered their meal. "Both you and I have been having some problems readjusting to civilian life, and I would be surprised if we were the only ones with this difficulty. It felt good the other day to talk to someone who understood what I was feeling. Perhaps a group of us could help each other."

Tom Stapleton looked at Alex for a long moment. "I'm drinking too much. Oh, I know a lot of chaps regularly get drunk, but I was never like that." He shifted his gaze to his almost-empty wineglass. "Now I am."

"It's easier," Alex said. He breathed in and out. "It keeps one from having to think."

"And it lets one sleep."

"Yes."

Tom raised his eyes and they looked at each other silently.

"I know it would probably sound strange to most people," Alex said. "We're not like those poor enlisted men who are coming home to face no jobs and economic destitution. We have money. We have fine homes. We have families who love us. There's no reason for us to be distressed. But there's no question that we are having some problems."

"I think a club for veterans is a very good idea," Tom said somberly. "I know it would help me."

They sat silently as their meal was served. Then, when the waiter was gone, Alex said, "We only want chaps who are having difficulties like us, though. Those men who have readjusted easily don't need a group like this."

Tom speared a slice of beef with his fork. "I know one other fellow who would be a good member. He's become my drinking partner of late, and things come out when a man is in his cups."

"I haven't spoken about this problem to anyone but you," Alex confessed. "But I'll sound out a few chaps that I know at the Horse Guards."

"How many members were you thinking of?"

"I was thinking of about eight or so."

The waiter came over to pour more wine into

their glasses. He asked if they wanted a second bottle.

"We'll have just the one bottle," Alex said.

"Yes," Tom agreed as the waiter walked away. "It's time we started to get well."

Diana's schedule was so busy the first few days that she arrived home from her visit to the Moultons that she didn't even have time to walk Freddie in the park during the afternoon. Mrs. Sherwood graciously offered to do it for her.

"The dog will be perfectly all right being walked by a footman," Lady Standish said impatiently. "Now that dear Diana is engaged to an earl, it is imperative that we improve her wardrobe. Don't you want to come with us, Louisa, and pick out her new clothes?"

Mrs. Sherwood looked at her daughter. "Do you want me to come, darling?"

"It's not at all necessary," Diana assured her. "I feel very badly about neglecting Freddie, and if you wish to walk him I'd rather you do that than come with me. A footman is all right, but Freddie would prefer one of *us*."

So Mrs. Sherwood was walking, leash in hand, along her usual path in Hyde Park when she was met by Sir Gilbert Merton, who was walking his dog, Caleb.

The man's face brightened when he saw her. "So, you have returned from your visit, ma'am," he said. "And a brilliant visit it was. We read all about it in the *Morning Post*."

"Yes, my daughter is to marry the Earl of Rumford."

It still sounded strange to Mrs. Sherwood's when she said that.

"It is a splendid match," Sir Gilbert said. "Will you be living with them at the earl's estate?"

Mrs. Sherwood nodded. "Yes, they seem to want me."

They both bent to let their dogs off the leashes.

"Who wouldn't want a lovely lady like yourself?" Sir Gilbert said.

Mrs. Sherwood flushed lightly. "It is all Diana's doing, I know that. But the earl was very kind to agree to her request. Not every man wants to inherit his mother-in-law along with his wife."

Freddie and Caleb were doing their usual sniffing ritual, as if they had never met before.

"You will be an ornament to the earl's home," Sir Gilbert said soberly. "You would be an ornament to any man's home, Mrs. Sherwood."

Mrs. Sherwood's flush deepened. "Thank you. You are very kind." She drew a deep breath. "And how does Miss Merton go on?"

"She seems to be having a good time for herself, but I do not perceive any particular suitor who seems really serious. In fact, without Lord Standish around to dance with her and encourage others to do so, Charlotte has been less on the dance floor than she was wont to be. She will have a respectable portion, but we are not wealthy people, Mrs. Sherwood. My estate supports itself and the people who live upon it, but there is not a lot left over for fripperies—like this Season. But I could not say no to my only remaining child."

The two dogs dashed off down the path, and their owners followed at a more leisurely pace. Mrs. Sherwood said, "From what you said to me earlier, you will not be all that unhappy if Charlotte returns to Sussex unwed. You said you would rather keep her close to home."

"That's true," Sir Gilbert said heartily. "There are several fine young men for her to choose from in Sussex. Perhaps she will appreciate their solid worth better after a Season spent with the light-weight beaux of London."

Two thrushes rose from the bushes into the air above them. Sir Gilbert looked up at the birds silhouetted against the blue sky. "I miss home, and that's a fact," he said nostalgically "London is too crowded and dirty and smelly for my taste."

"I prefer the country myself," Mrs. Sherwood agreed. "It was very pleasant visiting Lady Moulton's estate for a few days. The house was situated right on a river, Sir Gilbert. It was a lovely setting."

They walked in silence for a few moments. The dogs scampered back and then darted off again. Freddie spotted a squirrel and chased it up a tree. Both dogs stood at the base of the tree, looking up, hoping the squirrel would come down so they could chase it again.

Sir Gilbert said gruffly, "And your girl is all right with marrying a man old enough to be her father?"

Mrs. Sherwood didn't answer right away and he said hastily, "Forgive me if I was impertinent."

She gave him a faint smile. "It's all right. In fact, I was worried about just that thing myself. But now I think that Lord Rumford's maturity is one of his attractions for Diana." Her face became grave. "You see, Diana grew up without a father, and I think she sees a steadiness and stability in Lord Rumford that appeals to her very much. And I think he will take good care of her." Her smile reappeared. "In fact, I have come to believe that they have a very good chance to have a happy marriage."

"I am delighted to hear that," Sir Gilbert said. "I had a happy marriage myself, and I know what a blessing such a state can be."

"You must miss your wife very much," Mrs. Sherwood said softly.

He nodded. "I'm getting used to being on my own, but I still don't like it much. It will be harder still when Charlotte gets married, I'm afraid."

"How long has your wife been dead?"

"Going on three years now."

"Have you never thought of marrying again?"

"I've thought of it, of course, but I've just never met anyone I wanted to spend the rest of my life with."

There was the sound of a splash in the distance.

"Oh dear," Mrs. Sherwood said. "The dogs have gotten into the river again."

"It'll do them good," Sir Gilbert said as they strode along together toward the sound of the splashing.

"I know," Mrs. Sherwood said. "This walk in the park is the highlight of Freddie's day."

"It's the highlight of my day, too," Sir Gilbert said, looking soberly at the lovely profile of the woman walking beside him.

The faintest of color stained Mrs. Sherwood's cheeks.

Five days went by after Sally's return home from her visit to the Moultons, and there was no word from the Duke of Sinclair. He wasn't at any of the balls that she attended, she didn't see him at the opera and he didn't attend the meeting for supporting climbing boys. Then, on the sixth night, she saw him at Covent Garden. He was in a box across the theater from hers accompanied by a stunning woman with jet-black hair and a low-cut, clinging, black satin gown. As Sally watched, he bent his head to listen to something the woman said. There was something about the gesture that suggested intimacy. They were the only ones in the box.

The play was a comedy, *She Stoops to Conquer,* and the audience was uproariously noisy as it responded to the goings-on on stage. Sally sat quietly, her hands folded in her lap, with her mother and Mrs. Sherwood on one side of her and Diana and Lord Rumford on the other. The other four appeared to be enjoying themselves very much, but Sally scarcely smiled.

Who is that woman?

It was the thought that preoccupied her during the

entire first act. When the intermission came, and people got up and began to visit their friends, Sally kept her eyes on the box opposite. A few men had come in to speak to Sinclair and his lovely companion, and Sally watched as she threw her head back and laughed at something one of the men had said to her.

"Are you enjoying the play, Lady Sarah?"

It was Lord Dorset, giving her his sunny smile. His adoring brown eyes made him look rather like a puppy, she thought.

"It is very good," said Sally, who had not heard a word of it. She had to know who that woman was, and Alex wasn't here to ask, so she decided that she would have to ask Lord Dorset. "Who is that lovely woman with the Duke of Sinclair, Lord Dorset?" she asked. "I don't believe I've seen her before."

Lord Dorset didn't even have to look to know who she was talking about. His eyes became stern. "She is no one you will ever meet, Lady Sarah. Her sort do not frequent the ballrooms of the ton."

Sally's heart sank. *She's his mistress. And she's gorgeous and elegant and he looks as if he's enjoying himself with her very much. I wonder if he loves her.*

Sally rarely swore, not silently, but she did now. *Damn.*

This is what Alex was talking about, she thought. This is what it meant to be a rake.

"Do you agree, Lady Sarah?"

She realized suddenly that Lord Dorset was speaking to her.

"I beg your pardon," she said, "but I didn't hear you. It's quite loud in here, isn't it?"

He moved his chair a little closer to her and bent his head toward her ear. It was a gesture of intimacy, such as the one she had seen Sinclair make with his mistress. Sally didn't want such a gesture from Lord Dorset. She wanted it from the man with the dark gold hair and the enigmatic green eyes.

She had felt herself pulled toward the duke from the time that they had first met. She had sensed something in him that spoke strongly to something in her. She had thought that he was the man for her.

But now she looked across the theatre and saw him with that beautiful black swan of a woman, and she realized that she was only eighteen years old, and not very sophisticated. What did she have to offer a man like Sinclair?

Diana was much younger than Lord Rumford, she thought, trying to look on the bright side. But Diana was even more beautiful than the duke's mistress, and she was older than Sally, as well.

She smiled and nodded at Lord Dorset, agreeing with whatever it was that he was saying.

He isn't interested in me, she thought dismally. *He likes me because he saw me do a few charitable acts and he's a charitable man. He probably regards me as a kind of little sister.*

Damn, she thought again. *Oh, damn, damn, damn. I wish I'd never come to Covent Garden tonight.*

Twenty-Two

The day after Sally's visit to Covent Garden, Alex asked to speak to her after breakfast. The two of them went out into the small garden behind the Standish town house. It was mostly shrubbery, with a bench in the middle and a big circular bed of tulips. It was a chilly, overcast morning and Sally had put a wool shawl over her muslin morning dress. They sat together on the stone garden bench.

"Since you seem to be interested in Sinclair, I made it my business to find out everything I could about him," Alex said. "I know there are things men should not speak of to young girls, but I think it's important you know the truth about Sinclair before you give your heart away to a man who is not what you think he is."

Sally clutched her shawl tightly around her shoulders. "I know he has a mistress, Alex," she said in a low voice. "I saw them together at the theater last night. She is very beautiful."

Alex looked for a moment at her downcast profile, then he said matter-of-factly, "This is what I found out. When Sinclair was about four, his mother left his father. She ran off to Italy with an Italian count, in fact. I believe she is still alive, but of course he never sees her. After that, Sinclair's father became steeped in dissipation. He drank all the time, and he had his mistresses live in the house with his son. Sinclair grew up in an atmosphere of complete moral depravity, Sally. Of course, he went off to school, but what he saw at home has to have left its mark on him. He apparently has no desire to marry and has kept a succession of mistresses since he came to town when he finished Oxford. He is accepted by all the ton, of course, because of his exalted title and wealth, but he evinces little interest in good society. One rarely sees him at a ball—or at any other social function, for that matter. The one good thing I can say about him is that he is a genuine reformer in the House of Lords. Anyone trying to get some progressive legislation through can always count on his vote. And he actually shows up for debates, which a lot of peers do not bother to do."

Sally sat quietly, not saying anything.

Alex put his arm around her. "You're a wonderful girl, Sally. You were so good about writing to me the whole time I was in the Peninsula—it was always like a breath of home to get your letters. You have a huge heart. The man who wins your love can count himself one of the luckiest chaps on the face of the earth. Don't set your heart on Sinclair. He may be a duke, but he comes from bad stock. A man who was brought up like that—how can he possibly be a good husband to you?"

Sally said in a low voice, "I've only seen him a few times, Alex. He certainly hasn't asked me to marry him."

"But you're interested in him. That was very clear from what you said the other day. I don't want you to romanticize him just because he did a good deed for you. He carries a lot of baggage, Sal. A lot of baggage."

She stared at her lap. "For how long has he been a duke? How did his father die?"

"He's been the duke since he was twenty-four. His father got drunk and choked on his own vomit, Sally. That's the kind of man he was."

Sally made a small sound of distress.

"Pretty disgusting, eh?" Alex said.

She turned her head to look at her brother. "Is Sinclair a drinker, too?"

"I haven't heard that about him."

"Is he a gambler?"

"No more than is usual."

She nodded thoughtfully.

He squeezed her shoulders slightly then took his arm away. "I want to see you marry a nice young man, who will love you the way you deserve to be loved. I don't want to see you pining after a rake with a disreputable background who will probably never make you an honorable offer."

Sally smiled at him. "Thank you, Alex. You're a good brother. I appreciate that you told all this to me. I know a lot of people think young girls shouldn't be told anything about real life."

"You're not an empty-headed young miss, Sally, and I would never treat you as if you were." He stood up. "Now come along. It's chilly out here and you are only wearing that shawl."

Sally got up and accompanied her brother back into the house. Alex was going to the Horse Guards and gave orders for his phaeton to be brought around as Sally went upstairs to her room.

Once inside, she went to sit in the chair that was placed before the fire that had been lit against the chill of the overcast day.

That poor child, she thought as she stared into the flames. She was not seeing the fire, however, she was seeing Sinclair's face. *Deserted by his mother and left with a father who showed no concern at all for his son's needs. No wonder he doesn't want to get married. The example of marriage he grew up with would put anybody off.*

Alex had thought he was telling her something that would disgust her with the duke, but the exact opposite had happened. He had only confirmed Sally's feeling that Sinclair was a man who was harboring a deep hurt. Being a duke didn't shield you from the effects of a mother who had so little care for you that she left you to be brought up in an unloving, immoral household. His lofty status would have been no comfort to the deserted little boy.

The question was, was Sinclair so damaged, so

distrustful of women, that it would be impossible for him to fall in love? And if he were in fact capable of love, what made her think that his heart would turn toward her?

The image of the beautiful black-haired woman she had seen him with last night came once more to her mind. She stood up and went to stand in front of the cheval mirror.

She was a pretty girl. She knew that. She had thick blonde hair and nice blue eyes. *I wish I had Alex's eyes,* she thought as she met her own orbs squarely in the mirror. *They are something special. Mine are just ordinary.*

She wished she were older. She had always felt as if she were older than her years. Compared to some of the girls she had met this Season, she felt positively ancient. But she looked so young. Sinclair, she felt, would be attracted by a more mature woman.

I have to find a way to see him again, she thought. She must come up with a reason to ensure that their paths would cross again

Lady Standish had suggested an evening at Vauxhall, and her two children and Diana all agreed that it would be fun to see the famous Gardens, well known for their fireworks displays, their musical presentations and their food. Lord Rumford would go also, of course, to accompany Diana, and Alex surprised everyone by inviting Miss Charlotte Merton and not Lady Caroline Wrentham.

"Why on earth are you taking Miss Merton, Alex?" Lady Standish asked curiously. "She's a nice enough girl, I suppose, but there is certainly nothing special about her."

Alex shrugged. "She's pleasant enough, and I don't want to encourage any more gossip about me and Lady Caroline. I have no intention of making her an offer, and I don't want it to look as if I will."

Lady Standish looked disappointed. They were all sitting around the dinner table, dressed in formal attire. It was Almack's night. She said, "Why don't you like Lady Caroline?"

"I do like her, Mama. I just don't want to marry her. I don't want to marry anyone right at this moment, so don't get your hopes up."

He kept his voice light, but the underlying note of warning was very clear. *Don't trespass on my business.*

Mrs. Sherwood said softly, "I'm sure Miss Merton will be pleasant company for all of us, Amelia."

"I'm sure she will be," Lady Standish returned in a somewhat mournful tone.

"And don't invite Lord Dorset to accompany me," Sally warned. "I'm in the same situation as Alex. I don't want to do anything that will encourage him to make me an offer."

"Dorset will be the Earl of Winchester one day," Lady Standish said. "He is a very good catch, Sally."

"Then let someone else catch him," Sally said.

"But what is wrong with him?" Lady Standish asked with genuine bewilderment. "He seems like such a nice young man. And he is clearly interested in you."

"He is a nice young man," Sally returned. "But he reminds me of a puppy. And I don't want to marry a man who reminds me of a puppy."

Lady Standish sighed. "Then who shall we invite for you?"

"You don't have to invite anyone, Mama. I don't have to have an escort to see the Gardens. I will be with you and Cousin Louisa."

The last member of their party was another surprise. At Almack's that night, Sir Gilbert Merton asked if he could accompany the Standish party to Vauxhall.

"I have never been there myself, Lady Standish, and I will probably never have another opportunity to go. Would it be inconvenient for you if I accompanied you tomorrow evening?"

"Of course not," Lady Standish replied with a gracious smile. "Your company will only add to our pleasure."

Sir Gilbert looked from Lady Standish to Mrs. Sherwood, who wore the faintest of smiles on her face. "Thank you," he said. "May I get something to drink for you, ladies?"

They accepted and he went off to collect some of the atrocious orgeat that was Almack's idea of a tasty beverage.

Diana had not been able to stop herself from feeling delighted when Alex had decided not to take Lady Caroline to Vauxhall. She had developed the most unaccountable dislike of the girl. She was too aloof, Diana told herself. Too proud. Too obviously not the right person for Alex. She had been deeply relieved to hear Alex say that he did not have any intention of proposing to Lady Caroline.

It would be like marrying an iceberg, she told herself. Birth and beauty only went so far. It was much more important that Alex marry someone who truly loved him. Who that person might be, Diana couldn't say. She hadn't yet seen anyone among the season's eligible girls whom she thought would be good for Alex. But she absolutely knew that person wasn't Lady Caroline.

These thoughts were going through her head as she watched Lady Caroline and Alex on the dance floor at Almack's. It was true that they made a striking couple, her slender fairness in contrast to his tall black-haired self. *Thank God he doesn't love her,* Diana thought fervently.

She was standing by herself on the side of the dance floor waiting for Lord Rumford to bring her a glass of orgeat. When a feminine voice spoke from behind her, almost right into her ear, she jumped.

"I suppose you're feeling pretty triumphant," Jessica Longwood said bitterly.

Diana swung around to look at the other girl.

"I am happy," she replied quietly. "I am going to marry a very fine man."

"Did you compromise him?" Jessica demanded. "You must have. He wouldn't have offered for a nobody like you if you hadn't forced him into it somehow."

Diana fought off a strong urge to strike the other girl across her pretty sneering face. "You're a bad loser, Miss Longwood," she said with a composure she didn't feel. "Perhaps Lord Rumford discovered what a nasty person you really are. Perhaps that's why he rejected you."

Jessica's light brown eyes blazed with hatred.

"Here you are, my dear." It was Lord Rumford, returned with the orgeat.

Diana accepted it from him, grateful to be rescued from the venom of her erstwhile rival. Rumford looked at Jessica and a little color came into his cheeks. "How are you, Miss Longwood?" he asked courteously.

Jessica's smile was sweet. "Very well, Lord Rumford. Thank you for asking."

A young man came up to Jessica and said, "I believe this is my dance, Miss Underwood."

As he led Jessica away, Diana let out a sigh of relief.

"A little awkward that," Lord Rumford murmured.

"Yes," Diana said, and sipped gratefully at her cool orgeat.

Alex had hired a supper box at Vauxhall for the entire party, and Sally traveled with Lady Standish, Diana and Mrs. Sherwood in the Standish family coach. Alex drove himself in his phaeton, the Mertons came together and Lord Rumford also drove himself. They were all to meet up at the supper box, which was one of over a hundred that were located next to the Grove area of the Gardens.

Sally was awed by her first view of Vauxhall. She and the other ladies met up with Alex at the entrance, and after he had paid the entrance fee for them all, they strolled along the five famous walks that crisscrossed the extensive territory that made up the Gardens. Colored lamps glimmered among the elms and poplars that lined the walk, revealing mysterious alcoves and grottos on either side. There were a goodly number of other people on the path, and when they reached the section where the supper boxes were located, Sally saw that quite a crowd was seated and being served.

Their supper box was very pretty, adorned by a Francis Hayman painting of a maypole dance. Lord Rumford was already there and waiting for them, and Sally watched as he kissed Diana's hand gallantly and drew her to sit beside him. The Mertons arrived about fifteen minutes later. Charlotte was clearly a little overwhelmed at being part of such an illustrious company, and everyone did their best to make her feel more comfortable. Sir Gilbert took a seat beside Mrs. Sherwood.

Vauxhall was famous for its expensive suppers and the party partook of very thinly-sliced ham, chicken and an assortment of biscuits and fruit. Alex had ordered wine and lemonade, instead of the Vauxhall punch, which had an extremely high alcohol content.

People visited their box constantly as they ate. Lord Rumford and Diana in particular were besieged by people wishing to congratulate them. An orchestra was playing in the Grove, and people were dancing. When they had finished eating, Alex asked Miss Merton if she would care to dance with him and, blushing a fiery red, she agreed. Then Sir Gilbert asked Mrs. Sherwood, Sally and Lady Standish if they would care to stroll about the Gardens for a bit to see the sights. The elder ladies agreed, while Sally said she was comfortable where she was. She was hoping against hope that Sinclair might turn up—without his beautiful mistress.

The three older people went off, leaving Sally, Diana and Lord Rumford in the box. A man whom Lord Rumford introduced to the girls as his cousin, came up and began to talk to him. Sally's eyes searched the crowds which were flowing past their box. No distinctive blond head appeared.

Her head was turned toward Diana when she heard a familiar voice said, "How are you this evening, Rumford? I see that I must congratulate you for having won such a beautiful bride."

Sally's heart began to pound. She turned her head and found herself caught in an intent green gaze. "How are you Lady Sarah?" the Duke of Sinclair said. "Are you enjoying the evening?"

Sally hoped she didn't look as shaken as she was feeling. "Yes," she said. She swallowed. "Vauxhall is certainly very lovely."

"Would you care to go for a short stroll?" Sinclair inquired. "I found a place for your latest rescues on my estate and I thought you might like to hear how man and horse are doing."

"I would like that very much," Sally said with alacrity. She slid out of the box to stand beside the duke.

Lord Rumford was frowning. He said meaningfully to Diana, "Perhaps we should join your cousin." Clearly he did not feel it was appropriate to allow Sally to go off alone with Sinclair.

Sally cast Diana an imploring look.

Diana put her hand to her brow and said, "Do you know, I feel a trifle dizzy, my lord. I think I would be better off staying right here."

Sally rewarded her with a quick smile.

Rumford's frown changed to a look of grave concern. "Should I fetch your mother and Lady Standish for you, my dear? Perhaps one of them has smelling salts with them."

"That might be a good idea," said Diana in a failing voice. Sally silently congratulated her cousin on a splendid performance.

Lord Rumford looked sternly at Sally and commanded, "Stay here with your cousin while I fetch her mother."

Sally didn't appreciate being ordered about, but she didn't say anything, she simply slid back into the box and put her hand on Diana's forehead, as if she was checking for a fever.

"Are you really ill, Miss Sherwood?" the Duke of Sinclair inquired, one blond eyebrow raised skeptically. Apparently he was not as susceptible to Diana's performance as her fiancé had been.

Diana smiled and Sally took away her hand.

Diana said, "I know that Sally has been anxious to hear all about what you did with the man and the horse that she rescued. Go ahead and take your walk. I'll wait here for Rumford to return."

Sally said, "Are you certain you'll be all right?"

"Of course I'll be all right." Diane waved her hand at them. "Go ahead."

"I cannot leave you here alone," the duke said positively.

Sally tried not to look as disappointed as she felt.

"I shall be perfectly fine," Diana said. "No one will try to kidnap me, Your Grace. There are too many people around."

He shook his head. "You may not be kidnapped, but you could easily be the target of some drunken reveler. You cannot remain here alone."

"Then I'll come with you," Diana said. "If we stay here you'll be constantly interrupted." She glanced at Sally, a look that said clearly, *Don't worry, I won't get in your way.*

Sally said, "But what will happen when Lord Rumford comes back and finds you gone?"

"I'll leave him a note," Diana said. "I'll tell him I changed my mind and thought a walk would help to clear my head."

They waited while she wrote her note, and then the three of them left the supper box, the ladies on either side of Sinclair.

Twenty-Three

Sinclair chose the Hermit's Walk, the smallest and most private of all the walks at Vauxhall. On one side of the walk was a wilderness and on the other was an open area of rural downs. The three of them saw no one else as they traversed this path, which was dimly lit by lanterns hung from the trees. Diana tactfully dropped a little behind Sinclair and Sally, saying she didn't feel very sociable and wanted to enjoy the night by herself. She doubted that either of the others believed her, but neither of them challenged her excuse.

The scraps of conversation that Diana did hear were scrupulously above-board. The duke apparently was telling Sally all about her protégé and his horse and how they had settled in at Westover Hall, one of the duke's lesser properties in Wiltshire. Then they talked about the prospects for making things better for climbing boys.

Diana could tell, just from the way that Sally looked up at the duke, that she liked him very much. She had certainly never seen Sally look that way at any other man.

Don't let him hurt her, she prayed. *She's such a good person. She deserves someone who will recognize how good she is, who will understand that she is not just an ordinary young girl, with clothes and balls and other fripperies on her mind. She is a genuinely caring person. Please don't let Sinclair be playing with her. She doesn't deserve that.*

Suddenly, there was the sound of steps behind her. Before she could turn around, she was grabbed from the rear. In the brief second before the man got his hand completely over her mouth, she managed a muffled scream. She heard the duke curse and saw him whirl around to see what was going on, and she thought with great relief, *Sinclair will rescue me.* Then two more men rushed out onto the path behind Sally and the duke. Diana was incapable of warning them, and, as she watched in horror, one of the men hit the duke over the head with something in his hand, and the other man grabbed Sally.

Diana struggled madly to get free, but the man who had felled the duke came over to her and, lifting his fist, he struck her hard on her chin.

Everything went black.

The man who had felled the duke went back into the woods and returned with a lantern.

"What'll we do with this one?" the man who was holding Sally asked in a gruff tone.

"We'll leave the lady to summon help," the man with the lantern replied. "She won't try to follow us, and I don't want no nob's murder on my head."

"Give us a few minutes," the man with the lantern said. The other man bent and picked Diana up from the ground and slung her over his shoulder. Both men started across the downs. Sally watched helplessly before she looked at Sinclair, to see if he might be showing signs of revival. He never stirred.

The next few minutes were the longest of Sally's life. The man restraining her was holding her so tightly that she would have bruises on her face and across her ribs the following day. Finally, when the lantern was just a glimmer in the distance, he said in her ear, "You'd better get some help for the gentry cove, miss. He got hit on the head pretty hard."

He removed his hand from Sally's mouth and shoved her hard, so that she lost her balance and fell to her knees. She turned her head to see her captor disappearing across the downs. Her heart was beating frantically. Diana was gone and the duke lay sprawled on the ground. Sally regained her feet and ran to kneel beside him. He was lying perfectly still with his eyes closed. Gently, she put her hand to the back of his head. It came away sticky with blood.

Terror closed like a fist around Sally's heart. What should she do?

We have to get Diana back. God knows what

*those men will do to her. I have to try to find out
which way they went so Alex can follow them.*

The duke would have to wait.

Lifting her skirts, she raced across the downs in
the direction she had seen her captors take. Far
ahead of her, she could see the dim light of their lantern. But she had no light herself, and she tripped
and fell several times on the uneven ground.

Abruptly, the light ahead of her disappeared.
Sally had no idea what was on the far side of the
downs, but she kept on going until she was surprised to find herself standing on the bank of the
river. About a hundred yards away from her, down-
stream, a boat was moored. Sally was just in time
to see one of the men hand Diana to someone already aboard. Then the man who had been holding
Diana hopped on board himself. Sally started to
run, but before she could reach the boat, it drifted
out onto the river. It was illuminated by the lantern,
which the men had hung so that the craft could be
seen by other boats, and the light the lantern cast en-
abled Sally to get a clear look at the name that was
painted on the boat's side.

I have to get help, Sally thought, and, lifting her
skirts, she retraced her way over the uneven ground
of the downs, praying she would not get lost in the
dark.

She actually came out onto the dimly lighted
walk about fifty yards from the duke's prone body.
Two people were bent over him. As Sally rushed up
to them, she recognized the young man as a friend

of Lord Dorset. She didn't know the woman, who was wearing a very skimpy and revealing dress.

It took Sally a mere two seconds to realize that she should say nothing to these people about Diana's being kidnapped. She had been in London long enough to know that, even though Diana was the injured party, the gossip that would ensue over this could harm her reputation irreparably.

"Is he drunk?" she heard the woman asking her companion.

"No. There's blood on the back of his head. It looks as if someone hit him," the man returned.

Sally arrived at their side and said breathlessly, "It's the Duke of Sinclair." She put a hand to her heart. It was hammering. She had not been allowed to run since her illness and she was out of condition for the effort she had just made. She took a deep breath. "We were walking along this path when we were attacked. They hit the duke over the head and tried to kidnap me, but I managed to run away. We need help immediately. I'm Lady Sarah Devize. Can you find my brother for me? I will remain here with the duke."

"You had better come with us, Lady Sarah," said the young man, whom Sally recognized as a Mr. Bingham. "Clearly it isn't safe to leave you alone."

"The men got away," Sally said impatiently. "I'll be perfectly safe. Don't just stand here talking! Go!"

Mr. Bingham hesitated, then he said, "Stay with her, Florrie." He turned and started away down the path.

"Go as fast as you can!" Sally called after him. She saw him break into a run, then she knelt beside the duke.

She badly wanted to lift his head off the hard ground and cradle it in her lap, but she was afraid to move him. What if he was dead? She bent her head to listen to his heart and was reassured when she heard the strong, steady beat. She picked up his hand and held it.

The woman called Florrie started to ask her questions, but Sally just shook her head and said, "I'm sorry, I can't talk just now. I'm too upset."

It seemed like an eternity before Sally heard footsteps pounding down the path. It was Alex. He wasn't even breathing hard as he fell to his knees next to her. "My God, Sally, what happened? Where is Dee? Wasn't she with you? I sent someone to find Rumford. He should be just behind me."

Sally put a finger over her lips and looked meaningfully at Florrie.

Alex stood up and said to her, "Thank you for your assistance." He fumbled in his pocket and handed her some money. "Bingham should be here momentarily. Please step away now and let us help the duke."

The woman obediently moved a little way down the path, where she was in sight but out of earshot.

"The men took Diana, Alex," Sally whispered tearfully. "They hit her on the chin to make her unconscious."

Alex swore.

Sally nodded her agreement. "I chased after them. They had a boat moored on the river. They were moving away by the time I got there, but it was one of those rental boats you often see. It had a small cabin. The lantern on it showed its name—*Caprice*."

The duke stirred. He half opened his eyes and groaned. "Christ," he said. "What happened?"

Sally bent over him. "We were attacked," she said. "You were hit over the head. Don't try to move just yet."

Alex said, "I'll check the boat rental places and see if I can find out who rented the *Caprice*. What color was the boat, Sal?"

"Green and white."

"It might have come from that place near the Tower. That's where I'll go first. Tell Rumford when he gets here. Tell him to check the rental place by Westminster. It's imperative that we move quickly."

"How am I to get the duke back to his carriage?" Sally asked shakily.

"Bingham is coming back to collect the woman he was with. Enlist his services," Alex recommended. "And then have him tell Mama and the rest of them what happened to you and Sinclair. So they won't alarm the security people to look for us."

"They will wonder where Diana is."

"Don't tell Bingham anything about Dee. Just tell him that you and Sinclair were attacked and that they all should go home—including the Mertons." Then he was gone. Sally turned back to the duke, who was now struggling to sit up.

"I don't think you should move," Sally said, alarmed. "You were hit very hard."

"I can feel that," he said. Ignoring her advice, he managed to get himself to a sitting position. Wincing, he put his hand to the back of his head. "There's a handkerchief in my coat pocket, Lady Sarah. Would you get it out and hold it against the wound? Perhaps we can stop the blood from getting all over my new coat."

Silently, Sally did as he instructed. She was pressing the white cloth to the duke's head, and telling him what had happened, when the Earl of Rumford came running up to them. He was breathing very hard and had to struggle to get his words out. "What happened?" He looked around. "Where is Diana?"

Sally repeated her story of the attack, then told him that Alex had gone to check the boat rental company by the Tower. "He suggested you try the place by Westminster, my lord," she said. "The more companies you cover quickly, the better the chance of finding Diana."

"I'll go immediately," Rumford said. "Bingham is just behind me. See if you can get Sinclair on his feet and off this walk." He turned away, then turned back. "Oh, Bingham doesn't know that Diana was with you and we should keep it that way."

"We've been careful not to mention her name," Sally said. She gave him a bewildered look. "I don't understand why anyone would do this."

"I don't either." Still breathing heavily, the earl

turned. He ran for a few paces and then, as Sally watched, he slowed to a fast walk. Sally turned back to the duke.

"They may be holding her for ransom," he said grimly.

She was silent for a moment as she digested this idea. "That must be the reason. Why else would anyone want to kidnap her?"

"I'm going to get up," the duke said.

"No, you're not," Sally returned authoritatively. She held her hand up in front of the duke. "How many fingers?" she asked.

"Two?" he said after a minute.

"No, four. You have a concussion. You can just stay where you are until Bingham arrives. He can go for a stretcher. You shouldn't even be sitting up."

"I didn't know you were a doctor, Lady Sarah," he said acidly.

"I am not a doctor, but I know quite a lot about illnesses and injuries. And I know that if you have a concussion, you should stay quiet."

"Concussion or not, I am not getting on a stretcher. I will make it out of here on my own," the duke said. He managed to lurch to his feet, but he immediately staggered and would have fallen if Sally hadn't grabbed him and slid her arm around his waist to give him support. She braced herself as his superior weight sagged against her.

The duke cursed again.

"I said you shouldn't get up," Sally said.

"Do you think you can walk me back down this

path?" he asked. "We don't want to call attention to this attack. If Miss Sherwood has indeed been kidnapped, we want to keep it quiet."

At this point, Mr. Bingley appeared on the path. He stopped for a moment to talk to Florrie, then he came over to the duke and Sally.

"I want you to help me walk back along this damned path," the duke told the young man.

To Sally's keen ears, it sounded as if were slurring his words. He hadn't been doing that before he was hit. She frowned. He shouldn't try to walk, but what was their option?

"Certainly, Your Grace." Mr. Bingham said, and he went to the other side of the duke and braced him with his shoulder. Slowly the three of them began to retrace their steps down the path, followed by Florrie, who was clutching her money in her hand.

Twenty-Four

Diana awoke on a hard floor and the feeling of being rocked. She was dazed and disoriented and her head and her chin hurt terribly. It was a few minutes before her memory returned and she recalled the scene on the path at Vauxhall. She put her hand up to her aching chin and winced when she touched the tender spot.

Someone hit me, she thought unbelievingly. She recalled everything that had happened up to the moment when the world had gone black.

She tried to sit up, which made her head feel worse. She remembered the sound of the weapon hitting the duke's head. Her own head was throbbing with pain. *I hope Sinclair's all right,* she thought anxiously. *I hope he and Sally were able to go for help.*

Giving into the pain, she lay back down, shut her eyes and tried to think. *These men wanted to kidnap me. It was the whole purpose of the attack. But why? Why would anyone want to kidnap me? I'm not an heiress. I'm not an important person. Why?*

After a few minutes of hard, painful thinking, she came up with an answer.

They're going to try to get money out of Rumford. That's what this is all about. They are going to make Rumford pay to get me back.

But will he want me back after I've been held hostage by men like this? I will be irreparably compromised if they keep me overnight. People would always wonder what they did to me.

Tears sprang to her eyes. *Dear God, this can't be happening.* Gritting her teeth against the pain, she sat up once again and looked around, but it was too dark to see anything. From the way the floor rose and fell, she recognized that she must be on a boat.

What am I going to do? Please help me, God. I have to get away from these awful men.

What if they tried to rape her?

She wasn't tied in any way, and she put her hands over her face in despair.

They hit Sinclair, so he couldn't help me. And another of the men held Sally.

Could Sally be in here in the darkness with her?

"Sally?" she said in a low voice. "Sally, are you here?"

No answer.

She tried again.

Still no answer. And she didn't have the feeling that anyone was with her. She felt alone.

Terribly, terribly alone.

She heard steps and immediately she lay back down and closed her eyes. The cabin door opened and a man entered. Diana could feel him standing over her. The scent of his body odor was enough to make her want to retch. She tried to breathe evenly and slowly.

"She's still out," he called up to the deck. "It doesn't look as if we'll have to hit her again."

"Good," a deep voice called back.

"Are you sure we're headed in the right direction?" a third voice asked worriedly. "It seems to me we should be there by now."

"It's a hell of a lot harder to do this at night than it was in the daylight," the deep voice admitted. "But no one knows what happened to her. We'll be all right."

The man in the room with Diana swore. She heard him mutter to himself, "We don't have time to be sailing all over the bloody river." The next thing she heard was the sound of footsteps moving away from her. The door opened and closed. After a few moments, Diana cautiously opened her eyes. Doing that made her head hurt worse, so she closed them again. There was nothing she could do right now.

It seemed a long time to Diana that the boat kept sailing. Twice more a man came down to check on her, and twice more she pretended to be unconscious.

Alone in the dark, she decided that her only chance of escape would be to continue to feign unconsciousness. They had to get her off the ship sometime, and when they did that, she would make a move to escape.

She knew how to shove her knee into a man's groin. Alex had taught her that after her earlier encounter with Hawley. And she could use her nails.

Go for the eyes, Alex had told her.

Be strong, Diana, she told herself. *Think positively. You can get away from these beasts if you try. You can. You can. You can.*

When finally they came to get her, she was ready. The man with the deep voice was the one who came to pick her up. She did her best to hang limp in his arms as he carried her onto the deck.

She could feel the man holding her rocking with the motion of the boat. Then he said, "Here, take her," and she was transferred to the arms of the man with the terrible body odor. It was hard to lie still, not to turn her face away so she would not have to breathe in his disgusting smell, but she didn't want to make her move on the dock. She would wait until they reached the street, where she would have more room to run away and hide.

Her captor began to walk down the dock.

"This'un has turned out to be a simple job," someone said.

"Easy as pickin' cherries from a tree," the man with the body odor agreed.

"We ain't finished yet," the deep-voiced man warned. "Hazlett toll us we needs to deliver her safely to him before we get any money."

Hazlett. Diana filed that name away in her memory. She opened her eyes in a narrow squint and saw that they were approaching a small hut, which must be the office for the boat rental business.

I'll give it another minute, she thought.

Then, to her utter amazement, she heard a deeply familiar voice say, "Unless you want me to shoot each and every one of you, you will hand the lady over to the boatman. Now."

Alex.

Diana's eyes popped open and relief flooded through every inch of her body. "Alex! It's you!" She shoved hard at the chest of the man holding her.

He was so astonished to hear her voice that he actually dropped her. She scrambled to her feet and ran to Alex, who was holding a pistol trained on her captors.

He didn't take his eyes off the kidnappers. "Are you all right, Dee?" he asked anxiously.

Her heart was hammering. She couldn't believe that he had actually come. "I'm fine, except for my jaw and a bad headache. Somebody must have hit me." She stood slightly behind him, so as not to impede his aim, and said fervently, "I am so glad to see you! How on earth did you find me?"

"Sally followed you and saw them put you on the boat," he replied, never taking his eyes off the men. Then he said to the boatman, who had been standing silently in front of the small office at the end of the dock, "Tie these fellows up and keep them here until I get hold of Bow Street."

"Aye, my lord," the boatman said, and disappeared into his office to get some rope.

Diana's heartbeat had finally begun to slow. She pulled herself together and said to Alex, "They talked about a man named Hazlett. Apparently he's the one who hired them to kidnap me."

"I never heard of him," Alex said, "but I'll bet Bow Street has."

The boatman reappeared with ropes in his hand and proceeded to tie up Diana's kidnappers efficiently.

"Thank you for your help," Alex said to the boatman. He lowered his pistol and turned to Diana. "Come along, Dee. My phaeton is parked up the street. I'll take you home."

Once she was safely on the high seat of the carriage and was moving away from the pier, Diana began to shake. Alex put both his reins in one hand and placed an arm around her to draw her trembling body against him. "It's all right, Dee," he kept saying. "You're all right. There's nothing to be frightened of any more. I'm here. Everything is going to be fine."

She started to cry. "It was like that time with Hawley," she sobbed.

He tightened his arm. "I know, love, I know."

She tried to stop crying because crying hurt her head. She pressed against him, feeling immeasurably comforted by the solid bulk of him, by the sound of his voice. She was safe. Once again Alex had saved her.

The horses moved at a walk as Alex drove one-handed through the narrow streets on their way back to Grosvenor Square.

At last she was composed enough to ask, "What about Sinclair? Is he all right? I saw one of the men hit him over the head with something."

"He'll have a headache for a few days, but he'll recover. He was awake by the time I got to him and Sally."

She looked up at him. He was hatless and his black curls had fallen across his forehead. He was looking ahead, through his horses' ears. "Did you say that Sally followed me?" she asked incredulously.

"Yes. She was amazingly brave. You owe your rescue to her more than to me, Dee. She saw those brutes load you onto the boat, and she got the color of the boat and its name. I thought it sounded like one of the boats from the rental place near the Tower, so that's where I went. The boatman there confirmed that he had rented out a green craft named Caprice to three men earlier that day. So I waited for you to get back. Rumford was going to check the boat place at Westminster. We'll have to get word to him that you've been found."

For the first time, Diana remembered her fiancé. She forced herself to move away from the comfort of Alex and tried to make her aching head function. "But why would someone want to kidnap me?" she asked in bewilderment.

Alex shrugged. "Perhaps they were going to try

to get money out of Rumford. Let's hope the Bow Street runners will be able to find out the truth."

Away from the warmth of his body, Diana began to shiver again. Alex stopped his horses, took off his coat and put it around her. Then he picked up the reins in two hands and the horses began to trot briskly forward.

When they finally reached home, Alex had one of the grooms saddle Sally's horse and ride to Westminster to find Rumford and tell him the news. He told another groom to ride Bart to Bow Street and get someone to the rental boat dock by the Tower to take the tied-up men into custody. Then he took Diana into the first-floor drawing room and sent for some tea. "You need something to warm you up," he said.

Diana was sitting on the sofa next to Alex, sipping tea, when the Earl of Rumford came in the door.

"Diana!" he cried. "Thank God you are all right!"

Diana jumped up and ran to him. He put his arms around her and held her close.

"Oh, Edward," she said. "I was so frightened."

He was holding her tightly. He had been truly frightened for her, she thought. He really did love her.

The earl bent his head and buried his lips in her hair.

She heard Alex get to his feet and she stepped back a little from Lord Rumford to turn to him.

Rumford looked at Alex, as well. "What happened?"

There was a very grim look on Alex's face. "One

of the brutes hit her on the jaw and knocked her unconscious. Fortunately, they got lost on the river, so I was in time to intercept them at the boathouse."

"Thank God," Rumford said fervently. He scanned Diana's face. "You have a bruise on your jaw."

"That's where I was hit," she said. "It's given me a bad headache."

"You should go upstairs to bed," he said. "This has been an unspeakable experience for you. You must be exhausted."

"I want to see Sally first," Diana said. "I want to thank her."

As Diana was speaking, there came a knock and the night footman opened the front door. Diana heard Sally say, "She's here? Oh, thank God! Where is she?"

"In the Red Drawing Room, Lady Sarah," the night footman said.

"Come along, Your Grace," Sally said.

Sinclair is here, too? Diana thought. She drew away from Rumford and turned to the door.

Sinclair and Sally came in, both looking excessively disheveled. There was mud along the bottom of Sally's evening skirt and her slippers were filthy. Diana ignored her pounding head, ran to her friend and embraced her. "Oh Sally! Thank you, thank you, thank you! Alex said that you followed me and got the description of the boat." She shuddered. "I don't know what would have happened to me if you hadn't been so brave."

Sally hugged her back. "I'm just so thankful Alex found you."

Diana heard Alex say, "Here, Sinclair, have a seat. I'd offer you brandy, but I don't think that's a good idea with a head wound."

Sally dropped her arms from around Diana and watched the duke as he sat down. She wore a concerned look on her face. Sinclair was very pale and looked as if he would faint any minute.

"We need a physician," Diana said. "The duke looks awful."

"You don't look so wonderful yourself," Alex said.

Sinclair protested, "I just had a bump on the head. I'll be fine. I don't need a physician."

Sally frowned in disagreement.

Alex said, "I'll go for the physician myself, Sal. Monty's the only riding horse left in the stable and I don't want to put a groom on him." He turned to Sinclair, "We're not telling anyone that Miss Sherwood was with you. The story of a kidnapping will not help her reputation."

The duke nodded, then winced at the pain the motion had caused. "I don't need medical assistance," he repeated.

"I know a bit about wounds, and I know they need to be cleaned out," Alex replied. "I also know you ought to be lying down." He looked at Diana.

"You too, Dee. You took a blow. I'll wager you have a giant headache right now."

"I do," Diana admitted.

Alex turned to Sally. "I'll help Sinclair upstairs to an empty bedroom before I go for Dr. Murray. He seems to be a good chap. I've talked to him at Brooks a few times."

"Thank you, Alex," Sally said warmly. "Come along, Your Grace, and we'll make you more comfortable."

Sinclair raised his eyebrows in a look of pure arrogance. His voice was cold when he spoke. "I'll allow the doctor, but I don't need to go upstairs to a bedroom. After he comes I am going home."

"No, you're not," Sally said, not at all intimidated by either the voice or the look. "You obviously have a concussion and will need to be still for a few days. I am not sending you back to your own house, where you will doubtless disobey the doctor's orders and get out of bed much too soon. Now, come along."

Sinclair stared at her in amazement. In all of his life he had probably never been spoken to like this.

Diana smiled for the first time since she had been attacked. "You had better go with her. When Sally gets it into her head that something is good for you, she's relentless. Don't let that sweet, angelic exterior fool you."

"It's for your own good," Sally said.

Suddenly, Sinclair went chalk-white. He bent and put his head on his lap. He closed his eyes.

Sally put a reassuring hand on his shoulder.

When Sinclair finally looked up again, Alex said, "Come along and I'll take you to a bedroom. Sally's right. You need to lie down."

Without any more protest, Sinclair got unsteadily to his feet and allowed Alex to put an arm around his shoulders to brace him. Sally ran upstairs to ready a bedroom, leaving Diana and Lord Rumford alone.

"Come and sit," he said gently, and she followed him to a sofa, where they sat side by side. He put an arm around her and she rested her pounding head on his shoulder. It was not as wide as Alex's shoulder, she thought, but her fiancé's obvious concern enveloped her like a cozy cocoon.

He had been looking for her, too, she reminded herself.

"I'm so sorry that this happened, Edward," she said. "I think someone must have had the idea to try to extort money from you for my return. The three men at Vauxhall were just doing a dirty job for pay. The man who hired them was named Hazlett."

"There is nothing for you to be sorry about," Rumford returned. "You did nothing wrong. And do not worry, I'll get the Bow Street runners on the job. We'll find the man who ordered you kidnapped. Never fear."

"Alex already sent for Bow Street," she said.

Once again there came the sound of knocking on the front door. A few moments later, Lady Standish and Mrs. Sherwood were rushing into the room. Rumford had taken his arm away from Diana when he heard the women's voices and now Diana's mother came over to embrace her.

"What happened, darling? Thank God you are here. Mr. Bingham told us about the attack on Sinclair and Sally, but he said you were not with them! Where were you? And where is Sally?"

"She and Alex took Sinclair upstairs to lie down," Diana said, then she proceeded to relate what had happened. She had just about finished when Alex came back into the room.

Mrs. Sherwood gave him a tremulous smile. "Thank you, Alex. Thank God you found her in time!"

"Sally is the one you ought to thank, Cousin Louisa, not me." He looked at Diana. "I'm going for the doctor. I think you ought to take the advice Sally gave Sinclair, and get into bed. Your head must hurt like hell."

"All right," she said in a resigned voice.

"I'll go with you, darling," her mother said.

Lord Rumford helped her to her feet and asked if he wanted him to carry her upstairs. She started to shake her head, then quickly stopped and said, "No. No, thank you, Edward. I can walk. I'm not feeling faint, you know. I just have a headache."

She reached up a little and kissed him on the cheek. "Come tomorrow morning. I hope I will be feeling better by then."

"I'll do that," he said.

He stood there and watched as Diana and her mother left the room.

Twenty-Five

It was almost an hour before Alex arrived back at Standish House with the physician, Dr. Murray. Sally and Lady Standish accompanied him upstairs. He saw both patients and pronounced the duke to be in worse case than Diana. She could get up the following day if she so wished, but the duke was to remain in bed for at least two days. The doctor cleaned the wound, said that the brain was probably swollen and the patient should remain quiet until the headache had reduced itself to reasonable proportions. He gave some laudanum to both patients to help them sleep and went home again.

Alex loaned Sinclair a nightshirt and helped him change. Sally wanted to stay to make certain that the duke went to sleep, but neither Lady Standish nor Alex would hear of such a thing. So she went off to her own room and worried for most of the night about whether or not the duke would follow the doctor's orders.

In fact, Sinclair's head hurt so badly the following morning that he had no desire even to lift it from the pillow. Sally, with a maid sitting properly in the corner, sat in his room for several hours and read to him from a book she had very much enjoyed called *Pride and Prejudice.* He seemed to enjoy it too, although he said very little. But he smiled several times at the more amusing parts.

When she was leaving him, Sally had to restrain herself from bending to place a kiss on his poor aching forehead. What she would have really liked to do was place a kiss on his lips.

It was a little frightening, she thought, as she went back to her own room to dress for dinner. She had never been this attracted to a man in her life. Of course, she was only eighteen, but she had met many men this Season and Sinclair was the only one who could make her heart beat faster. There was something about him...there was a current of awareness between them. She felt it, and she thought he felt it, too.

Not for the first time, she thought back on his words: *Why are you bothering with me?*

It almost sounded as if he did not think he was good enough for her, which, on the surface, was ridiculous. He was a duke, after all. But Sally could not help but think of the neglected child he had been. Some scars went very deep. He had not been good enough for his mother to love. Perhaps he felt he was not good enough for anyone to love.

If that was so, it was a terrible thing. She would have to convince him that it was not so.

* * *

Two Bow Street runners came to see Alex the next morning to report that her captors were in their charge. He received the runners in the library.

"They're only hired help, m'lord," said the runner who had introduced himself as Fred Nance. He was a bulky man of medium height with a face that was lined with broken veins. He looked like a heavy drinker, Alex thought.

Another reason to stop drinking too much. I most certainly don't want to end up looking like that.

"Aye," the other runner agreed. This one's name was John and he had a long, needle-sharp nose that rather gave him a weaselly look. "They toll us the name of the man who hired 'im and we sent someone to bring 'im along to Bow Street so's we can question 'im. But Hazlett is only a go-between 'imself. Someone paid 'im to arrange the kidnapping."

"Can you find out who that person is?" Alex asked.

"We'll try, m'lord," Fred said.

"I will pay a reward to the man who finds the person who wanted my cousin kidnapped," Alex said. "Tell that to your men, will you?"

"Aye, m'lord."

Alex had offered the men seats when first they came in and now, as he got up, they rose, as well. "Report back to me anything you find out," he said.

"We will, m'lord," the men chorused.

As he watched them leave, Alex's brow was furrowed in a frown. He wasn't so sure about the ransom motive, but he was having a hard time coming up with another explanation.

Who the bloody hell would want to kidnap Dee?

While Diana was sleeping that afternoon, Mrs. Sherwood took Freddie for his usual walk in the park. She met Sir Gilbert down by the lake.

"I was hoping to see you," he said as the two dogs jumped around each other in joyous greeting. "You all left Vauxhall so precipitously last night. What happened?"

"Didn't you get my note?" Louisa asked. "I did leave you a note in our booth."

They both unleashed their dogs, who immediately made a dash for the water.

"I got your note that an accident had occurred and you had to leave quickly. I thought of coming to pay a visit to Grosvenor Square this morning to see if everyone was all right, but then I thought you might not like company. I'm glad to see you. It must mean that the accident was not too serious."

"Someone tried to kidnap my daughter, Sir Gilbert," Mrs. Sherwood said. "Needless to say, we do not want this information going round the ton, so I must ask you to keep it to yourself."

"My God," he said. "Of course you may rely on my discretion, ma'am."

As Sir Gilbert threw sticks for the two dogs to retrieve from the lake, Louisa told him everything that had happened the night before.

"That is very worrying indeed," Sir Gilbert said when she had finished. He was frowning thoughtfully. "I think you must be right when you say that Miss Sherwood was taken for ransom money. There doesn't seem to be any other explanation."

"That is our thinking."

"Well, your secret is safe with me," he said. "I won't even tell Charlotte. She is a good girl, but sometimes the young ones are not as careful with their mouths as they should be."

"I knew I could trust you," Louisa said warmly. "I told you because I felt so badly about leaving you at Vauxhall like that."

Sir Gilbert put the stick down, signaling to the dogs that the fun was over. He and Louisa began to return along the path, with the dogs running in front of them.

"Have you got the runners on the case?" Sir Gilbert asked.

"Yes. Lord Standish hired them to find the culprit. I hope to God they can. My deepest fear is that whoever it is may try again."

"I have a feeling that they won't," Sir Gilbert said. "They tried, it didn't work, the runners are looking for them, the chances of getting caught are much greater this time around than they were at first. I think Miss Sherwood will be safe."

"Dear Lord, I hope so," she said earnestly.

"I hate to see you so upset," Sir Gilbert said. "It must have been a very frightening experience for Miss Sherwood, but she is all right. You must concentrate on that, not worry so much about the future. I doubt there will be a repeat of such an episode."

She gave him a tremulous smile. "You're right. But I own I will feel much more comfortable if the runners can find the man behind this!"

He agreed and they continued their walk talking about other matters.

Viscount Longwood went to his club the morning after the attempted kidnapping, and waited to hear what had happened. He had not been to Vauxhall the night before, not wanting to be associated in any way with the disappearance of Diana Sherwood.

"There should be some kind of check made on the kinds of people who can get into Vauxhall," one of the members was saying indignantly when Lord Longwood approached the group who were sipping sherry in White's comfortable leather chairs.

Lord Longwood took the last seat in the conversational grouping. "Did something happen at Vauxhall?" he inquired casually.

"Sinclair and Lady Sarah Devize were attacked last night on the Hermit's Walk," one of the men told him. "I understand that Sinclair took a nasty blow to the head. Luckily for the both of them, Bingham came along with his new inamorata. God knows what would have happened to Lady Sarah if he hadn't."

Lord Longwood felt a nasty shock of surprise. What the hell had gone wrong? Why was Lady Sarah attacked? He had paid for the Sherwood bitch to be taken.

"Where was Miss Sherwood when this was happening?" he blurted.

The men in the leather chairs looked surprised.

"She was somewhere else, I imagine," one of the men replied at last. "She certainly wasn't with Sinclair and Lady Sarah."

"That's an interesting pairing, isn't it?" one of the other men said. "What do you think Sinclair was doing with an eighteen-year-old chit on the Hermit's Walk? I can't imagine that Standish knew that she was with him."

"I heard Sinclair rode out to Richmond with her a few weeks ago and Standish was in the party," another man said.

"Hmm," said a third man. "Do you think the book ought to start taking bets on the likelihood of Sinclair's finally becoming leg-shackled?"

"I wouldn't bet on it just yet," the first man said. "Dorset looks to be the leading contender for Lady Sarah's hand."

"Yes, but Dorset is only going to be an earl. Sinclair is a duke. Not many of those available on the marriage mart these days."

Lord Longwood ground his teeth in silence as the talk went on about Sinclair and Sally. Something had gone wrong. He had paid good money— money he could not afford to spend—and he had not gotten results. He would have to see about a different plan of action. He would have a talk with the ex-runner he had hired to arrange things at Vauxhall for him. No matter how it was done, Diana Sherwood had to be removed as the fiancée of the Earl of Rumford.

Sinclair remained two days at Standish House and during that time Sally spent a great deal of time alone in his company—which she managed without her mother's or her brother's knowledge.

She and the duke had long talks. On the second day, he asked her what her life at Standish Court had been like when she was growing up, and she obliged with a description of what she did with her time when she was in the country.

"I suppose that what I like to do the best is help people," she said. "It was rather a miracle that I recovered from the rheumatic fever, and I have always thought that God spared me for a reason, that He counted on me to do good in the world. I especially like to help children. I believe that what happens in one's childhood inevitably affects the kind of adult one will become."

His golden brows drew together and a distant look came over his face. His green eyes were veiled. "That is very true," he said expressionlessly.

Sally wanted to reach out and gather him into her arms, as if he was indeed the wounded child he once had been. Instead she managed to say cheerfully, "I am very lucky to have a wonderful family that I am very close to. I have two sisters and two brothers besides Alex, you know."

"And where are they?" he asked.

"My brothers are at school and my sisters are at home with their governess. Mama thought it would be too distracting to have them in London right now."

"You and Miss Sherwood appear to be close," he said.

"Diana is my very best friend. She is as much a sister to me as Maria and Margaret are."

"You are fortunate indeed to have so close a family," he said. He still wore that distant look on his face.

"Were you an only child?" Sally asked, carefully treading on intimate ground.

"Yes," was all he said. His green eyes gave no inkling as to what he was feeling.

"That must have been lonely," she pressed.

He shrugged. "It wasn't so bad."

Clearly he wasn't going to talk about himself. Sally tried another tack. "When did you become interested in reform, Your Grace?"

She didn't think he was going to answer, the silence was so long, but at last he said, "A boy who lived in the village near my home was caught stealing a cake from the village bake shop. He was transported to Australia. I knew him. I met him one day when I was fishing the river that runs through Greyfriars, our estate. He was fishing, also—poaching, actually. He wasn't supposed to be on our property. But he was so thin and he looked so hungry. I fished with him and gave him my own catch to take home.

He lived with his mother—his father had died when he was small. He came back many times and we were—well, I suppose you could say that we were friends. I tried to help him when he was caught with the cake, but no one would listen to me. My father said that he was a thief, that he had his punishment coming to him." He looked directly into Sally's eyes and at last she could see some emotion. He was angry. "When I became the duke, and had some power, I tried to find out what had happened to him. He died on the ship. He never made it to Australia."

Sally's eyes filled with tears. "What a terrible story. That poor boy."

"Yes. Well, that was what got me interested in reform. The penal code is barbaric. Our whole system—parliament, the judiciary, factory conditions, poor laws, child welfare—all need to be reformed. And they will be some day. I am just doing my best to make it sooner rather than later."

Impulsively, Sally leaned forward and placed a hand on his, where it lay on top of his sheet. A charge went through her at the touch and she pulled her hand away, as if she had been scorched. Her eyes grew huge.

He said grimly, "You should not be here with me alone, Lady Sarah. I am not a fit sort of person for you to be alone with. What can your mother and brother be thinking to allow it?"

"They don't know," Sally admitted. "And *I* think it is perfectly all right for me to be here. From what you have just told me, I think you are the finest man I have met in all of London."

He moved his head restlessly on the pillow. He looked very handsome, with his tumbled golden hair and his striking green eyes. Sally thought he was the most beautiful man she had ever seen.

He said, "You know nothing about my life. Believe me, it is far from exemplary."

"On the contrary, I know quite a lot about you," she protested. She folded her hands quietly in her lap, trying not to let her tension show. She was going to make a very bold move.

"I know you keep a mistress," she said.

His eyes widened in shock at the words.

She plowed bravely on. "I saw her at the theater with you the other night. She is very beautiful. I know that you have kept other women—Alex told me when he thought I was becoming too interested in you." Her hands tightened with nervousness. "I also know that your mother ran away with another man when you were very young and that you were brought up in an immoral atmosphere by your father." She leaned toward him and said passionately, "I don't care about any of that! What I care about is the kind of person you are. And you are a very fine person, Your Grace. I *know* that. I'm very good about sensing that kind of thing. I sensed it in you the first time we met, when you helped me with Jem."

He looked utterly taken aback. He didn't say a word.

Sally took her courage in both her hands. "I wish

you would give up your mistress and concentrate on me. I know I'm not as beautiful as she is, but I'm a caring sort of person, and I think that is important to you."

Still the duke said nothing.

Sally could feel the color coming into her face. "Everyone says you will never marry, but do you think you might change your mind one of these days?"

He continued to look at her. Finally he said, "I might."

Sally gave him a radiant smile. She arose from her chair and went to sit on the side of his bed. He took her hand into his. She looked at him with her heart in her eyes.

"I fell in love with you the minute I saw you clutching that filthy little climbing boy to your breast," he said. "You looked positively ferocious. You didn't care about your clothes. You didn't care that people you knew might be passing by. Nothing but nothing was going to harm that child while you were there."

Sally's smile grew wider. "Did you say you fell in love with me?"

"Yes. That is what I said."

"Oh, I love you, too …" She gave him a stricken look. "Do you know, I don't even know your Christian name?"

"It's Robert," he said. "No one has called me that in over twenty years."

"Robert," she said. "That's a beautiful name. I

love you, too, Robert. I loved you the moment you rescued me and Jem from that horrible chimney sweep."

"Kiss me, Sarah."

She bent her head and touched her lips to his. The current that she had always felt running between them increased a hundredfold. He reached his arms up and encircled her shoulders. She relaxed against him and gave herself up to the kiss.

He was the one to break from her, placing his hands on her shoulders and pushing her away.

"This is definitely not a good idea," he said. "I'm not *that* incapacitated."

Sally sat up straight and looked at him. She could feel her blood humming in her veins.

"I had better have some words with your brother," he said. "Is he going to object to your marrying me?"

"Alex just wants to see me happy. When I tell him that I will be miserable if he objects, he will accept your suit." She bounced a little on the mattress. "This is so exciting! I am so happy! Wait until I tell Diana!"

"Wait until you tell Dorset," he said dryly. "I thought that he was going to be the one you chose."

"He reminds me of a puppy," Sally said dismissively. "Puppies are cute and fun, but one doesn't marry them."

He grinned. She had never seen him do that. It made him look so much younger.

At this moment, the slightly open door was

pushed in farther and Lady Standish came into the room. She frowned. "Sally! I didn't know you were in here! It's not proper for you to be alone with the duke."

"I have asked Lady Sarah to marry me, ma'am," Sinclair said. "If Standish can spare me some of his time, I will do the proper thing and ask him for her hand."

"Actually," Sally said to the duke, "I think I was the one who asked you."

He grinned again.

Lady Standish looked a little shocked.

Sinclair's face sobered. "All I want for Sarah is that she be happy, and I promise you I will do my utmost to make certain that she is. She is a very, very special young woman and I am a very, *very* lucky man."

Lady Standish's face relaxed into a smile. Her eyes took in her daughter's face and became very bright. "I believe Alex has just come in, Your Grace. I'll send him to you right away."

"Thank you, Lady Standish."

"Come along, Sally," her mother said. "Alex and the duke will need some privacy."

"All right," Sally said reluctantly. Before she got off the bed, she and Sinclair exchanged a look that burned deep into her soul. Moving slowly, she left the room after her mother.

Twenty-Six

The Bow Street runners interviewed the man called Hazlett, who was a middle-level operator in the underworld of London criminals. After some persuasion, Hazlett admitted to having engaged the men who had tried to kidnap Diana, but claimed he didn't know the man who had paid him for the job. It wasn't anyone he had ever seen before.

Alex was stymied.

"There doesn't seem to be anywhere else to look," he said to Diana as they rode out one morning several days after the kidnapping episode. Her engagement hadn't stopped her early rides with Alex. Rumford had shown little interest in getting up at six in the morning. He had offered to go with her at ten, but Diana preferred the early morning, when the park was quiet and she could feel as if she was back in the country again.

She also liked being alone with Alex now that all

the stress of a romantic tie between them had been removed. After all, she told herself, he was her oldest friend. She didn't want to cut him out of her life completely.

They galloped the horses around most of the Serpentine, as usual, and were walking back toward the gate, letting the horses catch their breath, when Diana noticed a dirt mark on Monty's neck that had been partially hidden by his mane. Frowning, she leaned forward to rub it out, promising herself that she would have words with the groom who took care of him when she returned to the stable.

She had just reached forward, with her head alongside Monty's neck, when a whizzing sound passed just behind her. Then there was a *thump*. Monty jumped sideways and, because she was already unbalanced, Diana fell off.

Before she realized what was happening, Alex was beside her, pulling her and the horses into the cover of the thin line of trees that lay between the path and the Serpentine.

"My God," Diana said, white-faced. "What was that?"

"Someone just shot an arrow at us," Alex said incredulously. "Are you all right?"

"I think so." She rubbed her shoulder where she'd landed.

About three feet from where they were concealed, an arrow protruded from one of the trees that lined the path. Diana stared at it.

"It was meant for me, wasn't it?" she said in

shock. "If I hadn't leaned forward to brush that dirt away from Monty's neck, it would be buried in my head."

"I'm afraid so," Alex said very grimly.

Terror flooded Diana's heart. She could hardly breathe. "But *why?* Why would anyone want to kill *me*, Alex? Who could possibly benefit from my death?"

"I don't know, Dee," he said in the same grim voice as before.

He was standing in front of her, shielding her with his body from the view of any potential assassin.

"Do you think he's still out there?" she asked fearfully. Her heart was beating so hard it felt as if her chest was vibrating.

"He could be." Alex turned toward the path, cupped his mouth with his hands and called loudly, "Whoever you are, if you will come forward and tell me who it was that hired you, I won't press charges. In fact, I'll give you the reward money that I posted. Think about it. It will be well worth your while to give yourself up. There can't be many men in London whose weapon of choice is an arrow. We'll find you, and then you'll hang."

Silence.

"Perhaps he's gone," Diana said in a trembling voice.

Alex called again, "It's your choice—freedom with a reward or being hunted down and thrown into prison."

Again, only silence was the reply.

"It's probably the same as with the kidnapping," Diana said, struggling to think rationally. "These hired men don't know who is behind the attempts. They are contacted by a go-between."

Alex turned back to face her. His blue eyes were glittering in a way she had never seen before. "I'm afraid you're right."

Diana began to shiver all over. "Oh God, Alex. Someone wants me dead! How can that be?"

He reached out and pulled her into his arms. She pressed against him, soaking in his warmth, his strength, taking comfort from the feeling of his hard body against hers. He held her tightly and eventually her shivering slowed. She took a deep uneven breath and realized that she wanted to stay right where she was and never move.

The treacherous thought galvanized her into action and she pulled away. He looked down into her face and his forehead was lined with worry.

"This is damn peculiar, Dee," he said. "The kidnapping we could rationalize as a possible play for a ransom, but this makes no sense at all. I'd say it was the random act of some demented idiot if it wasn't for the kidnapping attempt. Or perhaps that wasn't for a ransom, after all. Perhaps the kidnappers were supposed to kill you."

She shuddered. Her chest felt tight and her stomach was churning. Her eyes scanned his face. "Oh Alex, I am so scared. I can't understand this at all! I have done nothing to make someone hate me like this!"

"It seems insane," he agreed, his eyes searching the trees opposite the bridal path. "but there has to be a motive somewhere. These can't be unconnected acts. They were obviously planned."

The horses had been standing quietly and now Monty nudged Diana with his nose. She caressed his forehead below the brow band of the bridle. She looked around nervously. "Do you think it's safe for us to leave?"

"I think we should walk the horses and keep them between us and the shooter, just in case he's still there."

Diana summoned all her courage. "All right."

It took them twenty minutes to reach the busy street. Then they both swung into their saddles and finished the ride home.

At eleven o'clock in the morning, the Earl of Rumford was admitted to Standish House. He found Diana waiting for him in the upstairs drawing room.

"What happened?" he demanded as soon as he saw her. "Your note said someone shot at you?"

"Oh, Edward!" She ran toward him and he opened his arms. "Someone shot an arrow at me while I was riding with Alex this morning. Right in the park! If I hadn't just bent forward to rub a spot of dirt off Monty's neck, I would be dead."

"Dear God," the earl said. He held her close. "What is going on here? Why are you all of a sudden a target for violence?"

She shook her head, her copper curls brushing

against his cheek. "I have no idea! All I can think of is it's some maniac. There simply isn't any rational explanation."

They went to sit on the sofa, Diana cuddling against the earl. He had an arm around her shoulders. "You have no idea who might be behind this?"

"None."

"There has to be a reason. Twice an attempt has been made on your person. There has to be a reason, no matter how far-fetched."

"That is what Alex says as well. But we can't think of anything." Her voice was deeply bewildered. "I haven't any enemies, Edward. How could I? I'm not an important person. I'm just an ordinary girl."

"You're not ordinary, my dear," he said as he rested his lips on her hair. "Could it be a spurned suitor, who is so madly in love with you that he'd rather see you dead than married to someone else?"

She shook her head. "No one else proposed to me." She managed a weak chuckle. "You're the only one who cared enough to do that. I'm quite sure this was not the work of a disappointed suitor."

"Then who can it be?"

"I don't know!"

There was the sound of a step on the uncarpeted floor near the door and Alex appeared. Diana hastily pulled away from Rumford and passed her hand over her hair to smooth it down.

Alex wasn't looking at her, however, he was looking at Rumford. "Dee has told you about what happened this morning?" he asked.

"Yes, and it is very worrying."

"There's got to be a reason behind these attempts, we just haven't found it yet. In the meanwhile, I think it would be a good idea if you took Dee to Aston Castle. She should be safe there. I'll stay here in London and see if I can discover a motive for what has been happening."

"An excellent idea," Rumford said heartily. "Diana, my dear, do you think you and your mother could be ready to leave this afternoon? We want to get away as quickly and as privately as we can."

At that moment, Mrs. Sherwood and Sir Gilbert Merton came into the room. "I have told Sir Gilbert about what happened in the park this morning, Diana," her mother said, "and he has a suggestion."

"Why don't you come on a visit to Hatton Manor, my home in Sussex?" Sir Gilbert said to Diana. "I think it is vital for you to get out of London quickly."

"We have already decided that my fiancée should come to Aston Castle with me," Rumford said. "But thank you for your offer, Sir Gilbert."

"I think it would be wiser if she came to Hatton Manor," Sir Gilbert said bluntly. "If you and Miss Sherwood disappear together, everyone will guess that you have gone to Aston. I realize that it would be much more difficult to get at her once she goes to Aston, but if she goes to Hatton no one will know where she is. She will be much safer. Of course, you are invited, as well, Lord Rumford."

Diana automatically looked at Alex. "What do you think?"

He said, "I like the idea." He turned to the earl. "You will be able to keep her safer at Merton's place than you will at yours. In the meanwhile, I will remain in London and move heaven and earth to find out who is behind these attacks."

Mrs. Sherwood said, "I think it is very kind of Sir Gilbert to offer his assistance in this way, darling. You can visit Aston Castle once this evil man has been caught."

The earl did not look happy, but he had to concede the practicality of the suggestion. "Thank you, Merton," he said. "This is very good of you."

Alex said, "Dee and her mother should go in your carriage, Rumford. Anyone watching the house will assume you are taking her to Aston. When you don't show up there, it will be too late to find out where she has in fact gone."

"An excellent idea, Alex," Mrs. Sherwood said.

"I'll leave for Merton immediately, to make sure all is ready to receive you," Sir Gilbert said.

"Will Charlotte be going with you?" Diana asked.

"I don't think so. I think it will be better if I just tell her and her aunt that I am tired of London and need some time at home. Since that is the truth, they will have no reason to question me."

They spoke for a few more minutes, then the group split up and Diana went upstairs to pack. Half an hour later Sally returned from a shopping expedition with her mother and came into Diana's room. Diana told her about going to Hatton Manor.

Sally was as horrified and bewildered as everyone else by these attacks on Diana. "I think it's a good idea for you to get away," she said. "But *who* could be doing this, Diana?"

Diana sat on the side of her bed. She was whiter than she usually was. "I can't even begin to imagine," she said. "Oh Sally, I was so happy. I am going to marry a wonderful man, everything seemed to be going so well, and now this...."

She began to cry.

Sally went to sit beside her and put a comforting arm around her shoulders. "It just seems unbelievable that this is happening," she said worriedly. "But you are doing the right thing. Get away to the country and leave it to Alex to do some investigating. Sinclair can help him."

Diana fought to compose herself. After a few minutes she managed to strike a lighter note. "I wanted to be here with you, to help you get through all the fuss that your engagement has created. Mine was nothing compared to yours! The untouchable Duke of Sinclair is actually getting married!"

Sally laughed. "Poor Robert. He tells me that the members of his club are furious that they never had an opportunity to make a book. He surprised everybody."

"Well, if an earl and a duke can't find out what is going on with me, then I suppose no one can," Diana said.

"They'll find out, don't you worry," Sally said. "Alex has offered an enormous reward, so you can be certain that Bow Street is highly motivated to catch the culprit."

Diana looked at Sally with wide, frightened eyes. "But what if they don't catch him, Sally? What if I have to spend the rest of my life in fear?"

"Don't think that way!" Sally squeezed her shoulders. "Where is the old fearless Diana?"

"I can throw my heart over any fence," Diana said, "but this situation is different. I'm angry and I'm scared all at the same time."

"You'll be safe at Hatton Manor."

Diana sniffed. "I hope so." She swallowed, trying to get rid of the lump of fear that was in her throat. "It was extremely nice of Sir Gilbert to invite me."

"Yes, it was." Sally slid off the bed and went over to the window. She looked out for a moment, then she turned back to Diana and said a little hesitantly, "Do you think there might be something going on between your mother and Sir Gilbert?"

Diana stared at her incredulously. "Do you mean something...*romantic?*"

"Yes."

"Good heavens," Diana said. Her brown eyes were wide. "I never thought about such a thing."

"As you said, it was extremely nice of him to offer to shelter you at his home. Someone who didn't feel personally involved with the family would hardly have done that."

Diana frowned, not at all sure she liked the idea Sally was proposing.

"I like him," Sally said. "He seems very unpretentious, very solid. It would be wonderful for Cousin Louisa to have her own home and a husband who loves her—particularly now that you are getting married yourself."

"But she would live at Aston Castle with me!" Diana cried. "Rumford has said that she would be very welcome."

Sally left the window and returned to Diana's side. "I know, but it's not the same as having your own home, Diana."

Diana's frown deepened. "She walks Freddie every day. I have been so busy, but Mama has not missed a single day of walking Freddie. Three o'clock in the afternoon, out she goes with Freddie. You could set your watch by her."

"And Sir Gilbert walks his dog, as well?"

"Whenever I've gone, he's been there."

"At three o'clock?"

"At three o'clock."

Sally said humorously, "Wouldn't it be funny if you and I *and* your mother all found husbands this Season?"

Diana didn't return her smile. "I'm not sure I like the idea."

"If it is the case, you should be happy for her," Sally said kindly but firmly. "Life has not been easy for Cousin Louisa. If a kind, well-off baronet loves her and wants to marry her, then be happy for her, Diana. Don't make her feel guilty about leaving you."

Diana had been staring down at her lap. Now she lifted her head and looked somberly at Sally. She drew in a deep, quivering breath. "You're right. You're always right." A faint smile flickered across her face. "How is it that you're not unbearable?"

Sally bent and kissed Diana on the cheek. "Your mother will always love you, even if she does get married."

Diana sighed a little mournfully. "I know. I suppose that if Mama wants to marry Sir Gilbert, I will give them my blessing. He *does* seem to be a nice sort of man." She sighed again, even more mournfully. "But I will miss her."

"I'll miss my mother, too, that's only natural. But that's what marriage is, Diana, giving up one's mother and father and cleaving to one's husband."

Diana laughed. "We just have to find a husband for *your* mother and the Season will have been an outstanding success."

"We have to find a wife for Alex before we can proclaim total success," Sally said. "I was really worried about him for a while, but he's looking better lately."

All the humor fled from Diana's face. "Alex doesn't need a wife to heal what's wrong with him," she said. "He needs to do that himself. And he won't do it by drinking."

Sally sat beside Diana and said softly, "He saw so much death in the war, Diana. I think he carries that around inside him. He probably always will."

Diana bent her head and once more stared at her

hands in her lap. "Yes," she whispered. Then, a little more strongly, "But that's what he wanted, Sally. He *wanted* to go to war."

"He was just a boy. He saw the drums and the uniforms and the horses charging gallantly into battle. He had no idea of what war really is."

There was a long silence. Diana had always known that war was about death. But perhaps Sally was right. Perhaps Alex hadn't really understood. She had always thought of him as older and wiser than she was. But perhaps he hadn't been.

Sally sighed. "I think you're right, I think he has a lot of healing to do. But I also think the right woman could help him."

Diana's mind shied away from the thought of Alex with the "right woman." It was just something she couldn't picture. She was relieved when Sally changed the subject by saying, "Ring for your maid and I'll help you pick out what clothes you want to take to Hatton Manor."

Twenty-Seven

Hatton Manor sat on top of the South Downs in Sussex with the green turf coming right up to its walls and a view that took in the sea in the far distance. The house itself was a silvery pink brick with white wooden trim and a central pediment. Indoors, Hatton Manor was a peaceful harmony of gently faded ivory, crimson, pink and blue, all lightly dusted with gold. It was much smaller than Standish Court, but Louisa Sherwood liked it better. It felt like a home.

"I can see why you hated to leave here to go to London," she said to Sir Gilbert.

He looked pleased. "It's not very grand, but it suits me."

"It's better than grand," she said. "It's soft and pretty and so very welcoming."

"*You* are welcome, dear madam," he said. "My house is all the more lovely for your presence."

Louisa blushed.

Louisa, Sir Gilbert, Lord Rumford and Diana were all waiting in the main drawing room for the housekeeper to show them to their rooms. Diana was holding Freddie on a leash and she looked at her mother blushing and thought, *She looks like a girl. I've never seen her look so pretty.*

After they were all settled in their rooms, it was time for dinner and the party of four met in the dining room, a lovely room paneled in ivory-painted wood with an assortment of landscapes on the walls. The meal was very good and very well served. Diana watched her mother, with Sally's observation in mind, and for the first time she saw how her mother bloomed under the attention of Sir Gilbert.

I have been so involved with my own affairs that I never noticed that Mama and Sir Gilbert were becoming close, she thought. *How selfish of me. Leave it to Sally to be the one to notice.*

She looked at Sir Gilbert, at his graying hair and his steady gray-blue eyes. *He seems like a good man,* she thought. *And this is certainly a very lovely house. I can picture Mama living here.*

She couldn't deny that part of her didn't want her mother to marry and leave her. It would be hard enough to adjust to marriage herself; she had counted on having her mother with her. But she hoped she was decent enough to feel happy that her mother had found a man who valued her and would take care of her.

Of course, he hasn't proposed yet, she thought a little hopefully.

But as she watched them during dinner, and afterward in the drawing room, she was certain it was only a matter of time before Sir Gilbert posed the all-important question.

It happened the following morning, while Louisa and Sir Gilbert were together in the garden admiring a brilliant array of multicolored spring tulips.

"Louisa," Sir Gilbert said. "You must be aware of how very dear you have become to me."

Color flushed into Louisa's cheeks. Her heart began to beat faster. "I have grown fond of you as well, Sir Gilbert," she said a little shyly.

He took both her hands into his. His hands were big and strong and warm. *These are hands I could trust,* Louisa thought. *Hands I could give myself to with confidence.*

He said, "I told you once that I had not remarried because I had never found a woman I wanted to live with for the rest of my life. Well, now I have found her. Will you marry me, Louisa? If you say yes you will make me the happiest of men."

Almost without volition, Mrs. Sherwood's hands returned his clasp. "Gilbert, it would make me very happy to marry you. But I worry about leaving Diana… I know she is counting on me to help her when she becomes the Countess of Rumford. And there is this awful threat to her life…"

His hands tightened reassuringly. "You are right to be worried about that, and we will do nothing until that particular issue has been resolved. And it will be, my dear. Both Standish and Sinclair are working on it, as well as the runners. They will find whoever is behind these attacks and stop them once and for all."

"I pray that they will," Louisa said fervently.

They were still standing hand in hand.

Sir Gilbert said, "As for your other concern about leaving your daughter on the brink of her marriage, you must accept that Diana has a very good man to take care of her now, Louisa. It is obvious that Rumford is head over heels for your daughter. She can go to him if she needs guidance. It's time for you to think about yourself and your own life. Marry me and you will be valued the way you deserve, I promise you."

Gilbert is right, she thought. *It might even be better for Diana's marriage if I'm not there. Then she will have to turn to Rumford for companionship and advice.*

A sudden, radiant smile transformed her into almost as great a beauty as her daughter. "All right, Gilbert, then yes. Yes, I will marry you."

His hands tightened even more, until they were almost hurting her he was holding them so tightly. "Thank you, Louisa," he said. "You won't regret your decision, I swear it." He loosened his hands and slid his hands up her arms until they rested on her shoulders. Then he pulled her toward him. She went easily, raising her face for his kiss.

It had been so many years since she had been kissed by a man that she had wondered if she still had it in her to respond or if the years of celibacy had quite quenched her sexuality. The rush of feeling and emotion she felt at the touch of Gilbert's lips, at the feel of his arms around her, laid that fear to rest. They stood for a long time, clasped in each other's arms, kissing as deeply and as ardently as eighteen-year-olds discovering passion for the first time.

Finally, Sir Gilbert raised his head. He looked deep into her eyes. "We are going to be very happy, Louisa," he said.

"Yes," she returned a little breathlessly. "I believe you are right."

"I'm truly happy for my mother," Diana told her fiancé as they strolled across the Downs that afternoon. "But the selfish part of me wants to keep her for myself. Isn't that shameful?"

"It's a natural reaction, I think," he replied. "It was just the two of you for so long. You are accustomed to relying on her for attention and love." He smiled down at her. "But now you have me for those things, my dear."

Diana smiled back. *What a kind and lovely man he is,* she thought.

"Look at the view," he said, and she stopped beside him and looked out over the horizon. In the distance, beyond the gently rolling Downs, she could just see the sparkle of the sea.

Mama will love living here, she thought. *It's so lovely. And, most importantly, she will be the lady of the house, not just a poor cousin who has fallen on hard times.*

"Look up at me, Diana," Rumford said, and obediently she lifted her face. His mouth came down over hers, and she slipped her arms around his neck.

His kisses had always been restrained, but today he kissed her deeply, thrusting his tongue into her mouth and asking for a response. She forced herself to give it to him, closing her eyes and trying hard to feel familiar sensations that had so far been absent whenever they had kissed.

I don't need that sort of passion anyway, she thought, as she kissed him back with all the sweetness she could muster. *All it ever brought me was heartbreak. What I need is this good, loving man who will take care of me and be a wonderful father to my children.*

Rumford was the one to break the embrace and when he did he was breathing quickly. "I know we set the date of our marriage for June, but that is looking very far ahead right now," he said, trying for some humor.

Diana said quickly, "I can't even think of getting married until this maniac is caught!"

"I know. I know." He pulled her close against him and wrapped his arms around her. "We will find the beast, my little love. Don't worry."

"I love you, Edward," she said.

"It is the greatest joy of my life, to hear you say that," he replied.

Diana closed her eyes and burrowed closely

against him. She liked being held by him much more than she liked kissing him. He made her feel safe. That was what mattered, she told herself, not physical attraction. The thought of Alex flickered in her mind, and she pushed it away.

Back in London, Alex met with the Duke of Sinclair to discuss the attacks on Diana. The two men sat in the privacy of the Standish House library on a beautiful sunny morning. The duke was sipping a glass of port and Alex was drinking coffee.

"Bow Street has come up with nothing," Alex said. "They have the names of a few go-betweens whom they can prosecute, but the originating party still remains obscure."

"They couldn't find the bowman?"

"They know who the fellow is, but he's left town. He probably doesn't know anything useful anyway."

Sinclair looked at the empty fireplace with a slight frown on his face. "What's strange is that Miss Sherwood was in London for quite a while before she was attacked," he said. "What could have happened to all of a sudden make someone think it was imperative to get rid of her?"

Alex took a swallow of strong coffee. He had been strictly adhering to his club's rule that wine should be drunk only with dinner. He thought for a moment then said thoughtfully, "The only change I can think of is that Dee became engaged to Rumford. There were no attacks before the engagement…they started afterward."

"Hmm." Sinclair maintained his slight frown as he rotated his wine glass in his hands. "I can't see how that would have anything to do with it. I can't see any of Rumford's relations trying to do away with Miss Sherwood because they thought she was unsuitable."

"Wait a minute." Alex put his coffee cup down on the table that was between them. "There *is* someone who was hurt by Dee's engagement," he said excitedly. "Jessica Longwood. Everyone expected that she would marry Rumford. Then he came to London, took one look at Dee and dropped Jessica like a hot potato."

Sinclair frowned slightly. "That's true. But what would killing Miss Sherwood accomplish?"

"Obviously Rumford is looking for a wife. Once Dee was out of the way, chances are good that he would turn to Jessica again."

"She can't be *that* desperate for a husband," Sinclair objected. "She's a nice-looking girl, the daughter of a viscount, surely there will be other men for her. Unless she was so in love with him that she would do anything to get him back, but somehow I don't think that's the case."

Alex jumped up and began pacing back and forth in front of the fireplace. "For some reason, it was imperative for her to marry Rumford. That must be it. It's the only explanation that I can think of."

Sinclair looked at him as he paced back and forth. After awhile he said slowly, "You may be right."

Alex came back to his chair, sat down, leaned

toward Sinclair and said urgently, "We have to figure out why it was so important for Jessica to marry
Rumford."

"In a case like this, there can be only one answer," Sinclair returned. "Money."

Alex raised questioning eyebrows.

"Most murders are done either for love or for
money," Sinclair said. "And we have ruled out love."

"Does Longwood need money?" Alex asked.

"Not to my knowledge. He has always been
thought to be financially sound," Sinclair returned.
"But that can change. Perhaps he made bad invest-
ments, perhaps he gambled too deeply on the
horses."

"We have to find out for sure," Alex said. "Who
can help us do that? Not the runners, that's not their
kind of job."

"My man of business is a very knowing chap
with a lot of connections in the financial world,"
Sinclair said. "I'll have him try to find out what he
can about Longwood's finances."

"I would appreciate that, Sinclair," Alex said.
"The sooner we can solve this mystery, the sooner
I will be able to sleep at night."

There was a balloon ascension from Green Park
later that afternoon and the duke took Sally to see
it. The weather was perfect and she enjoyed watching the balloon go up very much. She had never seen
anything like it before. As they were coming home,
she thanked the duke for escorting her.

"I know it must have been boring for you, Robert," she said. "I appreciate your patience."

"Nothing is boring for me if you are there," he replied matter-of-factly.

She turned to smile at him. "What a nice thing to say!"

"I don't say nice things," he returned. "I say true things."

She chuckled. "Then that makes me thank you even more."

He pulled his horses up so a woman and child could cross the street. When the horses were once more moving forward, he said, "Your brother and I were talking earlier about your cousin's problem and I wanted to ask you—did you ever notice anything strange about the way Jessica Longwood treated Miss Sherwood after her engagement was announced?"

Sally stared at him in surprise. "Diana and I never had much conversation with Miss Longwood, either before or after Diana's engagement to Rumford. I can't imagine that Miss Longwood was pleased about the engagement. All the gossip was that Rumford would marry *her*. But she certainly never *threatened* Diana to my knowledge, if that is what you mean."

"Miss Sherwood was not attacked until after she became engaged to Rumford," the duke said. "That is the single possible cause that your brother and I came up with."

Sally's eyes widened, "You and Alex think the *Longwoods* might be involved?"

"It's a possibility. You're sure you never detected anything strange in the way Miss Longwood treated your cousin?"

"No," Sally said regretfully. "I didn't notice anything."

They arrived back at Standish House and the duke left a groom holding his horses while he went into the house with Sally. The drawing room was empty and Sinclair closed the door behind him. Then he took Sally into his arms.

The duke had kissed many women in his life, but kissing Sally was a totally novel experience for him. She was such a combination of innocence and passion, and his own carnal feelings were so tempered by feelings of protectiveness and love, that he might never have kissed anyone else in his life, the experience was so new.

He wanted her as he had never wanted any other woman, but he also wanted to take care of her, be kind to her, to love her with every ounce of love in him. And he had a lot of stored-up love to give.

He was the one to reluctantly break their embrace. Sally looked up at him, her mouth a little swollen from his kiss, her blue eyes hazy with passion, and he felt his need for her as an ache in his heart.

"Soon, I won't have to leave you like this," he said softly.

She smiled. "I know," she whispered.

"I love you, Sarah," he said, and wondered if she knew what an extraordinary thing it was for him to say those words.

Her smile widened. She knew.

"I love you, too, Robert," she said.

He believed her, that was what was so amazing. He knew she loved him. It was a miracle, this love of hers. How had he managed to inspire love in the most wonderful woman in the world? He still wasn't sure. But he would take it. Oh my, he certainly would take it.

"I'll see you at the opera tonight," Sally said.

One of the things they had found they had in common was a love of music.

"You will," he said. Reluctantly he stepped away from her. "Until tonight, my love," he said.

Her eyes were so blue, he thought. So honest and kind and loving.

"Until tonight," she replied, and he turned and opened the door and went back to his horses.

Twenty-Eight

Benjamin Morse had been Sinclair's man of business for all the years that Sinclair had been the duke. Morse had been a brilliant scholarship student at Oxford during the time that the duke was there, and he had found a defender in Sinclair when the other upper-class boys had bullied him. He had been instrumental in setting up and keeping the books for all of the duke's estates as well as his many charities. Given the instructions to search out information on Viscount Longwood, he went to work with a vengeance.

Three days after he had been given the assignment, Morse had the information Sinclair needed.

"Viscount Longwood's son is a compulsive gambler," he told the duke as they met in the small room that Morse used as an office in the duke's London house. "Gerald gambled the whole time he was at school, and once he came down his gambling increased. His father has tried everything to stop him, unsuccessfully. Recently Gerald lost a huge amount of money in a card game at one of the more notorious halls here in London. The man he lost it to was Sir Rodney Henderson."

"Henderson! He's a hardened gambler. What the hell was he doing playing with a youngster like Longwood's son?" The duke frowned and drummed his fingers on the arm of his chair.

"Henderson doesn't care who he plays with as long as they have money. Gerald wanted to play and swore he had the money. When he lost, Henderson told him that if the money wasn't paid up, he would tell everyone in town that he reneged on his debt. The whole family's reputation would have been irrevocably blackened. Longwood paid the money, but I have every reason to believe that it bankrupted him. Longwood himself has been known to play deeply—the acorn doesn't fall far from the tree. I haven't been able to find out if he's mortgaged his estate yet—it's hard to get information out of the banks. But I feel safe in telling you that the Longwoods' financial situation is dire."

"Good job, Ben," Sinclair said. "That is exactly the kind of information I was looking for."

Sinclair wasn't able to catch up with Alex until he went to pick up Sally for their drive in the park that afternoon. Alex had just come in and he was still in the hall divesting himself of his hat and gloves when the duke arrived.

"I just this minute got your note, Sinclair," Alex said. "I was out all afternoon. You have news? Come into the library and tell me about it."

"I can't. I have come to take your sister driving in the park."

"Oh Sally won't mind if you cry off this once," Alex said.

"What won't I mind?" Sally said. She was coming down the stairs wearing a driving dress that exactly matched the color of her eyes.

"I have news from my man of business that may throw some light on the attacks on your cousin," Sinclair told her when she joined the two men in the hallway.

Sally's face lit up. "That's much more important than a drive in the park! Let's all go into the library and you can tell us."

The two men looked at each other, then Sinclair said, "There's no reason she shouldn't know about this."

"All right," Alex said. "Come along the two of you."

A footman appeared when they were all seated, the two men in leather armchairs in front of the unlit fireplace and Sally on an ottoman at the duke's feet. She spread her skirt carefully as she sat down.

"Would you like something to drink?" Alex asked the duke.

"A glass of your excellent port would be nice," Sinclair said.

"I'll have tea," Sally said.

"Bring two cups," Alex said.

Sally threw her brother an approving smile.

The wine and the tea were brought, and, after the footman had left, Sinclair told the brother and sister what Benjamin Morse had found out.

"It sounds to me as if they needed the match with Rumford badly," Sinclair ended. "Once the announcement of his engagement to Miss Longwood had gone to the papers, Rumford would have been caught. It's almost unthinkable for a man to back out of an engagement."

Sally said, "They must have been horrified when Rumford began to pay attention to Diana."

"It's bizarre, but it's possible," Alex said. "Longwood wanted to do away with Dee so that Rumford would go back to his daughter."

"If he was so broke, how did Lord Longwood finance the attacks?" Sally asked. "He had to have paid off the men who carried out his orders."

"He could have borrowed the money from the moneylenders here in town—at an exorbitant interest rate, of course." Alex said.

"But we can't prove any of this!" Sally said, a frown between her delicate brows. "How are we to proceed against Longwood if we don't have any proof?"

Alex said, "All we have to do is tell Rumford that we suspect Longwood is responsible for the attacks on Dee. Knowing that, he would never marry Jessica if something should happen to Dee. I will relay this information to Longwood. The whole point of these attacks is Longwood's hope that Rumford would turn to Jessica if Dee should die. Once Longwood knows that that will never happen, the attacks will stop."

"You're right," Sinclair said.

"I will make a call upon Longwood right now, then I will drive to Hatton Manor to tell Rumford and Dee." Alex put his teacup down and stood up.

"Good," Sinclair said. Then he added, "Although part of me is pained that Longwood is going to get away with trying to murder Miss Sherwood."

"I know," Alex returned. "But we will get nowhere by dragging this out into the public arena. Dee doesn't need to be the subject of speculation among the ton. It will be punishment enough for Longwood to be a bankrupt."

Sally said with pity, "Unfortunately, it will also be a punishment for poor Jessica."

"Jessica is not your problem, my love," the duke said firmly. "Do not fret yourself over her."

Sally sighed. "But it does seem unfair."

Alex said grimly, "Just think that if Dee hadn't bent forward to rub a dirt spot from Monty's neck, she would be dead right now. Then you won't feel so sorry for any of the Longwoods."

"I suppose you're right," Sally said in a subdued voice.

Alex headed for the door. "I will pay a call on Longwood at home. If he isn't in, I'll try to track him down at his club." He looked at Sinclair. "Come for dinner tonight. If I'm successful I'll have news you'll want to hear."

"I'd be delighted to come to dinner," the duke said.

Alex nodded and left the room.

Sinclair turned to Sally. "It's not too late for that drive in the park."

She smiled at him and rose easily from her ottoman. "Good. I think I need some fresh air to clear my brain after what I have just learned."

"You might kiss me first," he said, and she obliged with pleasure.

Sally had to go upstairs and fix her disarranged hair before they were able to get into Sinclair's phaeton.

Alex was lucky enough to find Lord Longwood at home and he met with him in the front drawing room of his house on Berkeley Square. It was not unlike Alex's own drawing room at Standish House, except for the absence of pictures. Alex wondered if they had been sold to pay Gerald's debt.

He refused to accept a seat and stood near the fireplace as he relayed to Longwood what the duke's man of business had discovered. "You thought that if my cousin died, Rumford would offer for your daughter," he ended in a grim voice.

The viscount denied Alex's accusation vigorously. "You have no proof of this and I am insulted that you should come into my house and make such a charge," he blustered. "I have a mind to have one of my footmen throw you out."

"I'll leave on my own," Alex replied coolly. "But understand that I will be telling Rumford of your vicious plot and you can be sure he will have nothing to do with your family in the future. Also, *should* something happen to my cousin, I will accuse you before the world."

"You have no proof to accuse me of anything!" Longwood almost shouted.

"I have enough proof to make a huge scandal," Alex retorted swiftly. "So don't make any more attempts on Miss Sherwood's life, or you will feel my wrath. Do I make myself clear?"

Longwood did not reply. But all of the angry color had faded from his face leaving it looking white and pinched.

Alex went on relentlessly. "I mean what I say. You are getting away easy because I don't want a scandal, but should anything happen to Miss Sherwood, you will wish you had never been born."

There was a long silence while the two men looked at each other. Then Longwood said quietly, "I'm quite sure that nothing else will happen to Miss Sherwood."

Alex's face relaxed a trifle. "Good," he said. "If I were you I would take my family and leave town. It won't be long before news of your financial situation becomes public and you will probably be more comfortable in the country than you would be here in London."

Longwood looked as if he had aged twenty years. He managed to nod in reply.

On this note, Alex left the room.

* * *

Alex reported on his conversation with Lord Longwood at dinner that evening and Sinclair, Sally and Lady Standish were all satisfied with the results of his visit. They all agreed that Alex should drive to Hatton Manor the following day to give Rumford and Diana the news.

It was an overcast day when Alex started out for Sussex. The weather had been beautiful for almost a full week, but it looked now as if it might be breaking. Lady Standish had wanted Alex to take the coach, so he wouldn't get wet if it started to rain, but he had insisted on driving his phaeton.

"A few raindrops won't make me melt away, Mama," he said. "I'll wear my driving coat. Don't worry."

In fact, it started to rain when he was an hour out of London and it continued to rain as he drove south, toward the sea. Diana was the first person to greet him as he came into the front hallway of the house. She had been sitting in the drawing room, and recognized his voice, and had come running to welcome him.

"Alex! What are you doing here? You're drenched!"

Freddie was with her and he went to sniff Alex and jump up with a greeting. Diana called him back to her side.

Alex let a footman help him off with his caped driving coat. He had been wearing a hat, but some of the rain had seeped through and his hair was damp. Raindrops even clung to his eyelashes.

"I've come with good news," he told her. "Where

is Rumford and your mother? They will want to hear this, too."

"You've found out who is behind the attacks on me?"

"Yes." He brushed the wet curls off of his forehead.

"Who is it?" she demanded.

"Wait until Rumford and your mother get here and I'll tell you all."

Diana looked as if she might protest, but then she said, "There is a nice fire in the drawing room. Come inside and dry off in front of it." She turned to the footman. "Please tell Sir Gilbert, my mother and Lord Rumford to come to the drawing room."

"Yes, miss," the footman replied and started toward the library, where Sir Gilbert was going over some accounts.

Within five minutes everyone had gathered. Alex stood with his back to the fire and told his rapt listeners all about Lord Longwood.

They were flabbergasted.

"Longwood!" Rumford said. He was sitting next to Diana on the sofa and now he put an arm around her shoulders. "To think that my love for Diana could cause such a reaction!"

Alex's jaw clenched. "It's almost unbelievable, I know, but when I talked with him I could see that he was guilty as hell."

"How clever of you to have figured this out, Alex," Louisa said admiringly.

"Sinclair and I put our heads together. And it was

his man of business who ferreted out the facts of Longwood's financial desperation."

"Lord Longwood tried to have me killed," Diana said slowly. She shook her head, her eyes on Alex. "It just doesn't seem possible."

"I feel terrible that my love for you put you in the way of such danger," Rumford said to her.

"You couldn't possibly have guessed what would happen," Alex said shortly.

"Mama is right," Diana said to Alex. "It was terribly clever of you and Sinclair to have found this out." A smile broke out on her face. "The runners will have to watch out or you'll be stealing their business."

He forced a laugh.

"Are you certain that Diana is safe now, Alex?" Louisa asked. "There will be no more attempts on her life?"

"Longwood told me there would not be."

"Thank God," Louisa said.

Rumford said expansively, "Now that it is safe, I would like to invite all of you to pay a visit to Aston Castle. I know you ladies are busy ordering new clothes, but I would like Diana to see her new home before our marriage."

Diana looked at her mother, who looked at Sir Gilbert. He smiled at her. "If you would like to go, my dear, of course we will."

"Thank you, Lord Rumford," Louisa said. "We will be happy to pay a visit to Aston Castle."

"The invitation extends to you, too, Standish," Rumford said. "I should love to show you my horses."

Alex hesitated.

"Do come, Alex," Diana said coaxingly. "You know you will love seeing the horses."

He looked at her. *This may be one of my last chances to be with Dee,* he thought. *Once she is married, God knows when I will see her.*

"All right," he said. "I'll come."

Twenty-Nine

Aston Castle was in Oxfordshire and Diana's first view of her new home was from the window of Rumford's carriage, when she looked across the shimmering Thames and saw a golden stone building, its roofline punctuated by weirdly twisted chimney stacks and a prominent octagonal tower.

"How beautiful," Diana said to her fiancé.

He smiled with pleasure. "I am very fond of my home. I hope you will be, too."

"I'm sure I shall be," she replied warmly.

The small house party was arriving at Aston in three separate carriages: Diana and Rumford in the earl's carriage, Louisa and Sir Gilbert in his carriage and Alex was driving himself in his phaeton.

Rumford and Diana were the first to arrive and he proudly gave her a tour of the house. He took Diana through all the public rooms, which were rich and beautiful and resonant of the family's long ten-ure in this magnificent home. The paintings were exceptionally beautiful and Rumford showed them off with obvious pride.

"I am very fond of landscape paintings," he said, as they stood looking at an oil by Claude which hung in the Green Drawing Room. "The ones on the other wall are by two current painters, Constable and Turner, who I think have enormous talent."

From the Green Drawing Room they walked to the lovely south gallery of the house, which was hung with portraits of family and friends. There was also a Van Dyke portrait of Charles I on horseback, which had been given by the king himself to an earlier Earl of Rumford.

Diana was accustomed to Standish Court, so she was not surprised or overwhelmed by the size or the magnificence of her new home. But as she walked beside her fiancé, she found herself engulfed by a strange feeling of loneliness. She would be leaving all the people she knew and loved and would be living here alone with this man. She would not even have her mother. It would be just she and Lord Rumford.

It will be fine, she scolded herself, as she walked back along the south gallery with her fiancé. *It naturally feels a little strange to think of marrying someone I don't know all that well. But Edward is such a good, kind man. It will be fine. I know it will be.*

Alex arrived as they were finishing their tour and Rumford invited him to accompany them to see the horses. Much as Alex disliked admiring anything that belonged to Rumford, he could not contain his enthusiasm for the earl's two stallions and eight beautiful mares.

"Do you know, I have been thinking about launching a breeding operation of my own," Alex said as the three of them walked along the graveled stable path on their way back to the house.

Out of the corner of his eye he saw Diana's head swing around as if he had startled her.

"Racehorses?" Rumford asked interestedly.

Alex shook his head. "No. I was thinking of breeding my own hunters, mixing thoroughbreds, for their courage and speed, with carriage horses, for their strength and solid bone and sensible brain."

"You never told me this," Diana said, almost accusingly.

"I thought about it a lot when I was in the Peninsula," he returned. "I used to lay in bed at night and plan out in my head how I would go about it." What he didn't say was that the planning had helped to get him through the nights when he couldn't sleep.

"It sounds like a splendid idea," Rumford said.

There was a pause. Then Diana said in a subdued voice, "Yes, it does."

"I'm rather excited about it," Alex confessed. "Once this Season is over, I'm looking forward to going home and getting started."

"Where will you get your breeding stock?" Rumford asked.

The two men launched into a detailed discussion about the business of breeding horses, to which Diana did not contribute. Alex, who had never known her to hold back from a discussion about horses, said at last, "You're awfully quiet, Dee."

"I've been listening," she assured him quietly. She lifted her eyes to his. "Your plans sound grand, Alex. If you have extra horses and want to sell them, I'll be your first customer." She smiled.

His stomach twisted with pain. *I shouldn't have come,* he thought despairingly. *It's too hard seeing Dee with this man. I am only making myself miserable.*

He wrenched his face into the semblance of an answering smile. "I'll hold you to that," he said.

The rest of the party arrived and were also shown around the house and the grounds. Dinner was served and Alex, Diana, Sir Gilbert and Rumford played at cards, while Louisa, who didn't play, sat on the sofa going through a book of prints from Rumford's vast collection.

Alex had taught Diana to play cards many years ago, when Sally was sick and the two of them had played whist with her while she was confined to bed. But Diana hadn't had much opportunity to play since, and she made the wrong discard, which Alex immediately took advantage of. She apologized to her fiancé for her misplay.

He was unperturbed. "That is perfectly fine, my love. You will get better as you play more."

My love. The words felt like a knife scraping

along Alex's frayed nerves. When the game was over he excused himself, not even waiting for the tea tray.

"Are you all right, Alex?" Diana asked in concern.

"Just a bit of a headache," he returned carelessly. "A good night's sleep and I'll be fine."

He knew, of course, that there would be no such thing as a good night's sleep, but he was prepared for that. He put on his dressing gown, took out the book he had brought for just this purpose and sat down by an oil lamp. He didn't open his book immediately, however, but sat staring into the glowing embers in his fireplace.

He had thought it was painful seeing Dee at home when he knew she could not be his, but seeing her here with Rumford was excruciating. He had tried so hard to resign himself to losing her, but it seemed that he had not been successful. He was still staring desolately into the fireplace when he heard a knock upon his door.

His heart jumped into his throat. It was Dee, he knew it.

"Come in," he called.

The door opened and she was there.

"Couldn't you sleep?" she asked as she saw him sitting in the chair.

"I don't sleep well in a strange bed," he replied. "What are you doing up?"

She came into the room and closed the door behind her. "I don't sleep well in a strange bed, either." Her eyes flicked across the table next to him.

"I'm not drinking, if that's what you're worried about," he said stiffly. "I've been more careful about that lately."

"I've noticed," she said. "I'm glad. I *was* worried about you, Alex."

She sat on the side of his bed and looked at him gravely out of large brown eyes. She was so beautiful, with her hair tied loosely with a ribbon and her silk dressing gown belted around her slender waist.

For some reason he found himself telling her about the veteran's club he had founded and the meetings they had held. He had never told anyone else about the club, and he didn't know why he was blabbing now to Dee, but he couldn't seem to stop.

She smiled when he had finished.

There was nothing in the world as beautiful as Dee's smile.

He waited for her to tell him that he had chosen to leave her and go into the army and that now he was going to have to live with the results.

She said instead, "I'm so glad you're getting help. It was very clever of you, Alex, to found that club. Is everyone benefiting from it?"

"I think so. It's just good to have a place to go where you can talk about things you saw and other men will understand because they went through the same experience themselves."

She nodded thoughtfully.

There was such sweetness to the curve of her cheeks, he thought. And her mouth…. Abruptly he brought himself back to the awareness of what she was saying.

He managed to answer her sensibly, but inside every piece of him was dying to lay her down on that bed and make passionate love to her.

She reached a hand up to push a stray strand of hair away from her eyelashes.

"You're going to have to go, Dee," he said, his voice sounding harsh even to his own ears. "Rumford would not like it at all if he knew you were sitting on my bed with the door closed."

She stared at him. They remained like that for a long moment, their eyes locked together. His whole body was taut and trembling, he wanted her so much. At last she said a little breathlessly, "He wouldn't care. He knows we're friends."

"My feelings for you are not those of a friend. You know that. It's not fair to Rumford for you to be here, and it's not fair to me. Go back to bed, Dee, and I'll see you in the morning. Your mission is accomplished. I am not drinking. Good night."

She looked at him with a strange uncertainty in her eyes.

If she didn't leave immediately, he wouldn't be able to answer for the consequences. "Good night," he repeated firmly.

She stood up. "Good night."

She tightened the sash around her waist, paused as if she would say something else, then turned slowly and went out the door.

* * *

Diana's sleep was restless, filled with troubled dreams that she couldn't recall when she woke up. She went down to breakfast heavy-eyed and a little late, and found herself alone in the dining room. When the butler came in with fresh tea, she asked him where everyone was.

He put the teapot down on the table and turned to her. He looked worried. "Oh, Miss Sherwood, there's a fire in the stable! That's where everyone has gone."

"Oh no!" Diana cried. She jumped up abruptly, knocking over her chair, and ran for the door. As soon as she was out of the house she could see the flames shooting up in the air from the stable area. The loft of the stable had been filled with hay, she remembered. They would never extinguish that kind of fire.

Dear God, she thought with panic. *I hope they managed to get the horses out!*

She began to run as fast as she could down the stable path. The smoke grew thicker the closer she got to the burning building. Some men had formed a line to the pond and were throwing water on the conflagration, but Diana could see that it was a futile effort. The hay and the wooden stalls would burn themselves out and leave only the stone shell of the building standing. At least some of the horses had been saved. Diana heard their terrified whinnying as grooms held them on lead ropes in the smoky courtyard. Diana's frightened gaze scanned the gathered faces, but she didn't see either Edward or Alex. Panic shot like a knife through her heart. She asked one of the grooms, dodging his horse's flailing hooves, "Where are Lord Rumford and Lord Standish?"

"They're in the stable, miss," the groom replied, coughing. "They went in to get the last two horses. But the fire has got so bad, I don't know if they're going to be able to get out. Part of the loft has come down."

Part of the loft has come down. No! Diana screamed in her head. *No! This can't be happening! It can't be!*

The smoke was so dense that it was becoming difficult to see. The stable looked like an inferno. She stared at it in frozen horror. *He's in there,* she thought. *Alex is in there. Dear God, dear God, dear God, what am I going to do?*

"Diana!" Her mother's voice seemed to come from a great distance. "Where is Rumford?" Louisa asked.

"He and Lord Standish are in the stable," the groom replied when Diana didn't answer. "They went in to get the last two horses."

"Oh no!" Louisa cried.

I told him I didn't love him. He's going to die and I told him I didn't love him. Diana couldn't turn away from the sight of the brilliant orange flames leaping high into the sky. *How can I live if I lose him? I can't lose him. Save him for me, God. Save him and I will be so good, I promise I will be so good, God. Oh please save him...*

She took two steps toward the barn, as if she would go in after him, but her mother grabbed her arm.

"You can't do anything, darling! The fire is too intense."

For a moment she stared at her mother's hand on her arm, not seeming to know where it came from. The horse next to her reared up and she didn't even try to get out of its way. Her eyes went back to the flames and she pressed her hands to her mouth. The smoke was growing thicker by the minute.

I don't even have his baby. He thinks I hate him.

There came the sound of a horse screaming from inside the stable. "Noooooo!" Diana screamed back in anguish.

Her mother put an arm about her waist, as if to physically restrain her. The flames were shooting impossibly high.

If he dies, then I want to die, too. How can I live without him?

Suddenly two loose horses erupted out of the stable, galloping hard. Grooms ran to try to catch them.

The horses made it out! Diana stared frantically through the smoke at the stable door. *Surely, surely....*

Then, holding their coats over the lower parts of their faces, two figures appeared, running through the stable door. Rumford and Alex had made it out.

His name tore itself from Diana's throat.

"Alex!" she screamed. *"Alex!"* She ran as if all the hounds of hell were at her feet and threw herself into his smoke-stained arms. "Thank God! I thought you were dead!" She began to sob, deeply and uncontrollably. "I thought you were dead."

He was coughing, but his arms came up to hold her.

"Dee," he managed to say thickly. "I'm all right, Dee. I'm all right."

Her arms were around his neck in a stranglehold. She said through her sobs, "They said the loft fell! I thought you were trapped!"

"It fell behind us. It didn't block our way to the door."

His voice was sounding stronger and he wasn't coughing so much.

"Thank God you're safe," she said. "Oh thank God!"

They stood locked together for a long minute, while the building burned and the frightened horses milled around. Diana continued to cling to him and sob. Over her head, Alex's eyes slowly went to Rumford.

The earl's face was as black with smoke as Alex's, and his stricken gaze was looking at Diana, whose arms were still wound tightly around Alex's neck.

There was a long silence as the two men regarded each other. Everything seemed to drop away from Alex; the fire, the horses, the bustling grooms. All he knew was the feel of Diana in his arms and the look in Rumford's eyes.

"Dee," Alex said softly.

Diana lifted her streaming face and followed the direction of Alex's eyes. She struggled to compose herself. "E-Edward." Slowly she relaxed her grip on Alex's neck, but her hand sought his and she clutched it tightly as she turned to face her fiancé. "I'm so sorry," she whispered. "I didn't know...I didn't realize...."

Rumford looked around at the fascinated grooms. "Turn these horses out in the paddocks and inspect every one of them for injuries," he snapped.

The stable yard emptied quickly, leaving only Rumford, Alex and Diana. Louisa and Sir Gilbert thoughtfully retired to the house. The fire continued to burn. The men had ceased their fruitless attempt to throw water on the raging flames.

Rumford said to Diana. "Standish is the man, isn't he?" His voice was hoarse from the smoke he had been inhaling. "He's the man you told me about."

"Yes," she said softly. "He is."

"And you still love him?"

"Yes," she said again. "I was so angry with him that I didn't know it. But now..." she looked up at Alex and tightened her grip on his fingers. "Now I do."

She had told Rumford about him, Alex thought wonderingly. She still loved him. His heart felt so full he thought it was going to burst.

"I see," Rumford said. The stricken look had not left his eyes.

"I wasn't lying to you, Edward!" Diana said passionately. "I do love you. You are so good and kind and steady. You are exactly the kind of man that I thought I wanted. I thought I was finished with Alex. I truly did."

"I thought that, too," Alex said. He made an effort to steady his voice. "Dee knew that I still loved her, but she kept telling me that we were finished. I never dreamed…" For a moment his voice broke. Then he said more firmly, "I'm only sorry that my happiness comes at your expense, Rumford."

"You don't deserve to be made unhappy again, Edward," Diana said tearfully. "I feel so terrible about this. But I wasn't lying to you. Truly I wasn't."

"I suppose it was better to find this out now, rather than after we were married," Rumford said bitterly.

God, yes, Alex thought.

Diana bowed her head.

"I will send a notice to the papers," Rumford said.

Diana said miserably. "I am so sorry to have made you the subject of gossip. All of this is my fault."

Rumford said even more bitterly, "It's my fault, for thinking a girl over twenty years younger than I am could love me."

There came a crashing sound as the whole roof of the stable collapsed. The heat and smoke in the stable yard intensified.

"Don't think that way!" Diana cried. "If it wasn't for Alex, I would have loved you very much. I still do care about you, Edward. And I am so very sorry to have brought this sorrow upon you."

Rumford shut his eyes, looking every minute of his age. He opened them again and said evenly, "Do you know, it's still early. I think it would be a good thing if you all left. You could be back in London by late afternoon."

"We'll do that," Alex replied quickly. He was as anxious to be gone as Rumford was to have them go. "You won't have to worry about having to face us any further, Rumford. Like Dee, I am sorry that you have been hurt. You're a good man."

He could say that now that Diana was no longer going to marry him.

"Before you go, let me thank you for helping to rescue my horses," the earl said painstakingly.

"I was happy to assist." Alex turned his head. "Come along, Dee. We'll tell your mother and Sir Gilbert and get packed up."

"Edward, I...." Diana looked at him, as if she wished there was something she could do or say that would make this easier for him. "Goodbye," she whispered at last.

"Goodbye, Diana," he returned steadily.

Alex tugged gently on her hand. "Come along, Dee."

Diana's fingers clung to his.

Together they left the stable yard and returned to the house.

Thirty

Diana rode home with Alex in his phaeton. The weather was a little overcast, but Diana's heart was so light that it seemed to her as if the whole world was bursting with sunshine.

They talked about the things that had kept them apart.

"It was all my fault," Alex said. "In my heart I knew I shouldn't leave you. I was just so damn determined to become a soldier. And I truly thought you'd wait for me." He turned his head to look at her, his crystal eyes very bright. "How stupid could I have been?"

"I *did* wait for you," Diana answered ruefully. "I didn't realize it, of course, but you were the reason I never accepted any of the offers that came my way. None of the men measured up to you."

"You accepted Rumford," he said.

"I truly liked him, Alex." She pressed her lips together and looked down at her gloved hands reposing in her lap. "I also think there may have been another reason for my accepting him."

He gave her a curious glance. "What was that?"

"I wanted to punish you."

Silence. Diana raised her eyes to his profile. It was unreadable.

Finally he responded. "Well, if that was your motive, you succeeded admirably. The pain I suffered from my wound was nothing compared to the pain I have been feeling over you."

She thought of the shadowed, strained look he had been wearing for so long and tears stung her eyes. "I'm afraid I'm not a very nice person, Alex."

"That's not true, Dee." A farmer's cart was approaching them, and he carefully steered around it. "I perfectly understand your feelings. You gave me your virginity and then I turned around and left you. And you were carrying a child! I would have wanted to punish me, too. I deserved to be punished."

She was deeply moved by the generosity of his statement. He had seen their past through her eyes; now, for the first time, she made a great effort to see it through his. "It wasn't entirely your fault. I never told you the truth about the baby."

He glanced at her, his eyes flashing blue in the sunlight. "I know. But still, I shouldn't have done what I did and then left."

She let out a long, slow breath, as if she was releasing a burden. When she spoke her voice was very soft. "You were still a boy. I know you loved me, but you weren't ready to marry and settle down. You had wanted to be a soldier for so long. If you had stayed, I think part of you would always have felt cheated. I would never have had your whole heart if you hadn't had a chance to follow your dream."

It was as if a weight had lifted from her with those words. For the first time she felt as if she had truly forgiven him. Her heart soared.

Alex's voice was thick with emotion, "It's very kind of you, Dee, to say that."

They drove for a while in comfortable silence before she asked quietly, "How was it, being a soldier, Alex? It seems to have left you with some scars."

He started to answer, then he stopped. She waited while he collected himself. When he spoke at last his voice was low, and she had to lean close to hear it. "Our cause was a noble one. Napoleon had to be stopped and I was proud to be part of that campaign. And there is nothing anywhere else like the camaraderie among men who are risking their lives together." He picked up his whip and carefully flicked a fly off of one of the horse's hindquarters. Then he turned his head to look at her. His eyes wore that shadowy look that so worried her. "But would I want to see my son go to war? No, I wouldn't. It was ugly, Dee. It was very, very ugly."

The tears that had threatened earlier now gathered and began to fall. She put her hand on his arm. "I'm sorry, Alex. I'm sorry I never wrote to you. I'm sorry I held a grudge for all those years."

"Don't cry, love," he said. "Please don't cry."

She made an effort and smiled at him through the tears that were raining down her face.

He said seriously, "Do you know what I think, Dee? I think we should try to put the past three years behind us. I think we should only look ahead to our life together. I think we should concentrate on being happy."

She rested her cheek against his shoulder. "I think that is a very good idea," she replied.

The family was stunned by Alex's announcement that he and Diana were going to be married.

"But what of Lord Rumford?" Lady Standish cried.

"I made a mistake," Diana said. "I have loved Alex for years, Cousin Amelia. I'm so sorry if you are disappointed that he is going to marry a girl with my poor prospects, but I will make him happy. I promise you."

"My dear girl," the dowager countess said, stretching out her arms. "Of course I am not disappointed! I have only to look at my son to see how happy he is. He hasn't looked like this since he came home from the Peninsula."

The two women embraced. Then Sally held out

her arms as well. "Just think!" she said. "You will be my real sister now."

Diana gave her a hug. "You have always been a sister to me," she said.

"Well, sister or no, you certainly fooled me," Sally said. "I always knew that Alex and you were best friends, but I never suspected this!"

Alex said, "You were too young to tumble to how we really felt."

"But what took you so long to become engaged?" Sally asked.

"It was my fault," Diana said. "I was angry at Alex for leaving me for the army. But now I know that I could never love another man."

Sally went to kiss her brother. "Well I am very happy for you both."

"What a success this Season has been!" Lady Standish cried. "Sally is to marry a duke, my dear Diana is to marry Alex and even Louisa has found a good match."

"We have to find someone for you, Mama," Sally said mischievously.

Lady Standish laughed lightly. "I am very well as I am, thank you. I am enjoying London enormously. In fact, I am thinking of bringing the girls to London and making Standish House my permanent home—if that will be all right with you, Alex and Diana."

"Of course it is all right," Alex said.

"Please don't think you would be unwelcome at Standish Court," Diana implored. "You have been like a second mother to me, Cousin Amelia. I would love to share a house with you."

Lady Standish shook her head decisively. "Two mistresses in one house is never a good idea. The staff and everyone on the estate must learn to look to you, Diana dear. And I am serious when I say that I would like to reside full-time in London, with an occasional visit back to Berkshire. And I think the children would like it, too. There is so much to see and do in London."

"Well, if you change your mind, know that you are always welcome at Standish Court."

"That is very kind of you, dear," Lady Standish said.

They were still in the drawing room talking when Louisa Sherwood came into the room. Diana's last meeting with her mother at Aston Castle had been hurried with the urgency of an immediate departure. Now she cried, "Mama!" and flew into her mother's embrace.

"I am so happy for you, darling," she said.

Diana fiercely returned Louisa's hug. Her mother was the only other person who knew the real story of her and Alex, Diana thought. She was the only one who knew what this reconciliation with Alex truly meant to her.

"I'm happy, too," she whispered into Louisa's ear.

Lady Standish asked, "How did you leave Lord Rumford?"

Louisa gave her daughter one last squeeze and released her. "Poor man," she said compassionately. "I saw him just when we were about to leave. He looked devastated."

A shadow passed over the shining brightness of Diana's happiness. "I don't know what made me accept him. I should never have done that."

Her mother touched her cheek. "I rather think you saw in him the father that you had always wanted. I have thought that all along and it worried me a little. But you seemed so happy."

Diana stared at her mother with dawning enlightenment.

Louisa smiled at Alex. "I am very glad that the two of you have finally come together. I don't think Diana has been truly happy since you left."

Mama knows me better than I know myself, Diana thought in amazement.

Alex said, "We are putting the past behind us and concentrating on the future, Cousin Louisa."

"I think that is very wise," Louisa said.

"We must begin to plan the wedding," Lady Standish said with relish. "Sally is being married at St. George's in Hanover Square in June. Do you wish to be married before or after her, Alex?"

Diana looked at her new fiancé. "We are going to go home to Standish Court and be married at our local parish church as soon as possible," he said firmly. "Dee and I have discussed this and we are in agreement. We'll have the banns called because I don't want any of the gossip that would invariably arise if I just got a special license. But once the banns are called, we're going to be married."

Lady Standish looked disappointed. "But you're an earl, Alex! You should have a big wedding."

"You're giving Sally a big wedding. That will have to be enough."

Lady Standish sighed. "Oh, all right. But there will be gossip whatever you do. Diana can't jilt Rumford and marry you without gossip."

"We won't concern ourselves with the gossip," Louisa said briskly. "But we will have to coordinate wedding dates, darling. I want to be able to attend yours and I want you to attend mine."

Diana hugged her mother again. "We are both so lucky, Mama."

Louisa hugged her back. "Yes, we are, darling. We certainly are."

That night, after everyone had retired, Diana was dressed in her nightgown and sitting up in bed with a book in front of her when a knock came upon her door.

"Come in," she called softly.

A thrill of excitement ran up and down her spine as Alex entered. He was dressed in just his breeches and a shirt that was open at the neck. His black hair was hanging over his forehead. He closed the door behind him but didn't advance into the room.

"Are you sure this is all right?" he asked huskily.

"Yes," she said. "It's the rightest thing that has happened to me since the day you left."

"God." He crossed the floor and sat on the bed next to her. She put her book down on the rosewood night table and looked up at him. Her hair was loose and streamed down her back in a fall of glorious coppery curls. He reached out and touched it.

"It feels just like I remember it," he said. "Like silk."

Her breath caught at his touch. She placed her hands on his shoulders and ran them over his upper arms, feeling the strong muscles. He wasn't the slim boy she remembered any longer.

"You've gotten bigger," she murmured.

"And you've gotten even more beautiful." His voice was huskier than it had been before.

She tilted her head back. "Kiss me, Alex," she whispered.

He bent his head and his mouth came down on hers. His kiss was like fire and she met it and matched it. All of the passion that she had so scorned with Rumford came rushing over her. She linked her arms around his neck and opened her mouth to him. The penetration of his tongue caused a throbbing to begin in her loins.

Alex laid her back upon the bed and swung his legs up to lie beside her. Their bodies pressed into each other and all this time they were kissing frantically. Finally he broke the contact of their mouths.

"Dee," he said breathlessly. "Do you think we could get rid of this nightgown?"

She didn't hesitate for a moment. She pulled the white cotton nightgown off over her head and her hair spilled down over her perfect white skin. He kissed her throat. "I thought only babies had skin as fine as this," he said.

She didn't respond. Her own fingers had felt something raised under his shirt and she frowned. "Fair is fair," she said. "Now you take off your shirt."

He looked at her for a moment, then he shrugged and pulled the shirt off over his head. She saw the scar on his shoulder immediately.

"You were wounded worse than we thought," she said accusingly. "That's a nasty scar."

"The scar makes it look worse than it was," he replied easily. "Don't fuss over it, Dee. It doesn't hurt anymore. I hardly think of it."

She reached over and pressed her lips against it. "Poor Alex," she said. "I hate to think of you being hurt."

"It wasn't so bad," he replied. "When I think of the men who were killed, or who lost an arm or a leg, I realize how lucky I was."

"Thank God you're all right," she said fervently. "Thank God you came home to me."

They began to kiss again. As they kissed Alex's hand moved from her throat to her breast and began to caress it. Diana's breath came faster. Then he slid his mouth away from hers and went lower, kissing first her throat and then her breast. After a few moments, he gently sucked on her nipple.

It was as if there was a nerve that went directly from her nipple to between her legs. Her hips arched involuntarily, searching for release from the building tension.

He moved to her other breast and started sucking there. She buried her hands in his thick black hair.

Finally he lifted his head and looked down at her. Her hair was spread out around her like a halo. "I love you so much," he said. "I was faithful to you, Dee. I want you to know that. There were available women around, but I never looked at them. I was always true to you."

Tears formed in her eyes. "I'm glad," she whispered. "I'm so glad to hear that, Alex."

He bent and kissed the tears away. "Don't cry, my love," he said softly. "I never want to see you cry."

"They're happy tears," she said.

He found her mouth and kissed her again. Then his fingers found the spot between her legs where her most intense feelings were concentrated. The shock of his touch ran all through her and once more she lifted her hips.

"Does that feel good?" he asked. "Do you like that?"

"Yes," she said breathlessly. "Oh yes."

He kept kissing her and moving his finger and all of a sudden a stupendous rush of sensation ripped through Diana, all emanating from that one single spot between her legs. Her body jerked again and again with the power of what she was feeling.

"Let me in, Dee," he said, and she opened her legs wider to give him access to the throbbing inside of her. She took him in deeply and closed around him, shutting her eyes, feeling that with this one act they could shed the lost years, shed the long loneliness, shed the pain. The heat between them was so intense, so deep. The feel of him inside her was so natural, so solid, so good.

She held him tightly, feeling the strong muscles in his shoulders and back, feeling the light sheen of sweat that clung to him.

He said her name as he reached his climax and she held him tighter, feeling the pounding of his heart and the laboring of his breath.

"Alex," she said. "Oh, Alex." And once again she had tears in her eyes.

Afterwards he lay quiet, with his body all along hers, his arms holding her close. He kissed her hair. "I love you so much," he said. "So much, Dee."

There was in his embrace a feeling of cherishing and protectiveness that was very sweet to her. She felt so safe, so loved and so very very happy.

"I love you, too," she said.

Time passed as they breathed together. Then he said, "I don't want to wait for the banns to be called. I want you to be mine right away."

"We have to wait," she said. "Our mothers would be very upset if we got married by a special license. It would probably cause a scandal, whereas our waiting for the banns will just cause gossip."

"Damn," he said.

"It's only a few weeks," she said.

"A day seems too long."

She kissed the scar on his shoulder. "I don't want to wait either, but we must."

He heaved a sigh. "All right. But I'm not ready to go back to my room yet."

"Who said you had to?"

"Will you kiss me again?"

She lifted her face to his and their lips met with great tenderness. "I will love you forever," she said.

"I will make you happy, love," he promised. "I swear it."

"I know you will," she replied softly. "You already have."

Epilogue

Diana and Alex were the first ones married. They spent a week at a seaside cottage that belonged to a friend of Alex's before returning to Standish Court. A week later they traveled to Sussex for the wedding of Diana's mother and Sir Gilbert Merton. Then, three weeks after that, they all removed to London for Sally's wedding to the Duke of Sinclair.

Sally and Sinclair would have been happier to be married quietly, with just family present, like Diana and Louisa had been, but Lady Standish had set her heart on a big wedding and Sally loved her mother too much to disappoint her. So they were married in St. George's, with the church crowded with all of their relatives and friends. The wedding breakfast was held at Standish House and even the prince regent threatened to attend. Fortunately, he did not, and Sally and Sinclair were able to get away to one of Sinclair's smaller estates, where they spent their honeymoon.

It took Sally two months to get with child. It took Diana four months. It took Louisa a year.

The most jubilant of all the couples was Louisa and Sir Gilbert. The younger people had always thought that, in the natural course of events, they would have children. But to Louisa and Sir Gilbert, a baby was like a small miracle.

Sally's baby was named Eleanor and called Nell. Sinclair was not at all perturbed at not having a son. In fact, Nell brought out a tenderness in him that touched Sally deeply.

Diana's baby was a boy whom they named William. The minute that Diana's son was born, she and Sally began plotting how the two children could marry each other. The fathers told them not to be looking so far ahead, but they went right ahead with their plans anyway.

Louisa also had a son, to Sir Gilbert's great delight. With the death of his first son in the Peninsula, Hatton Manor was going to have to pass into the hands of a cousin. Now he had another heir, and a new child to help ease the pain of losing his eldest.

Lady Standish remained single, thoroughly enjoying her emancipated life as a wealthy widow. She spent the summer in Brighton and the Christmas holidays and the occasional visit to Standish Court, but otherwise she was perfectly happy in London, where she had acquired a host of friends.

Sally and Sinclair were building an orphanage on one of Sinclair's lesser estates and they continued to work for improvement in the lives of climbing boys.

Diana and Alex started their horse breeding enterprise by acquiring three beautiful thoroughbred mares to breed to a stunning-looking draft horse stallion that they found at a sale in Derbyshire. Diana's riding had been curtailed somewhat by her pregnancy, but she was back in the saddle quickly after the baby's birth. Together she and Alex began some improvements upon their tenants' houses.

"We'll never be as philanthropic as Sally and Sinclair, but at least we can see to it that our people are comfortable," Alex said to Diana. He had spent months going over the books and the estates with his estate manager and he felt much more comfortable about what needed to be done on his property. He still had an occasional nightmare, and he still went into London once a month for a meeting of his veterans' club, but overall his mind was at rest.

As Diana said to him one night, as they were standing over the crib of their sleeping son, "It's so wonderful to be happy, Alex. How sorry I am for all the people in the world who aren't as happy as we are."

He reached over and took her hand into his own large, warm clasp. "We're very lucky," he responded soberly.

Diana raised his hand to her lips and kissed it. "Yes," she said softly. "We are."

New York Times **Bestselling Author**

KATHERINE STONE

Sixteen years ago, Snow Ashley Gable fled
Chicago. She ran away from the kind of loss
that comes from love and betrayal. Now thirty-
one, Snow is bringing her successful late-night
radio talk show, *The Cinderella Hour,* home
to Chicago. But not everyone wants her back.
There's the father she never knew, the mother
who acted out one dangerous fantasy after
another and Luke Kilcannon, the troubled
boy she loved. And it's Luke's own mystery
that may prove more devastating than
anyone would willingly believe....

THE *Cinderella* HOUR

"With this tightly woven, suspenseful plot,
peopled with memorable characters, Stone has
produced another surefire hit."

—*Booklist* on *Imagine Love*

*Available the first week of August 2006
wherever paperbacks are sold!*

MIRA®

www.MIRABooks.com

MKS2327

JOAN WOLF

32097 WHITE HORSES	___ $6.50 U.S.	___ $7.99 CAN.
22033 TO THE CASTLE	___ $6.99 U.S.	___ $8.50 CAN.

(limited quantities available)

TOTAL AMOUNT	$ _____
POSTAGE & HANDLING	$ _____
($1.00 FOR 1 BOOK, 50¢ for each additional)	
APPLICABLE TAXES*	$ _____
TOTAL PAYABLE	$ _____

(check or money order—please do not send cash)

To order, complete this form and send it, along with a check or money order for the total above, payable to MIRA Books, to: **In the U.S.:** 3010 Walden Avenue, P.O. Box 9077, Buffalo, NY 14269-9077; **In Canada:** P.O. Box 636, Fort Erie, Ontario, L2A 5X3.

Name: _____
Address: _____ City: _____
State/Prov.: _____ Zip/Postal Code: _____
Account Number (if applicable): _____

075 CSAS

*New York residents remit applicable sales taxes.
*Canadian residents remit applicable GST and provincial taxes.

MIRA®

www.MIRABooks.com

MJW0806BL